Acclaim for
HIDDEN CURRENT

"Hinck's intertwining of Christian theology and fantasy renders a thought-provoking tale, and readers will be challenged to question their convictions. Recommended."

—SCHOOL LIBRARY JOURNAL

"Both fantastical and a commentary on blind faith, Sharon Hinck's exquisite *Hidden Current* kick-starts a magical new series centered around the power of dance and staying true to yourself."

—FOREWORD REVIEWS

"Sharon Hinck's fantasy dances to the rhythm of our Creator's heart... the story moves well to the rhythm of an organic and necessary theme: the ultimate purpose of creative gifts, in a world that's guided not by human movers in a disordered Order, but by a divine and prime Mover."

—LOREHAVEN MAGAZINE

"Sharon Hinck has outdone herself with this tale of reclaimed mystery and redemption. As a dancer myself, I loved the rhythm and lyricism of Hinck's masterful prose and the perilous quest of her protagonist to learn Truth. *Hidden Current* dances on the page."

—TOSCA LEE, *New York Times* bestselling author

"Rhythm and dance can move a world, and *Hidden Current* shows how it might be done. A lovely story, told through the eyes of a character who must find her true strength in faithful, trusting service. *Hidden Current* combines a creative, sympathetic interweaving of the dancer's art with intriguing worldbuilding and a strong faith element. Well done, Sharon Hinck."

—KATHY TYERS, author of the Firebird series

"*Hidden Current* made me want to leap up and dance with joy. The characters, setting, and creatures were exquisite, and the Maker touched my heart. One of the most beautiful stories I've ever read."

—MORGAN BUSSE, award-winning author of The Ravenwood Saga

"Sharon Hinck's *Hidden Current* is absolutely beautiful! I was instantly drawn in by her intriguing island world held in place by dancers. This story is one of discovery, truth, and a lovely, fresh allegory that will touch readers' hearts. If you enjoy Christian young adult fantasy novels with danger, adventure, and a hint of romance, you're going to love it!"

—JILL WILLIAMSON, Christy Award-winning author of Blood of Kings

"*Hidden Current* enthralled me! Sharon Hinck brings characters to life like no one else! The characters' paths collide and propel them on an adventurous, imaginative quest. *Hidden Current* is bursting with intrigue, danger, betrayal, redemption and hope—everything readers want in an epic tale! *Hidden Current* is unputdownable!"

—ELIZABETH GODDARD, bestselling author of the Uncommon Justice series

FORSAKEN
ISLAND

Books by Sharon Hinck

The Secret Life of Becky Miller
Renovating Becky Miller

Symphony of Secrets

Stepping Into Sunlight

The Sword of Lyric Series
The Restorer
The Restorer's Son
The Restorer's Journey
The Deliverer

The Dancing Realms Series
Hidden Current
Forsaken Island

FORSAKEN ISLAND

THE DANCING REALMS

BOOK 2

SHARON HINCK

Forsaken Island

Copyright © 2020 by Sharon Hinck

Published by Enclave Publishing, an imprint of Third Day Books, LLC

Phoenix, Arizona, USA.
www.enclavepublishing.com

All rights reserved. No part of this publication may be reproduced, digitally stored, or transmitted in any form without written permission from Third Day Books, LLC.

This is a work of fiction. Names, characters, places, and incidents are products of the author's imagination or are used fictitiously. Any similarity to actual people, organizations, and/or events is purely coincidental.

ISBN: 978-1-62184-135-7 (printed hardback)
ISBN: 978-1-62184-137-1 (printed softcover)
ISBN: 978-1-62184-136-4 (ebook)

Cover design by Kirk DouPonce, www.DogEaredDesign.com
Typesetting by Jamie Foley

Printed in the United States of America.

for Ted, with all my love and gratitude

"For the LORD will not reject his people;
he will never forsake his inheritance."

—Psalm 94:14 (NIV)

ACROSS A SWEEP OF WAVES, THE NEW WORLD CALLED TO me. Sea breezes tickled my skin, stirring excitement and making my muscles twitch. What surprises might the unexpected island hold? The tangleroot shore of Meriel's rim rocked beneath my bare feet, daring me to leave its safety.

Beside me, Brantley rolled a cloak and stuffed it into his pack. "We should have left at first light." Wind brushed fair curls across his eyes, and he tossed his head like an impatient pony shaking his mane. A mottled brown tunic stretched across his broad shoulders, and a longknife rested at his hip.

I folded a sheet of parchment and tucked it into the tiny pouch hanging around my neck. "Saltar Kemp kept adding to the list of supplies she wants us to search for. She's hoping we can find seeds to bring back so the villages can develop new orchards."

The possibility of such bounty still felt surreal, the notion of an uncharted land like a child's fanciful dream. To think, for centuries we had believed our island floated alone on an endless ocean, and now a mere speck amid the vast expanse of blue had proven our wisest elders wrong.

We were not alone.

And the thought made me shiver.

Brantley leapt from shore onto his stenella, Navar. The graceful sea creature's sleek back provided enough room for us both, so why was I afraid to climb on? My companion's ocean-blue gaze held a challenge as he offered his hand. "Are you ready, Carya?"

Was I ready? After all the adventures I'd endured, you'd think I could face this trip bravely, but fear tiptoed into my heart and set up camp. Fear of the hungry ocean. Fear of threats we might face. Fear that we wouldn't find anything of use and our world would continue to suffer. I flexed my bandaged ankle and winced. Yet another reason many of the saltars had warned me not to make this journey.

Hiding my qualms, I forced a confident smile and accepted Brantley's grasp. Although we disagreed on many things, this man could teach me a lot about being fearless. He settled me in my familiar spot behind Navar's long neck, her gray-blue hide smooth and cool beneath my grip. She turned her head, making her floppy ears sway. Long-lashed, limpid eyes blinked over her perpetual grin. Then she wriggled against the makeshift harness Brantley had designed. If we found seeds, herbs, or wild grain, he'd assemble a raft, attach it to the straps, and tow back all we could carry.

Brantley lifted his fist and traced a tight circle. Then he pointed toward the distant land. Navar's spine rolled with enthusiasm, and she surged forward over the waves.

I squinted ahead. When the Order had shackled our world in place, it stopped traveling through the rich nourishment of various currents. Crops had been poor for years and fishing slim. A key point when we'd argued with Saltar Kemp.

Just two days before, we'd been up at the Order, sitting in her office and debating plans. I had chewed my lip but then squared my shoulders. "With respect, Saltar Kemp, you're isolated up here and well provisioned from the taxes levied under Tiarel. I've visited many villages. Several species of fruit trees have died off. Lenka trees all over the island are shriveling with disease. Tubers are stubby and gnarled. The people outside of Middlemost are suffering. They need our help."

Brantley crossed his arms. "I know the new current will improve fishing eventually, but rimmers are still going hungry. If the new land has resources to share, it will be worth any danger."

"I don't want to risk losing you," Saltar Kemp said quietly. Even as we argued, her eyes brimmed with warmth. "There has been so much change already, and the adjustment has not been easy. But I have to admit the saltars and rim leaders are leaning toward accepting your offer to explore."

Before Brantley could seize the tacit approval, an attendant had rushed into the office with news: Watchers at the telescope had seen the island shifting course. It was moving away.

"No more time for endless meetings and debate." Brantley stood, rocking side to side as if already riding Navar. "I'm going to find whatever the new land can offer."

Saltar Kemp twisted her hands together. "And you?" The gaze that had excelled at analyzing my dance technique now analyzed my soul. Did I have the courage and strength for this? Was I listening for the Maker's guidance or bounding ahead into folly?

"Would you rather send a dancer who is whole?" I asked. My wounded tendon throbbed in reminder of my weakness.

The High Saltar actually snorted. "Carya, there is no one I would trust with this more than you. If Brantley is determined to go, the other saltars will demand a representative of the Order to accompany him."

He had grinned then, and we left her office with her final words ringing in our ears. "Bring her back to us, herder."

Now my toes dangled, catching splashes of water, and I tasted sweet ocean spray on my lips. In spite of the possible perils ahead and the desperate need of our people, I stretched my arms in a happy sigh. After hobbling around the Order with its harsh walls and rigid cobblestones, riding the wild ocean set me free.

"Admit it." Brantley nudged my hip with his foot. "You missed this."

I grinned but kept my face forward so he wouldn't see. "I do like spending time with Navar." I patted her rubbery withers, and she whistled and chirped her approval.

Brantley barked a laugh. "Navar? And what about her herder?"

I glanced back at him. Knees slightly bent, he rode the waves as if he belonged to the sea. Though the shadows of injustice, violence, and death had cast hard lines into the set of his jaw, my heart warmed to see how wind and waves softened the edges. He was a good man with a noble heart, though he would probably scoff at me if I said such a thing aloud.

"I suppose I've gotten used to having you around too," I finally admitted.

He laughed again, his chest full of sea air and confidence.

I tightened my headscarf, tucking stray hairs back under control and wishing I could tuck my emotions away as easily. Though I was no longer in the Order, it still seemed wrong to even contemplate a life attached to another. Yet when I was with Brantley, he had a way of making the impossible seem probable. Which was why I had to find a better way to hide my affection for him. Letting him believe in a future to which I could not commit only fed false hopes.

As if reading my thoughts, Brantley leaned down and squeezed my shoulder. "Stop worrying. Everything will work out."

I looked over my shoulder again at safety and home. Meriel's shoreline undulated with the waves, then pulled away and grew smaller. The river that now led all the way inland to Middlemost cut a path through willows and ferns. Upland, taller pines painted dark green swaths. Higher ground offered glimpses of meadows and farmlands. Vertigo swept over me at being untethered from everything familiar. By the time we reached the foreign island, we probably wouldn't be able to see our home. We could be lost forever in the vast ocean. "Are you sure Navar will find her way back?"

"She's always brought me safely home." He whistled a signal to his stenella. "Hold on."

My legs tightened against Navar's sleek body. The folded fins along her side expanded into wide wings. She caught an updraft, and we rose. I sipped in a sharp breath and held it. The view was spectacular. I'd learned to enjoy short glides, but not when she rose this high above the water.

Brantley shielded his eyes. "Still quite a distance. I hope we reach it by nightfall."

I tried to follow his gaze, but the height created dizzying patterns on the waves, and I squeezed my eyes shut until Navar lowered back to the ocean's surface. Air exploded from my lungs. I collapsed forward to hug as much of her neck as I could reach.

Brantley chuckled, and I wished for something to throw at him. I'd like to see him take a pattern test under the unforgiving glare of the saltars. Then I could laugh at *his* fears.

We rode all the rest of the day, eating an occasional saltcake. Navar grabbed a few surface fish without pausing. I was grateful she refrained from diving deep for her lunch. The last time I'd ridden her during a dive, I'd nearly drowned.

The primary sun dipped into the sea, and the subsun cast long shadows before we drew near the new island.

"Look at the gulls." An eager lilt colored Brantley's voice at this sign of good fishing.

The birds danced their own pattern of hopeful swoops and circles. My misgivings slipped into the background as I appreciated their acrobatics. *Dearest Maker, thank You for designing so much beauty.*

My forehead bunched. Could I speak to Him out here? Did He abide on the currents this far away from Meriel? He was the One who had shaped our island and guided all her people—though that knowledge had been lost to us for years. But would this new place introduce me to a different Maker? A chill lifted the hairs on my arms, and I rubbed them.

The deep and silent voice for which I'd learned to listen gave a low chuckle. *"My child, I am the One. The Maker of all."* Awe sent a different kind of shiver through me.

"Are you cold?" Without waiting for an answer, Brantley pulled a cloak from his pack and draped it around my shoulders.

I stiffened against the warmth that his kindness kindled in my chest. My childhood in the Order had taught me to neither expect nor need compassion. Since meeting Brantley, I'd tasted the sweetness of another's support, and I feared I'd lean on it too much. Being cared for was too alluring. I needed to keep my focus on the purpose of our journey. "Do you think we'll find persea fruit?" I called over my shoulder. "Or tubers? Or stinging lanthrus? How much can we bring back before the lands are too far apart?"

"We'd have an easier time if the dancers would steer Meriel closer."

"Saltar Kemp has the dancers performing the old turning pattern to keep Meriel in place, but she won't use that for long." That pattern had bound our world for a generation. Kemp didn't want to make the mistakes of recent High Saltars. Meriel had new currents to follow, which made this brief opportunity even more crucial.

As we drew nearer, the subsun glinted off the water. My eyes ached from straining to see details of the island ahead of us. Instead of the gently sloping shape of Meriel, brown tangleroot vines wove upward around supple trees I'd never seen before. Thin, green trunks coiled toward the sky, covered with willowlike fronds that stayed in constant motion, stirred by the breeze. Multiple layers deep, the trees, vines, and branches created a vertical wall along the rim almost the height of the many-storied Order tower.

Brantley gave a low whistle. "Guess we don't have to worry about any inhabitants noticing Meriel. They couldn't see out through this forest."

I frowned. "But how will we find a way in?" As I spoke, the subsun dove beneath the horizon, transforming the ocean into a navy carpet studded with the crystal reflections of millions of stars. Any other day, I'd savor the beauty. But I was balanced on the back of a sea creature, out of sight of my home, facing a menacing wall of . . .

Something brushed against my foot, and I squeaked, yanking my feet out of the water.

"Told you there would be fish. Now if only we could find a spot to toss them." Brantley coaxed Navar into another upward surge, but this time she didn't find an updraft, so we quickly splashed back to the surface. With no place to go ashore, we skimmed along the foliage wall for what seemed like miles, a starlit carpet on one side and a black wall of trees on the other.

Eventually, Navar slowed. Brantley sank down and settled both his legs along the side of her body that faced the island. After another low whistle, she stopped swimming and stretched like a weary dancer after class.

Brantley patted her flank. "She needs a rest."

A knot twisted in my stomach. "Maybe we should go back."

"How does that give her a rest?" Brantley's chiding tone made me bristle.

I crossed my arms. "Maybe a slow swim . . ." As Navar relaxed deeper into the ocean, water lapped higher on my ankles. I bit my lip. "Will she sink?"

Brantley reached down and scooped up a drink of water, then offered his cupped hands to me. The honeyed flavor still startled me, since I'd been raised on the filtered water of the Order, but with my second sip I savored the milky, sweet liquid. It filled my stomach better than the saltcakes we'd nibbled throughout the day.

"She's not going to sink. Navar is a stenella, not a stone. You really haven't gotten over your fear of the water, have you?"

Fear? It was common sense to be intimidated by the vastness of the waves. I swung my arm outward. "All this emptiness."

"Exactly." His teeth flashed in the darkness. "Space to breathe. To think."

My lips quirked. "You would look at it that way. And what grand thoughts do you harbor when you're out herding?"

Brantley grabbed my arm. "Hush!"

I stiffened. Was he objecting to a little friendly conversation to pass the time?

He sprang to stand, every muscle tight and alert. "Hear that?"

Faint murmurs lifted from beyond the barrier of plants. Brantley crouched and tapped a silent signal to Navar. She eased closer to the island. A trilling laugh rose above the other sounds. None of the creatures in our forests made that noise. I leaned out, reaching toward the saplings. "It sounds almost like—"

A piercing melody skipped up and down a scale, while a drum added a beat.

"People!" Brantley gripped my shoulder so I wouldn't topple into the water.

We were drifting on a weary stenella, a half day from safety, with no way to retreat. Yet in spite of the way my heart pattered nervous triplets with the drums, I drew an eager breath. "We have to find a way through those vines."

THE LITHE TREES ALONG THE SHORE BRAIDED AROUND
each other, interlocking roots disappearing below the shadowed surface.
Was there truly no way past them? I eased onto my knees, then managed
to stand on Navar's back with precarious balance, fearful that in her
weary state a sudden wave might make her flinch or rock, plunging me
into the unending darkness below. My toes curled as if to dig in to her
smooth hide.

From deep within the island, another peal of laughter lifted toward
the stars. I faced the snarl of trees, confronting the impenetrable barrier.

Brantley drew his knife and grasped the closest sapling. "I'll get us
in there."

"Wait!" I grabbed his arm. "You can't start hacking at everything."

"Why not?"

I huffed. "Give me a minute." I leaned forward and touched one of the
trees, the trunk smooth and cool to my palm. A breeze tossed some of the
willowy branches, and they brushed against my face and the bare skin of
my arms. My nerves tingled.

Brantley shifted his position and held my waist with one arm, steadying
me. "What are you doing?"

"I'm not sure."

"That's helpful." His sarcasm bit, likely stirred by frustration, so I
forgave him. At least he fell silent.

Eyes closed, I felt the pulsing of the roots pulling in nourishment,
the swishing bend of branches, and the clenching grip of trees weaving
around one another. If this were a rhythm played out in the center ground
of Meriel, what would the dance pattern look like?

Encumbered by my wounded leg and the limited space on Navar's back, I began with a small gesture. I moved my free arm in sinewy shapes that curled over my head. Brantley gave me room but kept one hand on my hip to steady me.

Like a heartbeat, the gentle thrum of life provided a rhythm for the barrier trees and for me. I joined their subtle swaying. Part of me was still conscious of my narrow perch and the warmth of Brantley's body behind me, but I was also immersed into the foreign dance of this new world, as the trees played with the wind and rode the swells.

Instinct guided me more than dance training. When I released the tree, I still resonated to the deep, inaudible rhythm of the forest. Continuing to sway, my arms carved forward and open, all without losing the tempo of undulating life.

Before us, two of the saplings unwound and eased apart, revealing a mat of tangleroot. I smiled at the welcome and stepped forward. The rich, woodsy scent surrounded me.

"Hey! What are you doing?" Brantley yanked me back, almost casting me off the far side of Navar. The trees wove in and apart uncertainly but continued to beckon us forward.

"Stop that." I found my balance and brushed his hands away. "I'm finding a way in."

"You mean your"—he flittered his fingers in a mocking gesture—"dancer stuff works way out here?"

I pinched the space between my eyebrows. "I was about to find out."

"You can't plunge in there without me."

"I wasn't plunging anywhere. And there's nothing to be afraid of. The trees are welcoming us."

He scoffed but tucked away his knife. "Let me go first."

"Maybe you should wait with Navar. You make it harder for me to concentrate."

His teeth flashed. "You never mentioned that before."

Warmth flared across my face. I chose to ignore his teasing and stepped onto the waiting mat of weeds. The springy surface bounced, inviting me to join the playful actions of land and flora. In a few more steps, a cluster of saplings blocked my progress. I laid my hand on the smooth bark and listened again. Beneath the rhythms of living and moving, a deep and mournful voice called to me. "*Forgotten.*"

I gasped and pulled my hands away.

"What is it?" Brantley's whisper sent his hot breath across my ear. He had joined me on the path.

"Nothing." I didn't want to stop and explain. With most of my weight on my strong leg, I traced a new pattern, letting ripples roll through my torso and out my fingertips. More trees parted, and I limped forward. The tangleroot surface merged into a covering of dirt, and still I walked inland, Brantley a restless shadow at my back.

Once more, laughter rang out straight ahead. Through the thinning branches, hints of light flickered. I rested timid hands on the trees again. The inaudible voice repeated a distant thrum: *Forgotten, forgetting, forsaking.*

The ache of the Maker's heart pulsed through me, and I curled forward. Perhaps Meriel was not the only world that had made Him grieve. What would that mean for our expedition? Had He brought me here for a reason beyond providing supplies? I tucked the notion away to ponder later.

"What's wrong?" Worry wove through my companion's taut whisper.

Why hadn't he stayed with Navar? This wasn't the time or place to debate about the Maker's voice, so instead of answering, I crept ahead to a small gap in the underbrush. Brantley crouched beside me as we peered inland.

Several huge bonfires crackled and poured light onto a wide clearing covered with daygrass—an area large enough to hold half of Windswell village. A huge kettle hung over one of the fires, and even from our distance I caught the spicy scent of herbs mingling with savory meat and sweet ocean water. Sizeable buildings, mostly two-story, rimmed the clearing. Built from twisting tree limbs, they rocked gently as waves rolled underfoot. Unlike the rim cottages of our world, these didn't even creak from the constant shifts.

Near one of the bonfires, music makers played wooden pipes and drums on a raised platform. One man embraced a carved frame strung with thin boughs like those that dangled over our heads, but stripped of their leaves and stretched taut. He plucked them in an ever-shifting harmony, the tone rising sweetly over the other sounds.

My jaw gaped at the beauty and strangeness of the village, but the people themselves made me catch my breath. Men and women moved around the clearing in robes with wide sleeves that flared like wings. Golden embroidery caught the light and reflected against the rich crimson, azure, and emerald fabrics. No one wore the headscarf of a dancer, and their hair displayed a startling variety of shades and shapes. Elaborate braids framed the faces of many of the women, loops dangling down and pulled up again to pile atop their heads. A few children skipped around underfoot despite the lateness of the hour. Their cheeks were full and bellies plump, a startling contrast to the gaunt and weary faces we'd left on our world.

The musicians paused to confer about their next piece, then struck up a new song. Beside me, Brantley's fingers moved as if he were playing along on his whistle. The men in the clearing sang out, "No need for sadness, celebrate gladness, create and savor, taste every flavor." The deep voices made the whole forest resonate.

Because of my years in the Order, music still overwhelmed me, and I pressed my hands near my ears, not wanting to miss anything, but ready to mute the volume if needed.

A woman in the group selected one of the men and took his hands, her voice caroling above in an echoing descant. They moved in a mirror of each other, gliding to the side, circling, arms changing positions in unison. The wide, bright sleeves exaggerated the movement, creating the appearance of birds in flight. One by one the other men and women found partners until the whole clearing spun with glorious movement and song. I'd never seen anything like it. This chaos and color was a startling contrast to the white-clad dancers of the Order, who were carefully uniform. Nor was it like the gatherings in the rim villages, where the more daring indulged in a bit of playful music or dance.

My muscles flexed, and my chest expanded. After watching their patterns long enough to remember them, every corner of my soul drew me with a desire to join in.

Brantley's hand on my shoulder tugged me back; I'd begun to inch forward without realizing it. "What are you doing?" he whispered.

I dragged my gaze from all the beauty and crouched beside him again. We had no plan for this. We'd expected to gather a bit of food, load a raft, and bring it back to Meriel. "Let's go ask them for help. Clearly their world provides them with plenty."

Brantley snorted. "It's been my experience that those with the most wealth are least likely to part with it."

While we argued, the song ended. Laughter broke out, friendly embraces ensued, the musicians left the platform, and adults swept the few children into their arms and headed inland toward the tall buildings. A lanky man scooped remnants from the large kettle, while a woman banked the fire, leaving the last logs to glow and crumble. The tang of woodsmoke tickled my nose and stirred memories of camping in the midrim while fleeing the Order. The villagers' flickering torches illuminated teasing glimpses of their homes inland: gilded carvings, winding staircases leading to upper stories, hints of paths and gardens.

I straightened. "We're losing our chance."

Brantley yanked me down. "We'll wait until morning."

"Meriel is drifting farther away. The odds of finding our way back grow slimmer by the hour. And you want to delay? That's ridiculous."

"We don't know what weapons they have. We don't know how they'll respond to outsiders." His grip on my arm tightened, as if trying to infuse me with his memories of attacks and swords and death.

"Whatever we'll face, waiting won't help us."

"Navar needs rest. If we have to escape, we need her to be able to outrun any pursuit."

His worries coiled in my stomach and slithered up my throat. "Do you think these people ride stenellas too?"

"We don't know. That's my point. In the morning we'll be able to watch them and decide how to approach. Follow me."

He strode back the way we'd come, leaving cool air to swirl around me, raising goose bumps on my arms. I cast one last rebellious glance toward the fading flickers of torchlight and the villagers settling into their homes. His arguments were logical. Frustratingly so. I scampered to catch up to him. "Promise me you'll let me approach them in the morning. You're too . . ."

"Confident? Persuasive?" he asked helpfully, a swagger in his steps.

I fought back a grin. "I was thinking tactless and intimidating."

He scoffed but held back a low branch so I could duck through. "We'll stay on Navar for the night."

My shoulders slumped. Every muscle ached from riding all day, and the back of my ankle pulsed as if shards of glass slid back and forth across my tendon. "Couldn't we make camp on the—"

The howl of a creature overhead rose and then fell with gibbering cackles. My lips pressed together. No more arguments from me. I hurried after Brantley and scrambled onto Navar's back, tucking a hand under the harness. We would face the unknown when the primary sun appeared.

"You plan to sit like a High Saltar at the head table all night?" Brantley's husky voice indicated that he had settled close behind me.

I relaxed my spine a bit, keeping my death grip on the harness strap.

He wrapped his arms around me, coaxing me to lean back. His

chest welcomed my body with more comfort than a mattress ticking, and his warmth surrounded me.

What was I doing? I shouldn't encourage our growing closeness. He was an untamed rimmer who had spent his life herding fish. I had grown up as a novitiate in the Order, perfecting my skills as a dancer and pledging to forsake all attachments. He was bold and brazen. I was trained to follow instructions without question. Our one common bond had formed when we agreed the Order had become corrupt, but even then we'd pursued different paths to bring change.

Yet, sinking deeper into his arms, I felt a rare sensation of belonging. A happy sigh escaped my lungs, even as my eyelids drooped. *Dearest Maker, please, if there is a way to make this work . . .*

The strange noises from the island, the gentle rocking movement of Navar, and the scent of sweet ocean and unknown vegetation all combined into a disorienting lullaby. A soft smile curved my lips.

Brantley adjusted his grip on me and rested his chin against the top of my head. "I wish I'd brought more weapons."

Weapons? I bristled. More proof that our approaches to life were incompatible. After watching the villagers dance, I was positive the people of this island were friendly. Tomorrow I'd prove that to Brantley.

3

THE PRIMARY SUN DREW STREAKS OF AMBER AND MAUVE across the ocean, illuminating the trees and vines. What had appeared menacing the night before now seemed lush and inviting with its varied shades of greens and browns. Navar stretched her long neck upward, then swiveled to blink at me.

"Good morning to you too." I stroked her sinewy neck and offered my palm. She nuzzled my hand, her skin cool and smooth as leather. Then she chortled a greeting toward Brantley.

He groaned and rubbed his back. He couldn't have slept much, sitting upright on a stenella all night. Even so, his eyes brightened as he looked inland. He rummaged in his pack and handed me a saltcake. "No one attacked us in the night. That's a promising start."

I frowned at him as I chewed. "Why do you insist on expecting the worst?"

He reached down and scooped up a drink, then wolfed his saltcake in a few bites. "Expect the worst and you're ready for anything." Dusting crumbs from his tunic, he launched to his feet on Navar's back with the smooth balance born of a lifetime of riding the waves. Sunlight glinted off the pale stubble on his jaw, and he grinned. His hand slid reflexively to the longknife in his belt.

I rose awkwardly to my feet and faced him. "Or imagine the best and do all you can to make it happen."

"Sounds like one of the Order's proverbs."

The rebuke pinched. Had I really not shaken off their indoctrination? "I'm not in the Order anymore."

He pulled his gaze from the mysterious island and studied me. "I don't suppose you'll wait with Navar while I go in and scope out the situation?"

I stepped to the nearby tangleroot rim, grasping one of the saplings by the path for support. "You suppose correctly."

Instead of further argument, he laughed and joined me on shore. The trees had not knitted back together. They remained drawn apart far enough to provide a narrow path, although if they decided to close again, we'd never find a way back to the sea. Plant life barred us in every direction save this one, oppressive, humid, unyielding. If green had a scent, this was it. Rich, heavy, and salty, as if the plants were sweating. I quickened my steps to reach the clearing.

We stepped into the open field, expecting to greet those we'd seen dancing there the night before, but were greeted by silence. I took a few tentative steps toward the remnants of a bonfire. The sharp odor of burnt charcoal lingered. "Where is everyone? The primary sun has been up for a while."

Brantley scanned in all directions, even examining the sky above the distant buildings. "Maybe no one wakes until the subsun rises." He pointed to a grove of persea trees lining one side of the clearing near us. "At least there's fruit to gather."

I crossed my arms. "They don't belong to us."

"So what's your plan, dancer?" He rubbed the back of his neck, then rolled his head to one side, small bones cracking in protest.

I could show him a dancer exercise that would ease his stiffness, but I doubted he'd appreciate my suggestion. Instead, I waved toward the houses. "You wanted to lurk and observe, but there's nothing to watch. Let's walk to the buildings and look for a matriarch's home. We can introduce ourselves."

He grasped my elbow and drew me into the shadows under the persea trees. "If they react badly, we will be outnumbered . . . and surrounded."

"So what's *your* plan?" I shifted my weight to my good leg and jutted my chin at him.

He waggled his eyebrows. "Watch for the stray that leaves the herd." His eyes held the gleam of a forest hound on the hunt. I'd seen this man whittle toys for his niece, agonize over the wounds of his stenella, and tenderly embrace his mother. Yet the untamed wildness of his nature never fully left him. I shivered, unsure whether it was with fear or attraction.

He snatched a low-hanging persea, pried away the bumpy skin, and offered me a piece. Despite my earlier scolding, I was sure the villagers wouldn't begrudge visitors one little fruit. I savored the creamy texture on my tongue. The rich flavor was familiar, but an astringent aftertaste lingered that reminded me I was on a different world. "It tastes . . . younger."

Brantley swallowed his bite and met my eyes. Laugh lines deepened. "Look." He gestured past the first rows of trees. Stretching inland, every fruit-bearing tree I'd ever seen—and many I hadn't—flourished. Their limbs bent with bounty. Neglected fruit even littered the ground beneath.

My eyes widened. "How big of a raft can you build?"

He chuckled. "All we need to bring back are seeds and rootings. If the Order can find a way to steer our course closer, we could recruit every herder with a working stenella to make trips between—"

A door creaked in the distance. Brantley put a finger to his lips.

I hobbled behind one of the trunks, its bark as knobby as its fruit. Brantley, more able-footed, darted closer to the sound and ducked into the cover of shoulder-high ferns. A young man made his way down a winding staircase on the outside of one of the two-story structures. His long, fiery hair reminded me of my friend Starfire, though his plump physique bore no comparison to any dancer of the Order. He stretched his arms overhead with a generous yawn, then ambled toward the grove where we hid.

Brantley glanced back at me. "A stray," he mouthed. Then he signaled me to stay, as if he were directing his stenella.

I wasn't about to let him frighten someone who could be an ally. Instead I stepped from behind the tree. "Good morning."

The youth stopped several paces from me and tilted his head.

"Bountiful day to you and yours." His eyebrows gathered in an auburn bunch. "Have we met in this season? Be you recollecting?"

He spoke our language, although with a lilt that forced me to concentrate to follow his words.

"No, we're visitors." I glanced to Brantley, still crouched out of sight, his muscles tight and ready to spring. "Unsure of our welcome."

When the young man laughed, his cheeks rounded like ripe peaches. "Why unsure? Surely all be welcome. I'm Morra." He presented one leg and leaned forward, flourishing with his arm.

"I'm Carya of Meriel." I copied his movement.

That sent Morra into peals of laughter. Brantley eased to his feet, hand still resting on the hilt of his longknife. "We've come a long distance seeking supplies for our people."

Morra blinked at the sight of another stranger rising from the bracken but then grinned and bowed again.

My companion only glared in response. Why was Brantley still on guard? This youngling was close in age to Teague, Brantley's apprentice in Windswell. He was nothing but amiable. Certainly no threat.

Seeming unaware of the tension, Morra plucked a lenka from a branch overhead and popped the small yellow fruit in his mouth. He picked a few more and tossed them toward Brantley. "If supplies be sought, supplies be found."

The fruit lay where it fell. Brantley narrowed his eyes. "Are you saying your village elders won't mind if we gather fruit to take back to our people?"

Confusion knitted the boy's brow. "Why would they? There is always more." Then his face cleared. "Ah, you be newly disconnected, yes? I've heard tell that the newly disconnected are sometimes bewildered."

I had no idea what he was talking about, but time was wasting. "May we speak to your elders? Do you have a matriarch?"

Morra waved back toward the buildings. "Speak with whom you will. Elder or younger. Matters not."

Brantley rubbed his temples. "Who is your leader?"

The young man barked another laugh. "Any and all. Any and all." He sketched another bow and strolled away, singing a ditty of "any and all" over and over.

Brantley gave a low growl.

I bit my lip, trying to find something positive in the encounter. "Do you think we need to seek permission from everyone in this village? Whom do we talk to if there's no leader?"

"We need to find someone less addled." Brantley picked up a few of the fallen lenka and handed them to me. "At least we won't go hungry."

I stared at the unusual buildings and chewed thoughtfully. Tart juice trickled down my throat. My tongue worried the pit around my mouth, extracting every bit of flavor before I spat out the hard seed. "It doesn't look like anyone else is awake. Maybe I should collect all the lenka and persea I can carry. We were given an invitation to help ourselves to those."

"And I'll build the raft. We can take a load back today and let others know what we've found. If we can gather a dozen herders, each rim village can restock supplies before the lands drift too far apart." Brantley dropped his pack, pulled the knife from his belt, and hacked at a few saplings and vines. Now that we were making tangible progress, his whole body radiated new energy. His strong arms swung with the confidence of skill, almost like a novitiate performing an oft-repeated pattern.

I smiled, glad he couldn't read my thoughts. Being compared to a dancer wouldn't sit well with him. He'd thought of us as the vilest of enemies for too many years. With cause. I sobered. Even if I came to believe it possible, would he ever want to attach himself to a former dancer like me? I shook my head to dislodge the disturbing question and rummaged in his pack for a net bag to hold the harvest.

A few light shakes of the lenka trunks released a wealth of fruit, and I scurried around, dropping them into the bag. The netting stretched, and still I gathered more. I glanced over to where Brantley was already lashing branches together with the rope he always carried in his pack. "Make the raft as big as you can. I've never seen such a huge supply."

Brantley laughed. "Orianna will love you forever when you bring lenka to Windswell."

I grinned. His young niece knew how to enjoy a meal. And lenka had been a rare delicacy in recent years. Too many trees on Meriel had withered as our island spun in place, their roots missing the variety of nutrients they once absorbed from traveling across the ocean. How long would it take for them to recover? I scrabbled beneath more of the trees and gathered a variety of seeds in a cloth pouch, which I tied onto the net.

Brantley hefted the long, narrow base of his raft. "I'll finish constructing this at the shore. Let's bring what you've got so far."

I glanced again at the silent village, still nervous that someone would protest. "Good idea."

I dragged the bulging net of fruit and followed him as he made for the path.

Brantley stopped short, turned, and scanned the clearing. "Where did we come in?"

"On the far side of the largest bonfire pit." I limped past him toward the edge of the clearing, then released the heavy bag. No opening appeared in the tight wall of saplings and vines. "The path was right here, wasn't it?"

Brantley left the partially constructed raft and stalked along the edge of the clearing again for good measure. "I can't see a single opening now."

I placed my palms against two saplings that offered a space only a tiny child could squeeze past. "The trees must have reverted to their old places. Don't worry. I'll ask them for a new path."

After I pulled off my soft leather shoes, my bare feet embraced the warm earth. I closed my eyes, listening for the rhythm of waves rolling underfoot, branches bobbing in the wind, leaves rustling, and vines straining to hold the wall of foliage together. My toes flexed a few times in readiness. Despite my limp, my legs took up the swaying movement, and soon my arms repeated the languid pattern I'd used the day before. I smiled as I joined the dance of the forest.

When I opened my eyes, a wall of dark green still rose before me. I tried again. I felt no resistance, no argument from the underbrush. Simply no response.

A zephyr whispered across the back of my neck, sending a chill all the way down to my feet.

Brantley stepped beside me and touched one of the trees. "It's not working."

"I can see that. Give me space."

He lifted his hands and moved away. This time I danced with more force, praying with my side-to-side steps. *Holy Maker, open a way for us.*

The Maker didn't speak, and the forest continued to ignore me.

"Are you done?" Brantley met my bewilderment with a firm thrust of his chin. "I'll clear a path."

He hacked away several vines and bent smaller saplings to the side. At first I thought his efforts would work. We wouldn't be able to squeeze the raft through the opening, but we could at least return to the ocean rim. I picked up the net bulging with fruit, hoping I could maneuver it back to Navar.

But before we could move forward, the saplings sprang back. New vines erupted from the ground faster than Brantley could chop them away.

Sweat beaded his brow, and he tackled a new section. *Please work.* If he couldn't clear the way, what would we do? I leaned forward, wanting to urge him to chop faster, but I held my tongue. He created a tantalizing gap, but then the same thing happened. Plants grew back before either of us could step forward.

The chill running through my spine now wrapped cold fingers around my lungs and squeezed. "We can't get out," I whispered. "Could the forest be angry? I mean, you chopped down a lot of trees to build the raft."

Brantley swiped the heel of his hand across his forehead in an abrupt and irritated gesture. "Are you blaming me for this?"

"I'm only trying to figure out what changed."

He gestured at the beginning structure of a raft. "Well, I can't very well put limbs back onto the trees, can I? Maybe you shouldn't have gathered all the lenka."

I bit back an annoyed response and took a deep breath. "Let's not panic. Morra said we were welcome to the fruit."

Brantley directed his focus upward. The wall of trees was as tall as the Order with its many floors of dormitories, but he'd scaled those walls to rescue his niece. "Help me untie my rope." He slid a branch free from the frame he'd been creating and began to unwind the cord he'd used to bind the wood together.

I pried another knot free. "Are you seriously planning to climb? We don't know how stable those thin trunks are. And we've seen them shift position. What if they move while you're up there?"

His hands stilled, and he looked at me with one of the smiles that sent heat throughout my innards. "Are you worried about me?" His eyes warmed with understanding and affection. "I'll make you a deal. If you stop being overprotective, I'll do the same."

I returned a reluctant grin of acknowledgement. "We do tend to worry for each other, don't we?"

Still crouched across from the broken-apart raft pieces, he reached out and tapped my nose. "It's what folks do who care about each other."

Now the heat spread outward to my skin, and I dropped my gaze to the stubborn knot. I needed to set him straight. Our relationship held no future. But this wasn't the time for a heartfelt discussion. The fibers loosened, and I unraveled another section. "The Maker's letter reminds us to not give fear a place to bloom."

He chuckled. "Not bad advice, wherever the words come from."

As soon as the length of rope was free, he coiled it neatly and approached the nearest tree. "I'll climb to the highest point I can and see if I can find another path to the sea." The drooping branches were soft and pliable, making it difficult to toss the end over anything secure. Eventually he targeted a sturdier limb, caught it, and eased the free end down. He used the doubled cord to help him shinny halfway up the forest wall.

I held my breath as he gathered the rope and took aim at the treetops. Beneath my feet, a stronger wave rolled under the surface of the land. Brantley clung like a dragonfly on a wind-blown reed. Once the latest rocking eased, he climbed farther.

Dizziness swirled like star rain inside my head as I watched him. There were times I admired his boldness, but other times I wanted to scream at the risks he took. Yes, I worried about him. *It's what folks do who care about each other*, he'd said. How much did I care about him? Clearly too much. The Order had taught me that attachments were intrusions that hindered our work. Was that why my movements this morning had been ineffective at creating a path? Was I becoming too distracted?

"Do you see a way through?" I called to him. Did he intend to make his way across the upper canopy all the way to the ocean? What of me? With my wounded leg, I couldn't climb there.

He worked his way down to the end of his rope, then pulled it loose and prepared to continue the rest of the way to the ground. A gust of wind rocked the trees, and he fumbled for his grip. I hissed in a sharp breath, then held it until his arms found a sturdy trunk. When the movement slowed, he resumed his descent, then dropped to the earth and dusted off his hands. One of his palms was bleeding from all the sliding and gripping—or perhaps some of the vines hid thorns. Unconcerned, he blew over the tear in his skin, then shook it.

"Stop that. You'll make it worse." I pulled off my headscarf and wrapped it around his hand, securing it with a tiny knot.

He grinned. "Will you kiss it and make it better?"

I stepped back and crossed my arms. "Other than risking your life, what use was that climb?"

He tilted his head, brow wrinkling at my irritated tone. "It was worth checking for another path. Nothing the way we came in, so we'll need to search along the sides of the village. Let's avoid being seen by anyone else. We can look on the far edge of—"

Behind us in the village, a door slammed open. Two children raced from one of the houses into the clearing, then saw us and skidded to a stop. A large-boned woman stomped after them, then noticed us and backpedaled. She called to the row of buildings, and several other doors opened. More and more villagers emerged. A heavyset man in wide-legged trousers and an impractical gauzy cloak waddled toward us. His expression held much less welcome than Morra had offered.

A woman leaned out a window and shouted to her neighbor. More voices rose in a buzz of discussion that sounded hostile, even from our distance.

With our backs to the impenetrable forest, Brantley edged in front of me, hand resting on the hilt of his longknife. Dozens of strangers advanced toward us, and we had no way of escape.

4

THE LARGEST MAN ELBOWED PAST THE OTHERS AND stomped past one of the charred fire pits, his florid face glowering. "My favorite mug be missing. No doubt you be the thieves."

My eyes widened. The other villagers held back, but hostility painted their faces under the low angle of the morning rays. Brantley still stood protectively in front of me, but I sidestepped and put my hand on his fighting arm. A calm explanation could still diffuse this situation. I kept my voice level. "Morra said we could gather fruit. We're no thieves."

"Fruit?" The man's hairy eyebrows jutted outward like two alarmed hedgehogs. "It's me mug I'm missing."

Beneath my palm, Brantley's muscles tightened. "We had nothing to do with that." His arm flexed, and he slid his knife half free of its sheath.

Leaning into him, I whispered, "Sometimes bracing for battle can cause the battle."

He scoffed but pushed the knife back into its sheath.

A woman caught up to the man and put a hand to his arm. "Harba, it's too early in the morning for this bellowing. What be your concern?" Her soothing voice contrasted with her sharp features. Angular eyebrows, painted black, jutted down from the border of her white-blonde hair, which was cut in a jagged pattern around her face. A sky-blue robe enveloped her thin frame and trailed on the ground. A breeze riffled the fabric, and the tall trees behind us whispered.

At her touch, Harba transformed from snorting bull to placid lamb. He rubbed his belly. "Weren't finding my mug. Head hurts, and these be strangers."

She rolled her eyes. "Your mug be where you dropped it in the dirt after the revels. And your head hurts because it's nearing time for the convening."

His expression brightened. "Be there punch to tide me over?"

"Of course. Go ask someone." She gestured to the cluster of villagers. Most had turned back to their activities and resumed their conversations, with only a few studying us from beyond the empty fire pits. How odd that strangers should rouse so little curiosity.

Harba toddled off, seeming to forget us. The woman stepped closer, one dark brow lifting. "You must hail from a far village?"

I offered a tentative smile. "Actually, we're from another—"

"Village," Brantley said loudly. "As you already guessed. Our stocks are low, and we're seeking food." Why had he interrupted? I could see no harm in explaining that we had come from a different island world. They would surely be as enthralled by the discovery of us as we were of them. My companion's goal might be to gather resources with as little interaction as possible, but encountering people on this foreign world was too remarkable for me to ignore. I longed to share knowledge, experience—friendship—with the people here.

"My name is Carya. I'm pleased to meet you." I balanced on my good leg and attempted a small bow, imitating Morra's earlier greeting.

The woman's dark eyebrows disappeared upward under her fringe of white bangs. Apparently I'd used the wrong sort of gesture. She rose up on her toes, then lowered. "And I'm Trilia. You must gather at the red or blue convening. I don't be recalling meeting."

I was dizzy from my efforts to understand these people and their unfamiliar terms, from trying to avoid any offense, and from keeping Brantley's hand off his knife. Guessing at the best course to take, I copied Trilia's movements.

The moment my heels touched the ground, her expression cleared, and she smiled. "You've journeyed from beyond the lake, then?"

Brantley and I exchanged a look, and he shrugged.

"We've come a long way," I said. "But now we need to find a way back to the sea. Is it all right if we take home fruit to share with our people?"

The zigzag fringe of her hair shifted around the woman's face as she frowned. "You lack food? How can that be? Be you remnant?" She spat the last word as if it tasted vile.

Brantley likely didn't want me saying too much, but a bit of truth wouldn't go amiss. "Some of our trees have fallen ill," I said, hoping my tone reflected need but not desperation.

"Yes, of course. Take all you can use. But . . ." She glanced toward the orchards of fruit trees ranging inward from the edge of the clearing. When she looked back to us, her lips formed a circle of worry. "Could this illness be spread? Must we fear the Grand Convening?"

Brantley squeezed the bridge of his nose. "No, no. Our trees are a far travel from here. Now, can you guide us to a path to the sea?"

"The sea?" Trilia rolled one shoulder and rubbed her neck, as if she, too, were developing a headache. "Do you speak of the lake?"

Brantley gestured to the wall of foliage behind us. "We found our way in through the trees. Is there another way out?"

The woman stared as us blankly. Then she let out a shriek of laughter. She leaned forward and slapped her thighs, then cavorted in a circle, still giggling. A few of the disinterested villagers who had been lounging on stairs by the homes heard her and jumped up, racing over to learn the joke.

Through gasps of laughter, Trilia pointed to us. "They say . . . they came . . . through the trees."

One young man's jaw dropped open, then his expression shifted to a sly smile. "Oh, that be a new story. A good one."

An old woman snickered. "I don't recollect a tale like that before."

Trilia slapped Brantley on the back. "A fine joke, that one."

Brantley's fingers opened and clenched several times, as if wanting to wring a few necks.

Our efforts were producing nothing but a rising temper in Brantley. If she knew a way through the rim, she wasn't going to tell us. I rose to my toes and lowered, facing Trilia. "Our people will appreciate the fruit."

She shrugged. "Much enjoyment to you and yours." After a quick bob up and down, she and the others meandered off.

Brantley sank to the ground and braced against one of the smooth saplings. The neck of his tunic was dark from a line of sweat. Bits of vine and leaf still tangled in his hair and stuck to his linen trousers from his earlier climb. The lines on his face hardened as he frowned. "Carya, what sort of people care so little about strangers? They didn't demand to know more about us. They didn't seem threatened. They brought out no weapons."

I settled beside him and stretched out my sore ankle. "You say that as if it's a bad thing."

He lowered his chin, his piercing eyes confronting mine. "Even you must sense that something is strange here."

True. I'd heard the plaintive cry of the island the day before. Perhaps some darkness hovered inland, but we wouldn't be staying long enough to find out. Meanwhile the people seemed generous and good-humored, if odd. "It's just as well they aren't interested in us. Let's focus on finding a way out. We're running out of time before Meriel drifts out of reach."

Brantley's harrier-sharp gaze swept the edge of the clearing that we could see from where we sat. Thick foliage loomed dark and foreboding. "I agree. For now, we'll leave the harvest and find our escape."

His use of the word "escape" made my stomach muscles clench. The towering trees and vines seemed to bend inward, and the sense of being trapped heightened. Brantley sprang to his feet and offered his hand. "How is your leg holding up?"

With his assistance, I rose in one graceful motion. "It's healing." The last thing he needed was the added worry of my crippled state. Even his question stirred my deep humiliation. A hobbled dancer was a horror, a travesty. I had yet to come to terms with my identity, but I'd show him I could keep up. "I'm not sure we can avoid people if we're going to search for a path in other parts of the clearing."

Inland, the village buzzed with activity. More and more people had spilled from the buildings, their bright clothing flashing amid the equally bright homes and ornaments. Back home, our cottages were constructed from branch and thatch. These homes also seemed formed of wood, but the wood had been painted with curlicues, wave patterns, and even images of birds and rodents. Laughter dotted every conversation rising from clusters of people, while other individuals strolled along the village's daygrass-covered paths, pausing in front of one shop or another.

Brantley sighed. "We'll search the outer edges first."

His frustration with the villagers tugged a smile from my lips. "And if we don't find a path, I'll talk to more of the villagers so you won't have to."

He chuckled. "I admit I've no liking for the riddles of society. Not even those on Meriel. And these . . ." He swept an arm toward the stage, where three people had settled to play some sort of game, tossing carved wooden shapes and giggling as they landed.

"Perhaps the people of Meriel would be this carefree if not for the shortages and struggles we've faced."

He glowered at a group waving scarves and spinning along a path until they disappeared behind one of the tallest buildings. "Then I'm grateful even for the Order, if the suffering they inflicted on Meriel prevented us from becoming this mindless."

I grinned. Brantley would bravely ride stormy waves to herd fish for his village or rally an army to face down corruption, but he found conversation maddening, especially with people he didn't understand. I, on the other hand, saw the villagers as potential new friends and was intrigued to learn about their world. It was gratifying to know I could help our mission in ways he couldn't.

We left the net of lenka I'd gathered and walked, keeping as much distance as we could from the villagers. For now, we ignored the fruits and nuts and ample tubers sprouting from the rich soil. "Do you really think they have no leader?"

Another cloud passed over Brantley's face. "I'll wager they have a leader, but the person in control is clever enough to hide that fact."

"You're too suspicious. Look how happy everyone is." Back in the Order, every face was tight with fear, gaunt from endless striving to perfect our movements. Villagers of the rim bore dark rings beneath their eyes, drawn by deprivation and uncertainty. Here everyone looked well-fed and happy—if a bit unfocused. By the time we'd skirted the entire clearing in our unsuccessful quest for a path, my curiosity had only grown.

People wandered among the fruit trees, eating or chatting with no observable sense of plan or purpose. A man sat on the edge of the platform near the bonfire, idly plucking a stringed instrument, while a young woman spread parchments on the stage and drew pictures with willow pens of various thicknesses. No one seemed interested in what anyone else was doing, and no one showed particular interest in us. Their attitudes hinted at a peacefulness and security I envied.

"This place is making my skin crawl." Brantley stopped at a point on the far side of the buildings. A trail led inland, which would only take us farther from the sea and our journey home.

The land rippled beneath us, and Brantley softened his knees to adjust his balance. I stabilized myself with a nearby trunk. One of the buildings lurched at the motion, but the supple timber of the homes didn't creak.

We'd tried Brantley's plan, but now I needed to explore the village. "Let me go talk with people. If I can figure out their manner of speech, maybe we'll find someone to tell us how to get through the trees."

Brantley tugged at the makeshift bandage on his hand. "Or maybe someone is blocking our way. If your patterns made the trees part, what's to say someone else didn't make them close?"

He was right. Delving deeper into the village might lead us to people less carefree and blasé. Even people who would wish us harm. Branches rustled overhead, and my nerves prickled as if tiny insects scurried up my spine. I hid my unease under a deep breath. "Whether the village holds an enemy or a potential ally, either way, we can't keep wandering around."

Brantley's shoulders slumped, perhaps a bit of acknowledgement that his desire to avoid people wasn't working. Then he straightened and offered me his arm, probably aware that my limp was growing more pronounced. "Let's go," he said. Eyes alert, jaw set, he had conceded to get acquainted with the people, but he still approached the path as if a battle threatened.

I set a course for the heart of the town. In our world, the gathering lodges often formed the core of rim villages, with the Order poised in the middle of the entire island. A village center seemed a logical place to look for someone more knowledgeable than the people we'd met so far.

In spite of our urgent need to return to Navar, my steps slowed after we passed the outer homes. Beauty assaulted me from each direction. The next layer of buildings held even more elaborate carvings than the outer houses, with brilliant shades of paint and intricately woven vines. Some of the walls looked like a row of novitiates' braids. Others were planed into a smooth surface and bore images that seemed to tell a story. Delicious scents of flowery herbs and astringent lanthrus wafted from a building with a wide-open window, along with a salty whiff that made me lick my lips. I peered inside. A man shaped dough into forms of trees, animals, and humans. On a table, tiny bresh cakes—held together with honey and skill—formed sculptures of enchanted gardens and tantalizing landscapes.

From the second floor of the next building, several voices sang together, their harmonies vibrating enticingly through my bones. I took a few steps toward the outer stairway, but Brantley pulled me away. "Don't get distracted. Look for someone who can answer our questions—if that person even exists."

He was determined to be glum about our prospects. I was too excited by each new discovery to let him drag me into his worries.

"Look at that!" I hobbled away from Brantley's supportive arm to gaze into a gazebo that held display tables. A chandler had created designs in wax dyed with the colors of every fruit or berry I'd ever seen. One was so large that if all its wicks were lit, it would illuminate an entire longhouse.

A squat man with a neck like a tree trunk and a nose as bumpy as persea skin sat on a stool near a table, cutting and shaving a block of wax.

I traced a finger over a small candle in the image of a stenella. "Did you make all of these?"

The man's gaze skimmed over me, and he nodded. "Help yourself."

I pulled my hands back. "Sorry, I have no coin."

His head came up, so thick and heavy on his shoulders I expected it to make a grinding sound. "No what?"

"No way to pay you."

"What matters that?" He rubbed wax-coated fingers up and down his nose. "These be free for the taking."

"That's very generous." I reached for a sculpture of a forest hound beneath a maple tree. Wicks extended from several branches of the tree, and the hound's eyes sparkled with amber color.

A low sound of dismay rumbled in the man's chest. I quickly set the candle back on the table and gave him a questioning look.

"I be having a bit of attachment to that one." He added a heavy sigh. "Good thing tomorrow be the convening, right?"

Brantley cleared his throat to get my attention and cut his eyes to the street. "We need to keep moving."

"I know," I said softly. "One more moment." I moved closer to the man as his fingers continued to shape the wax. "Sir, do you perhaps know the Maker?"

His hands stilled, and he leveled puzzled eyes my direction. "Of course. We are all the maker." He chuckled, the sound like wood splitting, and then returned to his work.

My forehead puckered, but I allowed Brantley to lead me away. All the maker? It sounded like a lovely notion. Certainly it seemed that everyone we'd met was busy creating . . . music and clothing and art of all sorts. But the words prickled my heart like the unexpected brush of a nettle.

"Well, at least we learned that they know the sea. Those barrier trees and vines must have an opening."

Brantley frowned. "He didn't say anything about that."

"The sculpture of the stenella. They must see them."

"Or once did," he said darkly. "There." Brantley quickened his pace toward a three-story building surrounded by a plaza of stone sculptures and potted trees trimmed into triangles and diamonds. Huge carved doors opened outward, allowing glimpses of polished marble floors. "This is where we'll find someone in power," Brantley said and guided me to the yawning doorway.

INSIDE THE VAST LOBBY, TOWERING WOODEN PILLARS surrounded us, some carved and some gilded. A staircase wound along one wall, leading to an inner balcony with doors to rooms on the second level. Paintings and banners cluttered every surface of the walls. Embroidery drew images of clouds and water and copper fish leaping. In one faded corner of a tapestry, a stenella spread its fins and glided in shimmering colors. Another clue that these people had once known the vast ocean and the creatures that swam in it. The depiction made me long for Navar. Was she worried about us? Or when we didn't return, would she simply swim away?

I couldn't let the novelty of this place distract me. We had to find a leader who could answer our questions and help us get back to the sea.

Just as I was about to concede this point to Brantley, raised voices clashed from a side room. A deep voice rumbled, and a shriller voice cut it off. I tiptoed across the marble floor toward the inner doorway and hid to one side, peeking in. I didn't need to worry about being seen. The people inside were too preoccupied to notice us.

Men and women lounged on fabric-covered couches and overstuffed armchairs, their jarring red, orange, and purple robes creating visual chaos. Bowls of fruit and platters of cakes filled a low table. I spotted Morra sitting on the floor as he wove strips of vines together in a decorative basket.

"We can absolutely postpone the convening for a few days." Trilia, the woman I'd met earlier, plucked a lenka from a carved bowl, the angled cuts of her white-blonde hair swinging. "The weather will be better then."

A convening? Other villagers we'd met had mentioned the same thing. I strained to hear more. Perhaps this event would provide a leader, someone who could help us find our way off this island.

A shaggy-haired man with a gray beard lurched to his feet and paced behind the couches. "You're wrong. One of the musicians has grown attached to his latest composition. And at least three couples have been sharing star eyes and were overheard planning to leave messages for each other."

Morra blushed and ducked his chin lower, speeding up the work on his basket.

An old woman with looping braids bunched all her facial wrinkles together and pointed a gnarled finger at Trilia. "He's right. Far too dangerous to wait. I've seen this happen. Years ago—"

Morra raised his head and scoffed. "You be remembering too much. Not a virtue." The others cast the aged woman scornful sneers.

"Very true." She sagged back into the couch, suddenly appearing much older. "I were too ill for the last convening. Weighs on one." The old woman shrank in on herself.

It hurt me to see her disrespected by the others. On Meriel, matriarchs were given the greatest respect—whether in the Order, or midrim villages, or among the rimmers.

I'd watched long enough. I exchanged looks with Brantley, lifting my chin. He rubbed the back of his neck and shook his head but without much conviction. He knew he couldn't stop me.

I limped into the room, rising and lowering in a quick bob. "Greetings. My companion and I need to find a way to the sea. Can any of you help us?"

The old woman pressed a hand over her heart.

Morra grinned. "We be meeting again." He tossed aside his basket and looked at the group. "Forgot to mention we be having visitors."

"From where?" The old woman squinted at us.

Brantley stepped up beside me. "A far village. But now we must reach the sea."

The gray-haired man stroked his beard. "Never heard of that."

Trilia, who was still chewing her lenka, shook her head. "Perhaps they be meaning the lake?"

The rest of the group murmured agreements. "Strangers, if you be confused, the convening is needed. All will be well when you venture on the inland path."

Frustration pulsed against the back of my eyes. "We don't want to go farther inland. We need to reach the shore."

"Today," Brantley bit out. He slid a pouch from his tunic pocket. "Is there anyone who could guide us? We have coin to barter."

The bearded man marched over to us. "I misremember. Have I met a far villager with such strange speech?"

Brantley shook a few coins into his own palm, and the man poked them with little interest, then shrugged and turned away.

My turn to try. "Do you have dancers in your village?"

Morra laughed. "We all dance."

"Yes, I've seen you, and you all move with skill. But I'm asking after those who learn patterns and shape the course of the island." If Brantley's suspicions were right, someone might be preventing the vines and saplings from parting and letting us out.

A few of the people spared a blank stare our direction, then lounged back, dismissing us. "Enough distraction," one woman said. "I still say we must not delay." Immediately others picked up the debate again, brushing us off as if we were no more than annoying splatters of raindrops.

Having a dire need that others didn't even acknowledge was a sharply lonely sensation. The pain of being ignored tied a knot in my chest. "Excuse me," I said loudly.

The debate drowned me out. "Please!" I shouted, clapping several times. This time the room fell silent, and I clenched my hands together. "We have to find a way through the trees. Is there anyone in your village with knowledge of how to do that?"

The bearded man aimed his pacing our direction once more. "We've given our best wisdom. Be you addled to ask again? Leave. Our discussion here is important—"

Gasps rose around the room.

The man pressed a hand over his mouth, then stroked his beard, shame coloring his cheeks. "Apologies. Clearly we must delay the convening no longer."

Morra rose and ambled over, clapping the older man on the back. "Happens to the best of us. I'll see them out."

We followed Morra back to the massive lobby. The gilded pillars no longer stirred my admiration, and the tapestries and sculptures seemed to taunt me. Brantley leaned in. "I don't like this. They aren't merely obtuse. There are secrets here."

I agreed with him. Each hour that passed felt like a thicket closing in, the thorns drawing closer to our skin. I searched for a hopeful word. "At least everyone has been kind and pleasant."

"Better an enemy who declares his intent than one who hides behind a mask of smiles." Brantley spoke in a low growl, but Morra overheard him.

The young man clapped his hands. "Beautiful! Such a saying would be making a good song. Say it again."

Brantley rolled his eyes and stalked ahead. Morra's face fell, and I offered him an apologetic smile. "He's frustrated. We both are. We don't understand why the barrier let us in and now won't let us leave."

Morra barked a laugh, but when I didn't join in, he studied my face. "You aren't crafting a funny tale?" Pity formed in his eyes, changing them from vacuous to almost concerned. "Stayed overlong at your village's convening too many times? I've heard tell. There be stories. Or perhaps the opposite be true? You've missed a convening? You have that look about you."

My head drooped. Nothing here made sense, and I didn't know how to solve this puzzle. And now Brantley was striding far ahead, an angry cast to his shoulders as he brushed past shopkeepers and a girl hefting a basket full of rabbits.

"Hurry along to the furrier," Morra said to the child. "Else the welfen beast will find you and pick your bones clean."

The child paled and raced away, but Morra chuckled as if they'd shared a harmless joke.

"Is she all right?" I asked.

"Aw, she'll be fine. A cute one like that, some of the cloth makers be looking after her so they can dress her up and show off their wares. And tiny fingers be good for the weaving. Now give me another of your strange stories."

"Morra, we haven't been inventing tales. We truly come from far away." How much should I tell him? Would he understand our urgency if I explained that our home might be drifting out of sight this very moment? "If we can't reach the sea soon, it will be very bad for us."

The youth glanced down at my bandaged leg and offered his arm. "The convening is a place where questions be put to rest."

I accepted his help and limped alongside as we tried to catch up to Brantley. "How far is this convening?"

"It be a half-day journey for the fittest to reach the lake." Morra shot another look at my ankle. "And you . . ."

"I could manage. But we really can't head farther inland."

Ahead of us, Brantley stopped near a home that hosted a miniature garden. Flowers were planted in ways that created pictures with their colors. To one side, they shaped the outline of a crimson butterfly with green spots. Brantley's chest rose and fell in deliberate breaths, and his eyes were closed. He was probably reciting the names of rim villages or every subspecies of fish to get his temper under control.

"There be no answers for you here." Morra held on to a tone of sympathy for a moment longer. Then he tossed back his head and laughed. "So throw off your concerns and play until the morrow." He noticed a young chestnut-haired woman outside one of the cottages and called a greeting. After jogging to her, he grasped her around the waist and spun her. They laughed and headed down a path toward the orchard, their heads bent together. With Morra's vibrant auburn and her glistening red-brown hair, they looked like a crackling fire, sparking with life.

I had almost achieved a sensible conversation with Morra, but clearly I'd stretched his attention as far as it would go. I rested a hand on Brantley's shoulder.

He flinched, but then his back muscles loosened a bit. "Something isn't right here."

"Perhaps. But everything can seem dire when it's unfamiliar. What would a visitor to Meriel think if they happened upon the Order?"

"You prove my point. There are dangers here. We have to get out."

I ran a hand through my hair. "Say that ten more times and see if it changes anything."

He finally turned to face me, flashing a crooked smile. "Was I this cranky when we traveled across Meriel?"

I grinned. "Far worse. And me?"

"You bore every hardship like a soldier. Confused and irritated me to pieces."

My smile widened. "You underestimated the strength of a dancer."

He offered his arm. "I underestimated the strength of *this* dancer."

His words warmed me, once again fanning the spark of hope that perhaps we could find a way to connect our lives in spite of our differences. But as he led me down a path to the clearing, I sobered. So far, my efforts to part the trees or to understand the people had failed. When we reached my forsaken net of fruit, I released his arm. "Give me a bit of time alone. I want to talk with the Maker."

He scanned the open space before the village. "Agreed. I want to make another search of the barrier, and you should rest your leg. I'll keep you in sight. Call out if you need me."

I waved him away and sank to the ground, letting my torso relax forward over my legs. The familiar stretch brought relief to the aches that my back had gathered. My lopsided gait caused more than the burning in my tendon. Every joint in my body pinched and complained. The intent of hobbling was to ensure I could never dance freely again, and the punishment was horribly effective. I unwrapped the bandage and massaged the scarred skin, rotating my ankle gently as Ginerva had shown me. Without her help, I'd not be walking at all. Her salves and ministrations kept my ankle from tightening into a useless lump. She'd also advised me to rest my leg, but that wasn't going to happen today.

Brantley's figure shrank into the distance as he examined the edge of the woods, poking at underbrush with his longknife from time to time. Clouds hid both suns, casting a heavy shade over the clearing and village. I rewrapped my ankle and drew my feet close. *Maker, can You show me what we should do? We can't travel inland. We can't get through the barrier.*

Clouds hid both suns, casting a heavy shade over the clearing and village, yet still I turned my face toward the sky.

Did we make a mistake in coming here? Meriel seemed to be suffering so much that I thought You had provided this opportunity. But if You provided this, why are we trapped now? How does this help anyone?

Hopelessness rolled through me, even as a strong wave rippled the pliant ground, rocking. Strong gusts swept inland from the sea, and the whispering of the dangling tree limbs rose to a loud chorus. But I heard no direction from the Maker. A storm was brewing. This must be the expected bad weather Morra's friends had been arguing about.

I slid off my thin leather shoes, flexing my toes a few times. At least here was something concrete I could do. I rose awkwardly, but then found my beginning stance. Leeward pattern might be the best choice to coax the storm back out to sea. I glanced toward the village. A few people gathered near the bonfire pit, and others roamed the orchard and paths into the village. Yet they all ignored me with a disinterest that was so complete I felt invisible.

My toes curled into the soft daygrass, and I rode another swell, the earth as gentle as a mother's arms. I smiled and closed my eyes. No drums lifted the rhythm for me, so I clicked my tongue. Tee, tah, tah, tum. Tick, tick, tick, tick, tum. With the beat established in my head, I began the steps. I lunged and pressed my arms against the sky, as if pounding a huge door with both hands. I spun in a tight circle, hands pushing the hint of storm away. Small running steps came next, and my bad ankle made the movements uneven and awkward. I fought to shut out my frustration and pain. One lesson I'd learned as a dancer: give full focus to the work. No room for self-condemnation or doubt. No distraction.

Above me, the gusts tossed the branches again, then swirled upward. Soon the heavy, threatening pressure of the air lifted and dissipated. I continued to dance, sensing the leading edge of the storm curling and retreating out to sea. The clouds thinned and tore like much-washed fabric, allowing both suns to beam down. I finished the pattern with a shudder of exhaustion, welcoming the warmth and light on my face. I glanced toward the village. No one paid the slightest attention to me. I should be glad. Yet a part of me wished for some sort of acknowledgement. The effort had cost me, and no one even knew.

I sank back down, chiding myself for my selfishness. The Maker gave us the dance to serve others. "Thank You," I whispered. "Give me a heart like Yours that gives without demanding anything in return."

I took a lenka from the net and savored the fruit, resting my ankle and watching Brantley explore the barrier trees to the furthest edge of sight. He doggedly spent the afternoon checking and rechecking for any signs of a path. After I'd rested, I tried dancing a pathway again. Neither of us had any success.

As the primary sun sank beyond the village, more people gathered in the clearing. Bonfires blazed, kettles of stew simmered, and musicians took up places on the stage. The crowd grew until it seemed the entire village had assembled.

The small group from the meetinghouse stood on the platform, and the older woman called out. "We be leaving for the convening tomorrow!"

A cheer rose from the villagers.

Giddy music spun through the air, along with laughter. Folks brought out bowls and spoons and helped themselves to the stew, sitting on the sun-warmed daygrass to eat.

Brantley crouched beside me. "The only path I found is the one leading inland. Any ideas?"

Before I could answer, Morra jogged over to us. "You be here yet? I'm glad you stayed for the revels. Will you be traveling with us on the morrow?"

After feeling invisible, his acknowledgement tugged a smile from my lips. "Tell me about these revels."

"The night before the convening, we all share what we make." His auburn mop of hair caught light from the flames as he tilted his head. "So what will you be contributing?"

Brantley and I gave him blank stares.

Morra frowned. "Be you thinking you'll attend the revel and not participate? Would hate to tell you what happened to the last guests who failed to offer their work." He shuddered. "Tied to a tree and kept from the convening, they were. When we returned, the tree had sent branches straight through them."

He delivered this horrible tale with a grin, so I couldn't figure out if he was serious. Still, the threat hung heavy in the air, and my stomach sank.

LAUGHTER AND ANIMATED CONVERSATIONS FROM THE
nearby festivities spun toward the sky as long shadows of subsunset
painted the ground near where I sat. With my back propped against a
barrier tree, I looked up at the young man who had seemed amiable a
moment before.

"Well?" Morra's easygoing features darkened along with the dusky sky
as he loomed over Brantley and me. "What be your offering?"

I managed an uneasy laugh. "We have nothing to give, but we don't
need to join your revels."

The brewing tempest overhead had blown out to sea, but now a
different sort of storm gathered in Morra's eyes. "But you *have* joined us.
You be here."

Brantley rose from his crouch beside me, stepping closer to the young
man. "We've spent the entire day attempting to leave. We aren't here
by choice."

The portly bearded man from the meetinghouse strode up behind
Morra and clapped him on the back. "What be this lingering away from
the feast? Time passes."

"Merely asking what these guests plan to offer." Morra's chest inflated,
and he met Brantley's threatening stare with one of his own. "They claim
they won't contribute."

The low angle of the subsun deepened the glower of the man's eyes.
"What lack of courtesy is this?"

I maneuvered to my feet and rose to my toes and then lowered to my
heels, hoping the customary greeting would mollify the men. "No lack of

courtesy intended. We aren't familiar with your customs."

The bearded man boomed a laugh. "Customs? I care nothing for customs." His humor bled away, and his tone turned sinister. "But no one dishonors the revels and convening."

I cast a helpless glance at Brantley. A tendon flexed along his jaw, a sure sign his temper was fraying. We were outnumbered and had no way to escape, so we needed to do all we could to avoid a confrontation. I picked up our pack. "What do people share? I have a cloak, and we have a few saltcakes."

The older man leaned back and scratched his head. "We have no need of your . . . possessions." The word dripped disdain.

Brantley growled low in his chest. "Then what do you expect us to share?"

Morra chuckled. "Your poetry—"

"Poetry?" Brantley sounded as if someone was choking him.

"Or song, or sculpture, or fashion."

My companion's hand slid toward his knife again. "Wait," I whispered and stepped in front of him. "Morra, give us a few minutes to discuss our choices."

"Make haste, the feast begins."

The two men headed toward the nearest bonfire.

"Now what?" Brantley pinched his forehead, then tried to rub the frustration away. He only succeeded in smudging dirt across his skin. "We should never have come to this forsaken place."

Forsaken. The world had cried that word. Maybe the Maker had provided more direction than I'd thought. Perhaps we were here for a reason. "I memorized some of the Maker's letter. I could share that."

"I don't know. These folk seem odd enough without telling them the history of our world—"

"And you could play a tune on your whistle. Don't shake your head. I've heard you. If a melody keeps them from turning on us, it's worth the effort."

Brantley's face brightened. "That gives me an idea."

A woman approached before I could ask what scheme he was plotting now. "We begin. You must be joining the circle."

Dozens of villagers were now clustered near the stage. Others lounged near the bonfires. We were the last outliers. I smiled. "Of course. Where should we sit?"

She frowned as if I'd asked her how to breathe or where the sky dwelt. "Where you wish, of course. Amid the revel."

Brantley shrugged, and we followed the woman toward the group. Cooperating with the rules was problematic when no one explained them. As we reached the nearest bonfire, a child grabbed a bowl and spoon from a stack nearby, scooped up some stew from the cauldron, and offered it to Brantley. He sniffed it suspiciously, then tried a bite. His sour expression cleared. "Maybe this isn't such a miserable place after all."

The child offered a bowl to me, but I shook my head. I'd eaten my fill of fruit all day. Besides, anxiety stole my appetite. What happened to those who shared a gift that didn't meet the standards? Images of my years in the Order flashed through my mind. Harsh punishments. Brutal critique. Cast off. Hobbled.

The dull ache in my tendon flared a warning.

We settled onto the ground. I tucked my injured ankle into my lap and gently rubbed it through the bandage. Would they understand the Maker's letter? I could dance one of the patterns instead, but those were designed for a group of dancers—dancers at their peak and whole. I couldn't do them justice. If this world had no patterns, I would hate for their introduction to be the sight of me limping about, creating shapes out of context.

I chewed the edge of my thumb, silently reciting what I'd memorized of the first pages of the Maker's letter. Brantley could well be right. The story of how Meriel was created may be meaningless to the people of this world.

As I grew tenser, Brantley relaxed beside me. He leaned back on his elbows as a woman took the stage. She lifted a pot of wildflowers, arranged so the colors built to a cascade of brilliance. The group cheered and waved their hands in the air. I mimicked their gesture: a rolling of the wrists as if stirring the air overhead.

Harba, the angry man we'd met in the morning, sauntered to the center of the stage and turned, showing off a long robe with patches of shimmering fabric. At first I thought the garment was formed of random remnants, but as I looked closer, I saw a complex pattern to the positions of each piece. I gave an appreciative gasp and joined the cheers and hand waving.

Next Trilia told a story—much of which I couldn't follow—about a lake and a convening and two newly recollected who found each other and had a child, but a welfen beast stole it away. Trilia mimicked the gibbering cackle we'd heard the first night here while everyone shivered in mock fear. What a horrible story. Yet, unlike me, everyone around seemed delighted and entertained.

Then a lanky teen recited a poem about a harbinger. A creature from the sea who signaled the arrival of . . . something. I couldn't quite follow.

My head throbbed from concentrating on the lilting accents of each presenter, the foreign words, and the concepts that I didn't understand. Yet each performance was warmly welcomed, and I admired their work so much that when Morra came and offered his hand, I rose eagerly.

He helped me up the stairs to the stage. Faces gazed expectantly from between the bonfires. Where I'd estimated dozens of villagers before, now it felt like there were hundreds, thousands, all leaning forward and waiting. I swallowed, my tongue turning to baked clay.

From the side of the stage, Morra cleared his throat and gestured. With so many people taking a turn to share, lingering was clearly not appreciated.

I coughed, trying to get my dry throat to produce sound. "'One day as I danced to the music of the waves, the voice of the Maker spoke. He called me to record His words so that future generations would remember His great love.' So begins the letter the Maker gave us. 'He set our world amidst a vast sea, and directs its course . . .'"

A hiss of whispers broke my concentration. People turned to each other, gesturing, frowning. Morra rolled his eyes and shook his head, then beckoned me to exit. As I limped off, only a few hands lifted and twirled, but far more murmurs of displeasure circulated the clearing than the few feeble cheers.

Brantley shrugged. He could have gloated, reminding me that he'd warned the people here might not understand. Instead, he bounded past me and took the stage, brandishing his whistle. He played a brief bouncing tune. A cheer rose up, and every hand spun enthusiastically. But before he left, he played a few loud, slow tones. A code like the ones he used to call or direct Navar.

The crowd's arms lowered, their attention shifting to the singer who stepped onto the platform next. Brantley wended through the people and offered his arm. We moved to the edges of the crowd, careful not to draw attention to ourselves.

"What message did you send Navar?"

He grinned. "You caught that? In case she could hear my signal, I asked her to stay near."

The thought of Navar leaving without us sent a shiver through me. "Shouldn't we look for a path? Just one more time?"

A frown flashed across his face, but he quickly forced a smile. "Carya, we've looked and looked. For now, we need to fit in." He scooped some stew from a kettle and handed a bowl to me. "You didn't eat earlier. It's good. Try some."

I accepted the meal but not the plan. "Our world is drifting out of reach. We have to get back to Navar." The stew's unctuous gravy bound together root vegetables and mutton. Layers of herbs danced on my tongue. "Mmm."

Brantley smiled. "Told you it was good." He helped me settle on the ground. "We've tried everything. Tomorrow we'll travel inland. Unless you have any other ideas."

Even though the stew was delicious, it settled heavily in my stomach. My shoulders sagged. "I don't." I glanced at the stage where the last child was displaying a sketch and explaining it. One of the many oddities of this world. No one seemed to care that the younglings were staying awake far too late. I yawned. "At least the sharing time is wrapping up. We should find a place to make camp for the night."

Morra strode up behind us and overheard my last comment. "The revel is just beginning. Here." He pushed a jug at us, then lifted another one and took a long swig.

After a long day of exploration, tension, confusion, dead ends, and an exhausting dance to push away storms, I wanted nothing more than to curl under my cloak and sleep.

Morra studied me and smiled sympathetically. "The punch will help. No one sleeps the night before the convening."

"But if everyone has to walk so far tomorrow . . ."

Brantley wrapped an arm around my shoulder. "We'll be ready."

A group of musicians took the stage. Men backed away from the bonfires, clearing space. Women began to swirl in the clearing, arms spread, dipping first to one side and then the other. Butterflies. No. Exotic birds with plumage of lightning, their movements punctuating the thunder of drums.

The dance tugged me from my exhaustion and even distracted me from my need to find a way home. The movement invited me to cast off my cares. Without conscious thought, I was on my feet and limping into the fray. My tunic's simple sleeves couldn't produce the effect of the glittering robes, but my body copied the movements. No one seemed to mind the awkward stranger in their midst. Faces turned upward in blissful abandon.

Someone tapped my shoulder. Morra, his long, bushy hair catching the glint of flames, held out a robe for me. I smiled and slipped my arms into the sleeves. Now I was one of the birds. I swooped and dove, joining the pattern. We skimmed past each other in near collisions that somehow wove together.

As I'd seen the night before, men soon stepped in, choosing a partner. The pattern changed. Children romped across the open space, dodging the couples. Individuals without partners twirled in place. An old man with a twisted back that must hurt him terribly leaned against the stage, an empty mug drooping from his hand. He called out as a woman walked past with a pitcher, but she ignored him. Where were his people? It seemed the whole village was out here. Did he have no family? I snagged a pitcher and made my way closer to fill his cup. He thanked me with a painful version of Morra's bow from earlier, then hobbled away to sit near a fire.

Wincing at the throb of my ankle, I made my way to the edge of the clearing. I wondered if the old man would be my traveling companion on the morrow—both of us limping along at the tail end of the procession like lame sheep on the outskirts of the flock.

I stayed there, musing, until an arm came around my waist. Brantley pulled me close. "Remember, we need to fit in."

"You're going to dance?" I leaned away, studying his face.

His eyes twinkled. "Don't look so shocked. I've been known to join in during Windswell's festivals."

He swept me into the tide. Leaning against the force of our spin, we threw our free arms wide and pivoted around each other. His hold was so strong, my sore leg didn't even need to touch the ground. I was no longer limping, but flying.

I tossed my head back and laughed. This felt good. I'd spent too much of my life worrying. For now, I abandoned myself to the movement, the music, the flowing currents of people around us. Every care fell away, spun away.

The music slowed, and the patterns changed. Couples faced each other, holding both hands. Brantley lowered me to my feet. We watched the others until we could copy the movements, stepping close and then back out, then rocking side to side. With each drawing in and away, the dancers moved closer. Soon we were swaying with only inches between us. The muscles in Brantley's arms flexed and warmth radiated from him. Not the soothing warmth of a fireplace, but a heat that kindled an ache in me and pulled me toward him.

Firelight flickered in his gaze. "How is your leg feeling?"

"All . . . all right." I was grateful for the distraction of conversation. "Are we really going to head inland with these people tomorrow?"

"I don't think we have much choice."

"Morra said the journey will take all morning."

"I'll shape one of the tree limbs from the raft into a walking stick. Will that help?"

I shrugged and looked away. The reminder of my weakness cooled the strange yearning the dance stirred in me. I would never burden Brantley with someone as limited as me. Nearby, Morra partnered with the young woman with wild chestnut hair that we'd seen him with earlier. Her flowing emerald robe spun shapes in the flickering light. The young man leaned into her gaze, entranced. I smiled. "Looks like our young friend is smitten."

The musicians finished the song, and everyone clustered around the bonfires. A child handed a jug to me and I shared it with Brantley. Thirsty, we both drank deeply. A new group of musicians took the stage, and another round of dances commenced. Brantley cast a worried look at my ankle but took my hand to lead me into the group.

Harba lumbered over. "I know it's being close to the convening, but that's no excuse. No repeats."

I shook my head. "I don't understand." He gestured to the group. Everyone was grabbing someone new. Morra held the arm of Trilia, and Harba offered me his arm.

Brantley slid a protective arm around my waist. "She's injured. She needs to rest."

Harba shrugged and found another partner. Brantley settled me on the stair near the stage. He braced one foot on the step, watching the revels. "You were right. We need to win their trust. Friendship and not battle."

With laughter and music and feasting surrounding us, even Brantley couldn't hold on to his suspicions and distrust. Although the people of this world were difficult to understand, they were warm and friendly. And talented. I'd have so much to tell Saltar Kemp when we returned to Meriel. I hoped to bring back far more than seeds and fruit. I wanted to bring home the creative ideas I'd seen. Happiness welled up in me, and I leaned back on my elbows, feeling the vibrations of the music through the wood of the stage. The fun and play were as infectious as they were foreign.

Overhead, a cluster of stars sailed together and exploded in a cascade of glitter. "Look!" I pointed. "Star rain."

Throughout the clearing, others noticed and opened their arms to catch the fragments of light. As the glowing dust fell in piles, children raced around and kicked it up, reigniting the sparks. The noise and laughter rose to a crescendo.

Morra swept past, bowed, and released the woman he'd been partnering. Catching his breath, he noticed our perusal of the sky. "The Every be right. 'Tis past time for the green to convene. We should already be at the lake. The star rain be our last warning." Then his gaze swept toward the young woman in an emerald robe dancing with a blond man. Morra's placid face contorted as if he were fighting back tears. He sank to the ground near the steps and buried his head in his hands. "Crillo, you won't be remembering."

I rested a tentative hand on his shoulder. "Are you all right?"

He pulled in a long breath. When he lifted his head, he threw a knife-sharp glare toward the blond man. "No. But I will be." Fists clenched, he stormed into the dancing.

Brantley gave a low whistle. "Trouble brewing on your perfect new world."

"It's not *my* new world, and I never said it was perfect. Only that we could learn something from their . . ." My words trailed off as Morra reached the couple. He yanked the man away and tackled him to the ground in a flurry of punches.

7

THE ONCE GENTLE AND CAREFREE SOCIETY ERUPTED around us. As if Morra's attack had loosed a torrent, fights broke out all around the clearing. Even the logs of the bonfires seemed to crackle with rage. Brantley pulled me into the shadows. Shouts thundered. Children shrieked and tried to hide. The musicians continued to play, but the sound was drowned out by accusations, argument, and grappling bodies crashing to the ground. The beautiful last moments of star rain were ignored, and the falling glitter only added to the wild chaos.

Trilia grabbed fistfuls of Morra's robe to pull him off the man on the ground, but a wild swing knocked her back. Harba waded in, tossing aside those in his way. He wrenched Morra to his feet and dragged him toward the stage. The young man's knuckles bled, and his gilded robe was torn. Harba shoved a jug into Morra's hand.

Morra drank deeply and then swiped his arm across his mouth. His lips still curled and his chest heaved. Our winsome greeter had disappeared, replaced by this tormented and angry youngling.

Nearby, a boy snatched a flowered circlet from a little girl's head, pulling her hair in the process. She grabbed for him, but he scampered away. She collapsed to her knees with a wail.

I hurried to her and wrapped an arm around her shoulders. "Shh. It's all right."

She pressed her face into my shoulder. "I'm not supposed to care," she said between sobs. "But I do." The declaration burst from her as if she were confessing to murder.

"We'll make you a new one."

I scanned the crowd for the boy who'd stolen her treasured headband.

As quickly as it had flared, the fury of the crowd dimmed. Men and women sank to the ground, blotting blood off of knuckles and noses. Trilia ordered several youths to bring out more punch. With jugs in hand, fists stopped flying. The sound of sips and slurps replaced the shouts of anger. The girl lurched to her feet and meandered back into the throng. A woman—her mother?—gave her a mug of something to drink and smoothed her tangled hair.

Brantley and I watched the transformation in stunned silence. Trilia noticed us and shook her head. "I was wrong to think we could postpone a day. The rest of the council had the right of it." Then she frowned. "You aren't drinking?"

Brantley picked up a jug from the ground near the stage. "We have plenty, thanks."

A new dance began, trios holding hands, dipping and weaving. Trilia gestured. "Everyone must participate."

A trio of children swept past us. I was glad to see that only a few children were allowed to stay up all night. "Some of your people must miss these revels. Who is watching the other children?"

Trilia's chin drew back, making the edges of her white hair shift and resettle into new angles. "Other children? All be here. All must be here."

I cast my gaze around the clearing again. Dozens of families and only a handful of little ones? On Meriel, the poorest villages of the rim were still wealthy with children—even after the Order stole girls away. My confusion shifted into compassion. "I'm so sorry. Has your village faced illness?"

Trilia tilted her head. "You be strange guests. Be your village's people as lacking in health as your trees?"

"No, but—"

Brantley took my elbow. "Let's dance." As he led me closer to one of the bonfires, he leaned toward me. "I don't trust these people. Stop asking questions. We don't want them paying attention to us."

He was wrong. We needed to ask questions. We needed to win the trust of these people if we were to travel with them tomorrow and find a way home. But I was rattled by the strange outburst we'd witnessed, and I let Brantley lead me into the clearing. We had little opportunity to speak as dance followed dance. We studied the steps and participated enough to avoid drawing any ire. Eventually, Brantley led me to a step on the far side of the platform and coaxed me to rest my leg where we were hidden from view. The shifting shapes, the sour punch, the music that overlapped with laughter, and the bouncing thump of feet hitting the ground—all created a dreamlike fog until I wasn't sure if I was awake.

"Carya, do you agree?" Brantley shook my shoulder.

I blinked. "Wh-what?" My throat felt thick and dry, and I fumbled for a mug nearby.

"Are you listening? I'm going to explore the town while everyone is busy here. Rest as long as they let you. I'll be back soon." He shook me again. "Did you hear me?"

I rubbed my face, fighting to make sense of his words. Explore the town? What if Trilia was wrong? What if the buildings weren't empty? More crazy risks. "Wait. No—"

But he'd already jogged away, slipping into shadows between buildings. I braced a hand against the stage and stood. I wanted to follow, to help. But my knees buckled, and I sank back to the step. *Maker, protect him.*

Trilia appeared at my side. "There you be. Rested enough?" She cast a glance at my bandaged ankle and offered her hand. "At least come to the other side of the stage and watch. Where be your companion?"

I waved my hand vaguely. "Probably looking for more punch." I accepted her help and limped around the side of the stage. The sound of drums throbbed behind my temples, and the energetic reel of the pipes stabbed my ears. I winced.

Trilia frowned and eased me to the ground facing the clearing. "In your village, what do your unable folk do the night before the convening?"

Unable? I bristled. "We don't have a con—" I stopped myself just in time. "I'm not unable. Just a small injury."

Her mouth pursed, and for a moment I feared she'd insist I join the large circle dance that had just begun. Instead, she lost interest and walked away, joining hands with a tall man in a bronze robe and a robust woman who bounced through the steps on her tiptoes. I shook my head. The saltars would be appalled at the carefree movements and the untrained bodies as they moved around the clearing.

I studied their dance, a line that circled first one way and then another. Did their patterns influence their world in the same way that dance could shape life on Meriel? I saw no signs that their dance accomplished anything, other than play. A smile teased my lips. I could learn from them. But why did they insist on exhausting everyone with this revel throughout the entire night? How often did they do this?

During the next dance, I waved my arms and laughed along with the group, maintaining the impression that I was participating even though my leg couldn't support me any longer. A pile of stardust collected near my feet, and I tossed it in the air, reigniting the sparkling light. Even that small act took effort, my arms leaden from lack of sleep.

Song after song rang out from the rotating groups of musicians. Spritely, tender, rollicking, melancholy. If I didn't need to keep up the ruse of joining in, I'd have found a willow pen and parchment and made notes on the many different patterns. Instead, I watched carefully and tried to memorize what I was seeing. I might never have an opportunity like this again. Perhaps some of these alien dances could form the basis for new patterns on my own world.

A hint of blush touched the sky's face as the stars faded. The primary sun would be rising soon, and Brantley hadn't returned. I made my way to the edge of the impenetrable woods and selected a fallen branch. With that as a makeshift walking stick, I circled behind the platform and studied the buildings. Which way had he gone? My stomach tightened. No lights glowed from windows. The village truly seemed vacated for the revel. I glanced behind me, then scampered awkwardly around the first cottage, hoping to hide my exit from anyone in the clearing. I leaned heavily on my stick, letting my frantic breathing calm before continuing forward.

"Brantley?" I called softly. The only sound came from the music and laughter behind me, and a low moan of wind weaving between two shops. I shivered. The fingers of dawn threw unpredictable shadows. The dark forms of trees and sculptures cast onto the path became sinister as the light hit in odd angles.

I passed empty pavilions and gazebos, tables no longer full of merchandise. The two-story homes were quiet, abandoned. At last, as I reached the central hall, I braced my hand against the entry to rest a moment and again catch my breath. I limped past the towering entrance, trying to place my stick gently. It still clacked against the marble floor. The room where we'd witnessed the earlier debate was bare except for the low table, couches, cushions, and tapestries.

We'd been escorted from the building and never explored the upper rooms. Knowing Brantley, that was exactly where he'd go, in spite of the danger of discovery. I returned to the grand entrance, grasped the gilt banister, and headed up the stairs. I wasn't as brave or reckless as he was, but I had an advantage. I didn't share his paranoia. The people here were kind, if perplexing. I didn't believe anyone would harass me, even if I were found. At least I kept telling myself that as my stick clacked in the grand building.

In the upper hallway, the floor gave a subtle sway as waves coursed far beneath the land. I stumbled, scuffing the floor. The scrape echoed back from the end of the hall. Then it repeated. I froze. Not an echo. Someone else was up here.

My breath caught in my lungs, and I forced it out slowly. "Brantley?" I whispered, heading past several closed doors toward the sound, cursing my injury. In my old life I could glide silent as a feather; now my steps were heavy and far from stealthy.

Then behind me, air stirred. A swish whispered a warning. But before I could even turn my head, someone grabbed me and jerked me back.

8

"WHY BE YOU HERE?" A THREATENING VOICE GROWLED IN my ear, raising the fine hairs at the nape of my neck.

I twisted away from the sour breath and confronted my captor, who loomed large in the small room. "Harba! You startled me." I forced a smile and tried to free my arm from his grip.

He didn't let go. His furry eyebrows drew together in a fierce line. "You should be at the revel."

I floundered for a diversion. If I admitted I was searching for Brantley, that would only endanger him. I took a cue from the worry on Harba's face. I lifted my chin. "Shouldn't *you* be at the revel? Everyone is required to be there."

Color flared across his cheeks and bulbous nose. Then his broad shoulders sank, and he released my arm. "Please. Don't be telling anyone."

I peered past him into the room from which he'd emerged. A cot rested in the shadows, and a form stirred. I pushed past Harba. "If you've hurt Brantley—"

The person on the cot gasped and pushed up to her elbows. Not Brantley. A young woman with black hair tumbling around her pale face. Her limpid eyes widened at my entrance, her swollen belly at odds with her thin arms. She was with child.

Harba trundled in behind me, wringing his hands. "You won't be telling that she missed the revel, will you?"

I shook my head. "Of course not. I grew weary myself." I smiled at the woman. "I'm Carya."

She sat up with a groan, her round stomach declaring she was ready to deliver her child any day. "My name be Wimmo. And Harba fusses too much."

He knelt beside the cot and took her hand. Her delicate fingers disappeared inside his pudgy grip, and a connection flowed between them, infusing both their faces with adoration—and something more. An edge of yearning, desperation . . . fear.

"What's wrong?" I asked them.

Wimmo caressed Harba's cheeks, smoothed his bushy eyebrows, touched a tender finger to his lips. "This be a difficult time for a convening."

He kissed her hand. "We grew attached."

"We knew better." She pushed to her feet, drawing the heavyset man up too. "Now, no more regrets."

With Harba's arm supporting her, they walked past me.

"Wait. I don't understand."

Harba turned and blinked as if he'd forgotten I was there. "We be leaving for the convening. It's time." He waved to the window where morning light crept in and colored the walls, the floors, and the bedclothes.

Wimmo gave Harba a comforting pat. "And we'll enjoy our walk to the lake."

They left, and I walked to the window to watch them. Wimmo was in no condition to hike all day. And why did their love, or "attachment" as they called it, cause Harba so much distress? Was their match forbidden? An ache burned behind my eyes from too many questions, and I shook my head to clear it. Figuring out the culture of this village could wait. I needed to find Brantley. Soon.

I cinched the belt on my borrowed robe and headed from the room to continue my quest.

A quick search of the empty rooms on the first level revealed nothing. The upper floor yielded only increased throbbing in my overworked ankle. I left the central building and stood in the wide square. People had left the revel and were hurrying along the paths, dashing in and out of homes, tossing aside decorative robes, lacing shoes, and making other preparations for the day's journey. A pang of anxiety contracted my ribs. Where was Brantley? What would I do if he didn't return? Standing on this foreign world amid the swirl of activity, I'd never felt more alone and adrift.

In the distance, a mournful howl bid farewell to the night sky. A welfen beast? How close did they come to the village? Had Brantley ventured into the inland wood? That would be just like him. Morra's comment about bodies cleaned to the bone cast vivid horrors in my imagination.

I bit my lip, lingering under the eaves of one of the empty shops. Brantley could be injured or worse. I had to find him. Too much had remained unspoken between us.

I'd convinced myself that refusing his love was a sacrifice I must make to serve my world as a dancer. Yet he'd been a faithful presence almost from the time we'd met. He had resolutely and repeatedly rejected my rejection. And now as I opened my heart to the possibility of more between us, fear of his fate squeezed the breath from me. How foolish I'd been! I didn't want to lose him. Not to my stubbornness, and not to this odd island so far from home.

Ignoring the heaviness in my muscles, I planted my walking stick and limped at a near run, hurrying up and down each side street, peering into gazebos and shops. I knocked on cottage doors, stopped anyone who would pause in their preparations, and asked if they'd seen the stranger. No one shared my alarm, or even any interest in my search. I received shrugs and a smiling reassurance that everyone would be at the convening.

Brantley had completely vanished.

Panic swirled through my mind, ignited by exhaustion and an imagination far too vivid. I saw my entire life unspool before me without Brantley's crooked grin, without ever again watching him ride Navar over the waves, without seeing him swing his niece in a joyous circle of laughter. I'd grown to accept his place in my life in the way I accepted air and sunlight. Without it, my life would be a suffocating darkness.

I abandoned the village and aimed for the clearing. The bandage on my ankle unraveled, trailing in the dust of the path. I was forced to crouch down and secure it again. When I stood, I shielded my eyes against the primary sun, piercing the top of the tree line.

"There you are." Brantley jogged around the side of the musician's platform. He was coated with dirt, and a new scrape marred his face. "I told you to wait for me by the stage."

He was alive! Living, breathing, and irritated. I threw myself into his arms, squeezing him as if I could pour my affection into him through my grip. "I thought I'd lost you." I choked out the words, tears clogging my throat.

After a startled moment, he embraced me, then set me back to meet my gaze. Understanding and a hint of male triumph sparkled in the depths of his sea-blue eyes. "You certainly pick your moments, dancer."

I offered a watery smile. "It must be the punch."

"We'll have to ask them for the recipe."

Suddenly shy, I drew away, brushing mud and detritus from my palms. "What happened to you?"

He dragged a hand through this hair. "The barrier of trees. Couldn't go over or through, so I tried digging."

I raised an eyebrow. "And?"

His grin faded. "Didn't work. Maybe after everyone leaves, we can find some tools that would help."

"I thought we decided to go to—"

"There you be," Morra shouted over the clamor of preparations. "You will walk with me."

Brantley broadened his shoulders. "And if we remain here?"

Horror stretched Morra's features. "The Every must go."

A nearby woman overheard and sang out, "The Every must go." Soon more villagers gathered near us, bags of provisions slung over shoulders, practical cloaks and shoes replacing their decorative attire. Some of the adults wore longknives and swords. They chanted a chorus that grew louder and louder. "The Every must go."

I leaned in toward Brantley. "This convening of theirs might give us answers. We should go."

"I don't trust them." He took in the scene around us and frowned. "But we are outnumbered by far. And I've run out of ways to attack that barrier."

I touched his arm, wanting the reassurance of his tangible presence now that I'd found him. "If this is our only course, then this path may hold a purpose."

He tilted his head, his gaze sharp and searching. His lips quirked. "You may be right."

My brows lifted. "What was that? I didn't quite hear you."

He growled and pulled me forward.

The group set out on the trail leading inland from the village. Singing and chatter continued as if this was a part of the revel too. As the subsun joined the primary in the sky, the trees and vines glowed in a thousand shades of green. The plants near the path included fruit trees, tubers, and colorful mushrooms. Daygrass spread between, nibbled by occasional grazing animals and providing a sense of spacious beauty. Now that we'd moved away from the oppressive vegetation of the barrier trees, the landscape felt more similar to Meriel, although healthier and more lush. I could imagine I was strolling down a trail from Middlemost or exploring the fields near Windswell.

Morra strode alongside us, cheerfully grabbing persea, lenka, and kumquats from the trees and passing them to us. We ate as we walked.

"How often does the village travel for a convening?" I asked.

He tugged the neck of his tunic. It looked small for him, as if he were a child outgrowing his clothes. "We follow each green star rain, of course. You never told me. Which color be your village?"

I gave a noncommittal shrug. Morra was too engrossed in peeling a persea to challenge my vagueness. What he said about star rain intrigued me. As much as I loved the star rain, I'd never categorized them by color. Thinking back, dominant colors did flare in their displays, a convenient way to mark time. The star rains kept to a somewhat regular schedule. They usually came every few weeks, but occasionally closer together. I could tell when we were due for one by the swelling and pulsing of stars, and sometimes the taste of the air.

Not far ahead, Crillo, the girl that Morra had danced with, stopped to adjust her shoe. He ran ahead, crouched beside her, and offered her a choice fruit. Her warm smile sent a blush across his cheeks. They whispered to each other, but when they stood, they pulled apart. The girl hurried on ahead, leaving Morra slumped, his easygoing grin washed away.

Brantley and I caught up to Morra. "You can walk with Crillo if you'd rather," I offered. Was it my own newly awoken heart that made me want to encourage their young love? Or just compassion for the pain I saw on Morra's face?

He shook his head. "We've grown too attached."

Like Harba and Wimmo. Clearly there were restrictions in this world that I didn't yet understand. What would happen if these people realized that Brantley and I had a deep bond, newly acknowledged and potent?

I glanced at Brantley, but he'd strayed away, still hunting for an escape path. I stayed close to Morra. "Tell me about yourself. You were so kind to welcome us when we arrived, I'd love to know more."

The young man turned his attention my way, then pointed to my walking stick. "Give that to me."

I stopped and handed it to him, balancing on my good leg. He pulled out a knife and with swift movements reshaped the top. Then he handed it back. "I create beauty from wood and reed," he said. "And when needed, I be making a few practical things as well."

I tested the smooth grip he'd created, which better bore my weight. What talents these people had! "Thank you."

We strolled forward, keeping the bulk of the villagers in sight ahead of us. I wanted to glean information from my young friend but was distracted by checking on Brantley's progress. After my earlier panic, I didn't want to lose sight of him. "The people of your village have amazing talents. Do your parents live here, too?"

Morra shook his head. "You and your friend speak strange words. I once visited a village beyond the lake, and they were not like you."

Should I explain we were from a completely different island? Would that put us in more danger, or enable us to get the help we needed? I wanted Brantley's input, but he was poking into the underbrush several yards off the trail. He abandoned that effort, jogged past us, and darted into the trees on the other side of the trail. Where did he get his stamina? He paused in his search to check on me. Sunlight glinted from his hair, but shadows carved gaunt lines in his face. He was worried. With cause. When we hadn't returned to Meriel, had Saltar Kemp directed the dancers to keep our island in sight? Or had she consigned us as lost? Had our world already ridden the currents away from this one? How long could she wait for us?

I didn't believe Brantley's efforts would yield anything as we moved inland, but I was grateful for his dogged determination. In the meantime, I made my own efforts to find out what I could.

"Morra, the tall trees and vines around your village. They seem impossible to penetrate."

"That be the edge," he said. "You be slowing your steps. Do you want a second stick? We must keep up with the rest."

"I'll be all right." I quickened my pace. "So, has anyone tried to go through the edge?"

Morra chuckled. "Why?"

"I don't know. Curiosity?"

Now his face puckered, incredulous. "They be trees and vines. What would stir interest?"

"Well . . . what lies beyond?" Getting information from the man could drive me to madness, but whom else could I ask?

Morra shook his head. "You be full of worries and longings. Good thing it be convening time." He pulled a lenka from his pocket and popped it in his mouth.

"Can you tell me more about the convening? Why is it so important?"

Morra spat out the lenka pit. "Surely you know."

"Pretend I don't. Explain it to me."

His expression lifted. "Like a game?"

I nodded.

"We be makers." He cast a sideways look at me. "I've seen another village, and surely our people be the finest."

"What does that have to do with the convening?"

He paused and took a swig from a leather flask. "Else how could we bear our gifts?" A dark thread colored his tone, and a tendon flexed in his neck. "The ceremony frees us from pain."

"Pain?"

"The pain of love, of longing, of attachment. With those erased, our making thrives."

I struggled to understand. My brain throbbed from the long night of revels, but even so, his story felt wrong. "How do you know that?"

He faced me. "Everyone knows."

"But how? What happens if you don't go to this convening? Did someone teach you this?"

"The Every knows."

His resigned proclamation reminded me of the Order. The rules I'd grown up believing, the facts everyone knew, had been false. A shudder jostled my core. "I believe our gifts come from the true Maker. The Maker of all. And they are just that—gifts."

Morra didn't seem to hear me. He stared ahead at where the girl he loved disappeared around a bend. "We mustn't grow attached."

Like a lens turning in a telescope, I glimpsed the lines of this world more clearly. The sadness that hid behind the laughter. The lies beneath the surface. "Who says so?"

"This game be no fun. Find another."

"Who says you can't have attachments?"

"Did you not hear me? Everyone."

"Sometimes what everyone believes is true is still wrong."

As I was speaking, Brantley rejoined us, overhearing the last part of our conversation. "Morra, if you call a tail a leg, how many legs does a hound have?"

The young man brightened. "A better game. Five!"

Brantley shook his head. "Four. Calling a tail a leg doesn't make it one."

Morra barked a laugh. "That be good." He ran ahead and clapped a man on the back, repeating the joke.

I leaned heavily on my stick and trudged forward. "Find anything?"

Brantley rubbed the back of his neck. "No. Learn anything?"

In spite of the languid air, chill bumps rose on my arms. "Enough to know that this convening sounds like a bad idea."

9

BOTH SUNS BURNED OVERHEAD, UNRELENTING IN HEAT
and unyielding in their watching. I trudged forward, each step a small
stride followed by a painful limp. No matter how many times I repeated
the process, I never seemed to get anywhere. Step, limp. Step, limp.
More trees, more undergrowth, more trail trodden by all the villagers.
Unending. And every bit of progress took us farther from possible
escape. The thought of retracing this route after the convening provoked
shuddering muscle spasms in my weary, wobbly legs. I shut out that
dread and focused on the will required for one more step.

I stumbled. What now? No root rose above the path. No stone. No
rut marred the way. Nothing. I was tripping over my own feet, my
dancer-born determination no longer enough to overcome exhaustion.
Nor could it stop the new waves of pain spiking through my leg. Fresh
blood seeped through my bandage, leaving an irregular trail of red
behind me. Ginerva, my attendant back home, would be furious at
this latest setback in healing. But what choice did we have? We'd tried
every possible way to reach the ocean. We were committed now.
Determined to reach the lake and find answers—all while avoiding
the dangers raised by these people and their confusing customs.

Speeding my gait, I stumbled again.

Brantley caught me. "Let me carry you. Please."

I shook my head. I was already too much of a burden, and I was
determined to hang on to whatever independence I still had. My pride
wouldn't let me be carted around like an infant, no matter how many
times he offered.

Brantley slipped an arm around me, taking some of my weight. Even so, our pace dragged, placing us in a group at the rear. The old man from the revel limped slowly but with fierce determination. Harba and Wimmo waddled just ahead of us. She pointed out a gossamer insect flitting near a tree. He laughed and plucked a pink wildflower from the side of the path and presented it to her with a bow and flourish. They seemed determined to savor this time together. Crillo had hurried on ahead with the bulk of the travelers, leaving Morra moody and scuffing the daygrass as if it had become the target for all his frustrations.

Emerging from a bend in the trail, Trilia walked against the flow of travelers to check our progress. She frowned at my hobbling gait. "Stop. Sit a moment. I can help."

I sank onto a fallen log at the side of the trail. The relief was so exquisite, I feared I'd never convince my body to stand again.

Brantley crouched beside me and waved Trilia away. "I can wait here with Carya. We'll catch up later."

Trilia ignored that offer and dug through her pack, unearthing a small silk bag with a drawstring. After shaking dried herbs into her palm, she crushed them with her thumb. The fragrance of spice and shady groves and hope sweetened the air.

Bristling like a forest hound, Brantley edged closer to me. "What's in those dead leaves?"

"They be easing her pain." Trilia raised a brow toward me. "Yes?"

I nodded and leaned back against Brantley as Trilia unwrapped my bandage and cast it aside. The fabric was stained and torn, but I still couldn't afford to lose it. "Wait—"

"Hush. 'Tis fine. I've more." Her finger traced the scar where the High Saltar had sliced my tendon and cut away my purpose and identity in one cruel blow. Angry red skin puckered, and the wound leaked blood.

The sight drew a hiss from Brantley, but my weariness suppressed any urge to react. From her pack, Trilia unearthed a clump of moss tied in a bundle. She dabbed the cool, wet sponge over my skin, then pressed her herbs in place. They stuck to my damp skin while she rummaged again. Her head bent to her work with the same intensity that Ginerva had always shown when tending my injury back on Meriel. Ginerva. Her name made me homesick. Would I see her again? Was she worrying about me? I'd welcome her motherly scolding at the moment.

Trilia finished her ministrations by unspooling a band of clean, stretchy fabric and wrapping my ankle. Already, the herbs had dulled the pain, and the gentle pressure of the bandage brought further relief. "Thank you."

Brantley tightened his protective arm around me, clearly untrusting of Trilia.

She ignored him and met my eyes. The fringe of her white hair swayed forward as she dipped her head. "You have more distress to release than most, I'm thinking. Good thing the pain will soon end."

Did she mean because of the herbs? Or because of the convening that was supposed to solve every problem?

"She needs rest," Brantley ordered in a tone that had once commanded a ragtag army and guided his village.

Trilia's expression remained placid but unrelenting. She studied the arc of the suns overhead. "No. We be late already."

Brantley's arm flexed against my back, and his other hand gripped his knife hilt. For the tenth time since we'd landed here, I scrambled to forestall a confrontation.

I lurched to my feet, and Brantley sprang up as well. Resting a hand on his chest, I willed him to listen. "I'll be fine."

Trilia busied herself rearranging her pack, then hoisted it to her shoulder and headed up the path.

I leaned in to Brantley and whispered, "There may come a need to fight, but not now. Let's get along if we can."

His brow darkened. "This walking is too much for you."

"Didn't we already have this discussion?" I smiled, lightly touching the scrape on his cheek, then pointing to the bandage over the gash he'd received climbing trees. "I won't fuss about your injuries if you don't fuss about mine."

"It's not the same," he grumbled. His hand closed around my fingers, and he leaned in. Our faces inches apart, he searched my eyes. "You meant what you said earlier? In the village?"

My lashes swept down. "That I don't want to lose you?"

"Will the Order even let you marry—"

"I'm not in the Order anymore." I dared to look up, losing myself in his eyes.

"You won't change your mind?" His words breathed against my mouth.

The question stopped me. I'd committed myself to the Order but later fled. I'd determined not to saddle Brantley with a crippled partner but later cast off that noble intention. I had proved myself unreliable and fickle. He deserved so much better. Yet the love that swirled in the ocean depths of his gaze wooed me, won me, convinced me to let myself be loved.

A shadow crossed his brow. "Well? Are you sure?"

"Positive," I whispered.

His lips met mine, gently, with promise. Warmth surged through my spine. The earth seemed to not only rock but spin.

He pulled away reluctantly, blinked several times, and drew a shaky breath. "Then let's get answers and get off this island. We have a future to build."

He positioned my arm around his shoulders, grabbed my waist, and tried a few steps. My limp was less pronounced. The herbs were helping, but the giddy joy bounding around my ribcage helped even more. We moved ahead with new determination, and I barely felt my feet touch the ground.

We caught up to Trilia. Ahead of us, beyond a cluster of trees and shrubs, voices rose in argument. Trilia shook her head. "We cannot delay. Already the pain builds in some." She hurried toward the sound.

"Last chance." Brantley squeezed my waist. "We can turn back. If they try to stop us, I can fight them off."

"And do what? Sit around an empty village, trapped?" I urged him forward, and we continued up the trail. "Besides, I'm getting a sense that these people need help. We're here for a reason."

"Of course we're here for a reason. We're here to get supplies for Meriel and get home again." He tilted his head so it rested against the top of mine. "Besides, now that you're seeing sense about us, I'm eager to get back. Build a new cottage in Windswell. I thought you wanted that too."

A tingle of anticipation played through my chest. I could picture the cozy home we'd create, surrounded by the warm villagers and his family.

Family. I bit my lip. "How will Brianna feel about our marriage? About us?"

"Why?"

Was he really that oblivious? "She cares about you."

"Of course she does. We both loved my brother. She's like a sister to me."

My legs felt heavy again, but I told them to keep walking. "Are you sure the bond isn't more than that?"

He squeezed my shoulders. "You do get the oddest notions. How long has that thought been worrying you?"

"I've seen it in her face. And she hated me for a long time." I thrust my chin up.

A chuckle rumbled through his chest. "Because you were a dancer. You know she adores you now. So does Orianna. They'll both be thrilled to have you living nearby."

Another worry pinched between my eyes. "I did promise Saltar Kemp I'd help teach new patterns to the Order. I'll need to make regular trips to Middlemost."

He shrugged. "With the new river, it's but a half-day's journey on a stenella. You can visit whenever you wish." Muscles tightened across his back. "Are you sure about leaving the Order? Any regrets?"

A sigh soaked through me. "I loved being a dancer. I grew up believing only dancers of the Order could serve our world."

"And now?" A hint of endearing insecurity graveled his voice.

I stopped, turned, and hugged him. "I'm not called to live at the Order. Perhaps I can serve the Maker and still love a husband."

"A husband? I would hope you'd be more specific than that."

I suppressed a giggle. "All right. *This* husband. And his people. If I dance in Windswell, it may bring aid as truly as performing patterns in the center ground of the Order." I met his gaze and swam in the joyous light dancing in his eyes.

"You couldn't have come to that realization sooner?" He gave a groan of frustration. "First we have to get off this Maker-forsaken island."

Forgotten, forgetting, forsaking. The deep heart cry I'd heard when we arrived here. "These people are not forsaken by the Maker. They don't know Him. Much as our world forgot. We should help them."

Brantley snorted and turned us back to the path. We caught up to Morra, who was sulking again, his heels grinding into the ground as he walked. The careless foot placement made me shudder. Some dancer habits were so ingrained they'd always stay with me. Touching the earth with respect and care was one of those rules. I tried to engage the young man in conversation but couldn't budge his sullen mood. I eventually gave up and focused on the sensation of Brantley's strong muscles supporting me, the warmth of him at my side, and the wonderful hint of ocean and leather and salty sweat.

Fatigue dragged my eyelids down, and I sleepwalked for long stretches. The primary sun lowered toward the treetops as the trail unraveled into a vast open space. Brantley stopped and gave a whistle of appreciation.

Beyond the several dozen villagers, a huge lake spread under the glow of the subsun. Colors shimmered on the surface, and the honeyed scent of ocean rose like mist.

On Meriel, the center of our world was much thicker than the rim. Wells were dug many stories deep to reach the ocean below. Here the lake's surface was only a house's depth below the woods from which we emerged, and the wide fields surrounding the lake rolled gently down toward its shore, reminding me of soup in a bowl. The people who had arrived before us had strolled down the hill and congregated near the water. Some threw off their outer clothes and dove in, paddling around and emerging refreshed and grinning. The lake was so big the whole village could have fit within. A splash several yards out rippled the surface.

"Fish!" Brantley hurried me along, drawn toward the water like a child to star rain.

"Whoa." I untangled from his grip. "Go on ahead. I'll be fine."

He spared a quick nod and jogged to the lake's edge. A smile tugged my lips. There were times his nature reverted to that of a little boy. Eager, reckless. What was I getting myself into? My smile broadened. A life with the most noble and challenging man I'd ever met.

I spotted Morra. Perhaps now that we'd arrived at the lake, he'd be more forthcoming with explanations about what we could expect and where we would find a guide to get us home. I limped over to him. "Thank you again for reshaping this cane."

He thrust a leg forward and bowed. "Of course. You must be glad we're here."

"It was a difficult journey." A tired sigh shook the last bit of energy from my frame. "What happens next?"

Morra squinted at me. "Be you doing the game again?"

The game? "Yes. Please pretend I don't know anything about the convening."

He scratched his head. "I've told you all."

"So, what do we do next?"

He gestured to the shore. "Now we call on the Gardener, and then we sleep."

Sleep? The important convening had been the focus of the village ever since we'd arrived. The revel and lengthy hike had built to this moment. I rubbed my eyes and murmured, "Seems anticlimactic."

Morra didn't hear me. He walked toward the edge of the lake and grabbed the arm of the girl he'd pursued all day. Crillo shook her head, but he forced a small token of carved wood into her hand. She stared at it and nodded, then walked away. Morra looked back at me, a hint of triumph painted across his face.

Brantley strode toward me, light glinting off his blond curls and energy in his step. "I wish I hadn't left our net behind. There are signs of a large school. What I wouldn't give for a warm fire and hot coals to grill a fish steak. I'm starving."

"Morra tells me the first item on the agenda is sleep." All along the lakeshore, individuals spread blankets. "You can figure out how to fish tomorrow."

His gaze narrowed as he watched the villagers settle in. They didn't lie down, but sat shoulder to shoulder, staring out at the water. "Why are they so close to the edge?"

He was right. Even small children settled so near the water that a shift in position could send them tumbling into the lake. I started forward, but Brantley grabbed my arm. "Don't interfere. Let's find a safe place for you to rest."

"For us both to rest." My weight had dragged against him for hours as we walked. He must be exhausted.

He rubbed his shoulder. "I'll keep watch for a while. There's something very odd about all of this."

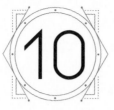

BEFORE OUR LONG HIKE, THE VILLAGERS HAD ADMONISHED us to participate in the revels and forced us to attend this convening, but now the people lost all interest in us, not caring that we stood back and simply observed. Men, women, and children perched along the edge of the lake. They swayed side to side, humming, their raised hands twirling in the air. Even though I'd lived my life moving in unison with other dancers, these odd actions disturbed and unsettled me with their detachment. Their eyes stared vacantly into nothing. Their expressions were entranced, completely oblivious to everything around them.

Without warning, the swaying shifted to a frantic forward and back movement. The humming rose to a clashing chord. My heart raced. Before I could blink, everyone fell over, sprawled along the tangleroot and as still as death.

I grabbed Brantley's arm. His face paled as he studied the strange sight, but then he broke away from me, jogged to the nearest man, and touched him. A shiver rode through my frame. Brantley had more courage than I did.

He strode back to me. "They're just asleep."

"That was . . ." I pressed a hand over my mouth.

He guided me up the slope to the trailhead, putting more distance between the unnatural scene and us. "I know. But now we finally have a chance to rest." Brantley rolled out a blanket under a tall pine where we could still see the gentle slope down to the lake.

Eyelids heavy, I collapsed to the ground and pulled a cloak over my shoulders. The effects of the sleepless revel and then the long hike asserted their power. "I can't stay awake."

Brantley settled beside me. "Don't worry. I'm sure nothing more will happen now. They're all too tired." Yet worry edged his voice.

I shared his apprehension. "I'll rest a few hours. Then I can keep watch for a bit." That was my valiant intention. But I fell into a heavy, intoxicating slumber and didn't wake until deep into the night. I sat up, glancing around to get my bearings.

Brantley snored softly beside me. A lock of hair fell crookedly across his brow. My fingers itched to brush it back, but I didn't want to disturb him. I couldn't remember when he'd last slept, and he'd half carried me for much of the day. Standing, I reached upward to the stars overhead, then bent and pressed my palms against the ground, relishing the deep stretch. Muscles, ligaments, tendons all relaxed as if sighing in appreciation.

Silence shrouded the lake. In the dim starlight, the lumpy silhouette of bodies looked like shrubs guarding the water. I rubbed my eyes and squinted. Perhaps it was a trick of shadows, but all the cloaks and blankets were deep green.

I picked my way with my walking stick and headed down the hill for a closer look. Morra's auburn hair caught a glint of starlight where he curled like a tiny child on a favorite blanket. Near him, Trilia's brilliant white hair stood out among the coverings of green. She rested on her back. One pale arm flung outward from the green covering her body.

My eyes widened. Tendrils of vines crept along her exposed arm, encircled her neck, and wrapped across her forehead like a crown. I turned to Morra. Foliage stretched around him, hugged him, entwined over him. Where it had easily coated others, here the greenery seemed to struggle, twist, and fight to encapsulate him. He whimpered and shifted, and more moss spread across him. I touched his shoulder. "Morra?"

"Don't wake the sleepers," a deep voice intoned behind me.

I spun, nearly losing my balance. A tall man stood a short distance up the rise that added even more height to his imposing presence. His sleeveless green tunic exposed spindly arms like twigs shorn of leaves. His frame was skeletal, his face gaunt. His angles felt out of place on this otherwise plump and jolly island.

"Who are you?" I blurted.

He stared down his narrow nose with a glare that rivaled the harshest saltar. "I am the Gardener."

At his voice, the earth quivered beneath my feet. Clearly this man demanded respect. I rose high on my tiptoes and lowered, hoping the customary greeting was appropriate. "I didn't mean to intrude. What's happening to them?"

The Gardener gave a dark chuckle, and all the foliage stretched and contracted in response. A sharp thrill ran through me, the sense of being in the presence of someone "other." I'd felt this same current sweep through me when I'd met the Maker. But when the Maker gathered me in light, the awe I experienced was wrapped with warmth and love. The man before me exuded age and power, but no warmth. Tiny hairs rose on the back of my neck.

Morra gave a low moan. More leaves crept across him, seeming to burrow into his skull. I reached out to pull them aside.

"Beware!" The earth shuddered again, tossing me back. Spears of thorny vines shot up, as tall as my head, blocking me from Morra.

I whirled to confront the Gardener. "What are you doing to him?"

His thin lips parted, revealing uneven, yellowed teeth. "Giving him what he desires."

Anger surged through my muscles. "Death?"

The Gardener's laugh was wheezy and warped like a broken flute. "Is that what upsets you? Perhaps you're right. Perhaps in his deepest being, that is what he most desires. But that isn't given me to grant." His face twisted. "Not yet."

Nearby, Trilia stirred and also moaned. My fingers clenched on my walking stick. "Stop it! They're in pain."

Another wall of thorns sprang up and kept me from reaching her. "Just the opposite. I'm repairing them."

"Repairing?" I sounded like a little girl in the first form, echoing questions, and I felt as inadequate and foolish. I didn't understand what was happening, and if this Gardener was harming the villagers, I had no way to stop him.

His smile twisted further. "These foolish mortals would destroy each other were it not for my help."

As he spoke, the vines and leaves continued to grow, reach, and tangle over each villager along the shore. One inquisitive branch slipped toward me, and I edged away.

"Carya?"

Up the hill, Brantley's silhouette parted from the pine tree.

Relief rose and filled my chest. I was no longer confronting this strange being alone. I waved. "Down here!" A tendril unfurled and splayed across my foot. I kicked it aside. The Gardener slid among the sleepers, waving his bony arms. Moss and foliage covered each face as he passed. Most succumbed easily, not even stirring as they were immersed in verdure. But a few seemed—even in their sleep—to resist. Harba and Wimmo tossed and turned near each other, as if trying to shake off the blankets of green. Yet soon even they stilled.

Longknife at the ready, Brantley bounded down the rise. He took in the green-covered shapes and the gaunt Gardener. He placed himself in front of me, facing the man, but spoke in an undertone to me. "Are you all right? What's happening?"

"I'm not sure. He says he's repairing them, but I—" Another root crept toward me, and I shoved it back with my walking stick. How to explain the murky darkness that emanated from the man; the frissons of fear that kept running through me; the worry I felt for Morra, Trilia, and all the rest?

As if conducting music, the Gardener waved his arms and guided the progress of the vines. Then he stalked back toward us.

Brantley's shoulders tensed; perhaps he felt the same dark impressions that frightened me. He stomped on a weed that wriggled toward him. "Who are you?" he asked in the same voice that had once confronted the past High Saltar. No reverence. No awe. No fear. Admiration muted my dread for a few heartbeats, until I peered around Brantley and gazed on the contorted features of the Gardener.

The odd creature rolled his eyes. "This grows tedious." He flicked a hand, and vines uncoiled from the ground and wrapped Brantley's ankles.

Brantley's knife flashed, and he cut himself free. Instead of backing away, he strode closer to the man.

The Gardener seemed to grow taller like the foliage, chest lifting and wrath stretching his face. "This is my island. Do not interfere."

"Looks like you're the one interfering." Brantley had to lift his chin to address the man, but nothing in his posture showed retreat. "Are you the one who kept the barrier from letting us out?"

I'd always resisted Brantley's attempts to teach me how to use a knife for hunting or fighting, but now I longed for a weapon. I gripped my cane like a cudgel, as if my slim presence could add power to his defiance.

The Gardener's eyes narrowed. Then a sneer curved his lips. He pointed a long-nailed finger toward the earth and the moss coating the ground. Green spores exploded in a cloud around Brantley. He choked, crumbled to the ground, and fell to his back, a look of surprise on his face. In the moment it took for me to crouch beside him, the moss spread and blanketed him.

"No!" I tore at the greenery, pulling off layers that immediately grew back. "Let him go."

Brantley groaned and writhed, resisting the plants. I tried to help, tugging at each vine, my palms soon blistered and raw. He freed one arm and began to rip off the binding moss. The Gardener grimaced, effort appearing on his face for the first time. Then a thorn shot up from the earth, curled, and pierced Brantley's chest. His struggle stopped, and he went limp. Choking out a cry, I dug at the root of the thorn and yanked it away.

The Gardener's jaw clenched. With another wave of his hand, vines left the bodies near the water and trailed toward me. One wrapped around my bad ankle. I hopped away, trying to tug myself free. Another creeper wriggled toward me. I flailed out with my stick. Nothing held back the tide. The earth rose and fell, and I lost my grip on the walking stick. This was a nightmare. I was drowning. Drowning in waves of green instead of the ocean waves I'd always feared. My only ally was already trapped in the eddy, and I would be next.

Dance.

The whispered word swirled in my heart. I wrenched my leg free and spun in place on my good foot, whipping my weak leg to help me turn again and again. My arms opened over my head. I was a cyclone, a child's top, a vortex of opposition. The vines near me fell back. *Loving Maker, this is Your battle.* My heart cried out as I continued to dance. *Help me! Help Brantley! Guide my steps.*

Fragments of patterns played through my mind. Would rainclouds inhibit the plants or only cause them to grow faster? Could a fog protect us all from the Gardener? I settled on movements that urged the wind to surge across the land. After my spins forced the vines to draw back, I turned to confront the Gardener, trying to block Brantley from him.

Rage contorted his features. He raised an arm, pointing one gnarled finger at me. "You have no right." He spared a glance at all the unconscious villagers, and then Brantley's inert body behind me, as if reassuring himself of his control over them.

Cold chills shook my bones, but I squared my shoulders and stood firm, fighting to hide my terror. Whatever he was doing to these people, I'd resist him with every ounce of my being.

As if he read my thoughts, a thin smile stretched his lips. "You've accomplished nothing here. You are too late for them. As for you, you'll pay for your interference."

My eyes widened. This was no empty threat.

Malice poured from him in waves. "Until now my power has been leashed, but the signs have shown my fulfillment approaches. Did you think I wouldn't sense the brief break in the barrier? Soon there will be nowhere in my world for you to hide." The hills rocked and moaned as if acknowledging his rule. Then he glanced at the sky, where a hint of dawn's light bled into the deep darkness of night.

He crouched and pulled up twining creepers, wrapping them around his arms. It seemed his evil bled through the vines and into the essence of the world. An ugly cackle burst from his throat. He turned, enrobing himself in the vines as they surged into leaves and thorns. Mossy spores exploded around him, and then all the plant life collapsed inward.

He had disappeared, but the danger had not. The foliage crept toward me again, so I began a limping run with wide sweeps of my arms. Too bad I didn't have all the dancers of the Order to join in the pattern. Yet even with only one hobbled dancer, the steps were effective. The gale buffeted any plants that stretched upward so they shrank and withdrew. The greenery closer to the ground clung to the bodies it covered until wisps of wind slipped under and fought it.

I closed my eyes and listened to the breath of the island, felt the struggle, and coaxed the plants to withdraw. I reached for the moss that coated Brantley, but as soon as I stopped dancing, the plants surged forward again. As much as I longed to free him, I needed to continue the pattern for wind.

I resumed a series of turns, wobbling when the earth shifted underfoot. My training served me well, allowing me to regain my footing and increase the pace of my frenzied dance. The wind grew in power. Light sparked at the sides of my vision. In the midst of my furious movements, it took some time to realize that the first fingers of the primary sun tickled the sky.

I gathered strength from the beauty, stretching my arms to welcome the many-hued light tinting the sky above the tree line. Hope helped me ignore the pain in my ankle and the exhaustion in my bones. The night was almost over. My dance shifted to passionate thanks for protection and rescue. I would dance as long as I needed to, to hold back whatever dark purpose the Gardener had been shaping.

In the growing light, the last of the smothering vines withdrew. Once again the lakeshore was rimmed only with sleeping villagers. I sank to my knees.

I drew in several deep breaths until I could still the trembles that quaked through my body. I crawled over to Brantley. "It's over," I whispered. "Wake up."

I smiled at the stray curl that once again rested across his brow. This time I brushed it gently to the side and replaced it with a soft kiss. "The moss is gone. You're free now."

Still he didn't move. I pressed a hand to his chest. Was his heart beating? Was he breathing? Fresh panic flared hot in my chest. Was I too late?

I grabbed his shoulders and shook them. "Brantley. Come back. Please—" A sob cut off the rest of my words. He remained lifeless, silent, rocked gently by waves coursing beneath the land. *Loving Maker, was I wrong to love him? Have You taken him from me because I turned from the Order?*

No. The Maker Himself had called me to challenge the Order. But perhaps I'd failed in some other way. If I were to blame, perhaps this could still be reversed. *Forgive me for whatever I did wrong. Please, don't take him. Whatever the Gardener did to him, You are stronger. You can wake him. Do something!* Hot tears stung my eyes.

A blush of dawn passed over Brantley's cheeks. A trick of light. But I grabbed at the slim hope and shook him again. With his muscles slack, his face no longer held the humor and determination that were so much a part of his nature. My heart ached to see his smile again. Or even his frown. I'd never before appreciated how much fun it was to quarrel with him. "You can win our next argument. I promise. And don't forget, we're going to fix up a cottage in Windswell. Think of it. I'll help your mother with her garden, and your village will never go hungry again." I stroked his cheeks, pressed my face against his, begged for a sign of breath. "We can build our home near the rim, so you can see Navar first thing every morning. We have to find a way home. Meriel is waiting for supplies."

I picked up his hand, rubbing warmth into it. "You aren't going to leave me here alone, are you? Not that I need your protection." I forced a gurgle of laughter. "Dancers are every bit as tough as herders. You've said so yourself. But I've gotten used to you. Come on. Stop idling about."

My fingers clenched around his cold hand, and I squeezed back tears. I would not cry. I would not grieve. That would be allowing for the possibility that he was gone, and I would not do that. The Order believed we could create our own reality. If I wished it enough, if I pictured his eyes opening and his lips lifting in a crooked grin, if I imagined his rumbling chuckle—I could bring him back.

Except I couldn't.

My body sagged, powerless against whatever held Brantley. I wasn't the Creator of life nor the Overcomer of death. But there lived a Creator and an Overcomer. He had shown Himself to me. *Maker, I need You. Help him.*

Along the lake, the other people remained in a strange torpor. Alive or dead, I couldn't say. A bird called a greeting from deep in the nearby forest. How dare he sing on such a dark dawning? The primary sun crested the treetops, blazing more warmth on the sparkling lake, the vibrant daygrass, the dozens of bodies. How dare it shine when the man I loved rested lifeless beside me?

Something inside me broke, and tears flowed hot and furious down my cheeks. I loosened my desperate grip on Brantley's fingers and bent forward, resting my head on his chest, letting sob after sob shudder through me.

One of the Order's teachings was accurate. The attachment of love could lead to pain beyond imagining. "It's worth it," I whispered. "I'm still glad I love you. Every minute we spent together was a treasure."

I strained to hear the reassuring drumming of his heart, but his chest was motionless beneath my ear.

11

A BREEZE SHOOK THE DISTANT TREES. RIPPLES SCUDDED across the lake. The whole world pulsed with life. The whole world but for the man I loved.

Was he truly gone? Lost to me forever? This wound cut more deeply than the High Saltar's knife. My entire body clenched against the pain. My heart contracted into a tight fist that hardly dared beat.

Maker, Maker, do not abandon me. Not here. Not now. Not like this. Breathe life into him. Please. I beg You. Help him wake.

I pressed my ear more firmly against his chest.

Thu-thump. Thu-thump.

I tensed. Was I imagining the sound? My fingers felt for a sign of life along his neck. Yes! A pulse beat against my touch—frail, but better than nothing.

"Brantley. Wake up." I sat back and willed him to respond with every ounce of my being. His features were lax and pale, as if all his vitality had bled from an invisible wound. I'd do anything to see the piercing light of his eyes, the lively quirk of his eyebrow, even the tight line of his lips when he frowned. "It's morning. Stop lazing about. I . . ." My voice broke, and I swallowed back the bitterness of my fear. "I need you."

Cupping my trembling hand against his face, I prayed the warmth would coax him out of this unnatural slumber. When he still didn't move, I grasped his shoulders and shook him. "Brantley. Wake up . . . please."

At last, he stirred. Lashes lifted, and eddies of blue and green swirled in his unfocused eyes. He squinted, then met my gaze and cleared his throat. "What are you doing?"

Relief poured through me. "Only waiting for you to wake up. Are you all right?"

"Why wouldn't I be?" His voice held a curt edge as he propped up on his elbows.

I eased away and sat on my heels to give him room to stand. He stood but didn't offer a hand to help me up.

"What happened last night?" he asked. This wasn't his familiar grumbly tone, the one I could always provoke with a bit of teasing. This morning he sounded cold and distant. Not annoyed, but coolly disinterested.

"I met the Gardener. Remember?" I struggled to my feet, suddenly embarrassed at how I wobbled. He didn't reach out a steadying hand, so I found my footing and faced him.

Frown lines pulled together on his forehead. "The what?"

"A strange man. He made the plants cover everyone. Consume them. I tried to beat them off. You collapsed. I was afraid—" I caught my breath. Fear knocked the wind from me again at the memory of Brantley's lifeless body on the ground. I clasped my hands together to still their shaking.

His expression cleared. "The convening. I understand now."

"You do?" I wanted to run into his arms, feel the reassuring warmth of his muscles—alive and moving. Yet his stance was remote and held me at a distance.

He glanced at me with something close to disdain. "Of course. Morra told us. You just didn't understand. The convening removes the pain."

"Pain? What pain?" I took a step back, my heart contracting at the stranger standing before me. He was Brantley, but Brantley without the warmth, the passion, the connection that had crackled between us.

He shrugged. "Longings unmet. Free of them all." He stretched and grinned.

"Do you remember me? Remember why we're here?" I watched closely for recognition to flare in his eyes.

Instead, he turned away. "To gather supplies and bring them back. But we can't."

His flat tone made me angry. "You're acting like you don't care. We have to find a way home." A dull throb took up residence behind my eyes.

Instead of arguing, he walked closer to the lake edge. The people who had slumbered there and been covered by the Gardener's vines were waking. Wimmo was still curled on the ground with her arms protecting her swollen belly. Beside her, Harba snorted, then sat up. He glanced at her, then shoved to his feet and wandered away. Morra sprang to standing, his auburn hair catching the rays of the subsun as it rose.

Brantley ignored them all and went to the shoreline. He pulled off his vest, tunic, and boots, tossed his longknife carelessly onto the clothes, and dove into the water. I knew he loved the water, but this was an odd time for a swim. We needed to make plans. Find a way home.

I limped over to Morra, hoping to glean helpful information. I executed the customary bob up and down, fighting to be civil and not take my frustration out on him. "How are you?"

He presented his leg and bowed. "All is being well." He spotted a young raven-haired woman nearby and smoothed his tunic. "She looks in want of company."

I pressed the heel of my hand against my forehead. "Morra, what changed? She's not the girl you were pining after yesterday."

"Pining?"

"Don't you remember? Crillo. You gave her flowers."

He chuckled. "But now I care not. Though flowers be a fine idea." He plucked a few yellow blossoms scattered among the daygrass and carried them to the girl who had newly caught his fancy. I shook my head. Such a fickle nature didn't bode well for his future relationships.

Wimmo woke, and I offered my hands to help her up. "Harba is around here somewhere." Why wasn't he hovering protectively near her as he had been?

"Who?" she asked.

"Harba. Your mate. The father of your babe."

Her confusion cleared, replaced by the same strange disinterest the others wore. "It matters not. Be you hungry? I recollect some persea trees nearby." She waddled toward the edge of the forest.

I stood watching the unnatural interactions as the rest of the people woke. They had seemed strangely disinterested before, but now their faces were vacant, empty of expression. Something inside them had changed in the night. I cast an uneasy glance toward Brantley, then back toward the others.

One small child toddled too close to the water's edge. I hurried forward and scooped her into my arms. Looking back to those awakening on the shore, I expected to see the relieved faces of the child's parents. Not one eye looked our way. All readied themselves for the day ahead. Strange people. "Who does she belong to?" I called.

No one answered. A shock of white hair caught my eye, and I carried the child to Trilia. "She almost fell in the water. Where are her parents?"

Trilia pulled her cloudy gaze from her feet and looked at me. "Any and all," she said at last.

I bounced the girl on my hip, my frustration mounting. "Well the 'any and all' are doing a poor job of watching her."

She tilted her head and stared at the child, then offered her arms. "She be pretty enough to show off designs. Perhaps a worker of fabric will take her." The girl reached out in return, so I surrendered her to Trilia's care. Trilia seemed to fill a sort of leadership role in the village. I hoped she'd be able to get the girl to the right people.

The atmosphere along the lake took on the spirit of another revel, though more subdued. Many men and women swam, paddling around along the lake's edge. Considering they only encountered the ocean here in their world's center, they all seemed comfortable in the water. Others gathered fruits and vegetables from the nearby forest. Still others constructed fire pits. One man pulled in a net of fish from the lake, and soon the scent of roasting filled the air. I wandered from one cluster to another, trying to have a sensible conversation. I received only blank stares, vague gestures, unhelpful shrugs.

At last I cornered Morra once again. He was the first I'd met, so we had a small connection. Perhaps if I pushed harder, he'd be able to help.

"You said the convening would give us answers, but I'm more confused than ever. Please. Tell us how to get to the sea."

He rubbed his eyes. "You be having trouble seeing?"

"No. Not 'see.' Sea. The ocean."

He laughed. "You be a good spinner of tales. Be that your gift?"

I raked a hand through my tangled hair. The snarls caught and added to my headache. I wished now that I hadn't used my headscarf to bandage Brantley's scraped hand. "I'm not a storyteller. But I am out of patience. Is there anyone who knows why the trees let us in but not out? Anyone to tell us how to free ourselves from this place?"

He rested a hand on my shoulder. "You be too full of care. When the rest of us leave, you should spend another night. Some be needing more help from the Gardener to be at peace."

I pulled away from his touch and crossed my arms. "I don't want to be at peace." Not if it meant being an empty-headed child sleepwalking through life.

He dusted his hands. "Untrue. All seek comfort."

"Some things are worth discomfort." How could I get any straight answers out of him? "Think of it. You stayed up all night and walked here all day, though you were exhausted. You chose discomfort to come to the convening."

His eyes lit. "A riddle. But we must."

I looked at the amiable but vacant faces eating their breakfast feast. "Why? What happens if you don't come to the convening?"

His brow wrinkled. "I know not. Ask another."

I limped from campfire to campfire until I found Trilia. She no longer held the little girl. I hoped she had found the child's parents and not just abandoned her. "Trilia, you're a leader among your people. I'm sure you can help me. What happens if you don't come to the convening? Morra couldn't explain to me."

A dark cloud settled over her, and I almost rejoiced to see a mixture of annoyance and disquiet touch her features. Anything but the numbness that painted the others. She sank to the ground and patted the spot beside her. I sat with straight legs, stretching forward and easing the soreness from the rigors of the past days.

"Fine. If that is the only way to stop you from pestering everyone. I'll retell the tale." Trilia stared at the water. "Long ago, our people created beautiful things but grew too attached. We built bonds with others that were too long-lasting. Jealousy, greed, possession became rampant." She shivered, even though the full warmth of both suns poured down on us. "Violence and destruction infected us all. So the Gardener gave us an answer."

"But he—" I bit back my words. I wanted to argue, to tell her about the Maker's love, His plan for those He'd created. A life so much better than the numbness the Gardener offered. Yet my disagreement could push her away, and I didn't want to risk interrupting her story. This was the closest I'd been to learning how this world worked.

She rested back on her elbows and smiled blandly up at the dazzling light. "As the vines be twining us, we be connected. All one. No person more cherished than another. We are free to be makers of all that is beautiful. By attaching to all, we detach from the pain of love and longing, of bonds and vows."

My heart recoiled. "What art is worth making apart from love?"

She turned toward me. "You visited our village. Were not the buildings and music and sculpture and dance of the highest beauty?"

I rubbed my forehead. A fair question. "The work I saw was gorgeous. Beyond anything my people have made."

"So, what be your concern?"

I had no answer and didn't try to stop her when she sprang up and stalked away. Only weeks ago, I would have agreed with her. Sacrificing everything to create my art had been the central truth of my life. If the novitiates of the Order had discovered a means to disconnect our hearts fully from all attachments, we would have welcomed it. To our detriment. For most of my life, I hadn't realized the pain and emptiness that came from pursuing dance apart from the Maker of all beauty and truth.

I flexed my feet and pointed them a few times, pushing against the soreness in my bad ankle. My conversations with these people kept going in circles. And at the moment, I had a more urgent problem. Our journey to the convening hadn't given the answers we'd hoped for, and Brantley and I needed to decide what to do next.

Except Brantley hadn't returned.

With the help of my stick, I pushed to my feet and walked along the lakeshore. Here, inland, the water was far more placid than the ocean's frightening waves. As placid as the tranquil expressions on everyone's faces. Yet the scent of honey and citrus wafted toward me. This was no basin of rainwater, but a fragment of ocean surrounded by land, and it could still swallow me if I fell into its depths. I eased a few paces away from the shore. If only a stream wound from this lake toward the rim. My swimming ability was weak, but I'd take the risk if it provided escape. Perhaps that's what Brantley was searching for, though I couldn't see any break in the surrounding slopes.

Scanning the water, I found nothing of Brantley, so I lifted my gaze to the opposite shore. There he was. He strode up the hill and disappeared into a break in the trees that appeared to be a path. My throat tightened. Was he leaving without me? I forced a slow breath. He would never leave without his clothes and knife. Maybe he was searching for an escape route. I limped back to his possessions and settled on the ground to wait.

A man strolled past. "Hungry? I have extra." He offered a broad leaf that held roasted fish.

"Thank you." I accepted the food, though I wasn't hungry. I would rebuild my strength so I'd be ready for our next step. Without so much as a sideways glance, the man ambled away as if we hadn't spoken. I felt invisible.

As I ate, I glimpsed Brantley's tiny shape again, then watched him slip in and out of view as he investigated the far side of the lake. At last, he dove back into the water, as fluid as a stenella at play. Strong arms propelled him across. Water glistened in his hair, and confident energy poured through his torso. But the usual light in his eyes seemed flat and lifeless, as if part of him still hadn't awoken.

He hefted himself onto the tangleroot not three feet from where I sat and grabbed his tunic, blotting his face, then dressing. He pulled on his boots, still not acknowledging my presence, not meeting my gaze. When he reached for his longknife, I grabbed it. That would get his attention.

One of his eyebrows rose in question.

"It's time to make a plan, Brantley. We can't stay here any longer."

He shrugged. "Plan whatever you like. I found a path to explore."

I scrambled to my feet. "That's wonderful news. Did you find a stream leading away from this lake? Could we follow it to the rim? Navar may be waiting for us."

He snatched the knife from me. "Didn't look."

Maker help me. Would I have to do the thinking for both of us? My heart stuttered. He would shake off the effects, wouldn't he? I didn't dare believe differently, the idea too horrific to accept. I'd treat him like the Brantley I knew, and eventually he would be. I leaned toward him. "Let's take that path. Perhaps we'll find a more helpful village."

He frowned. "Do what you will."

Then he strode away at a pace I would never be able to match, around the lake toward the path he'd discovered on the far side.

My mouth gaped, and pain tore through my heart, almost as bad as the brutal ache when I feared he would never wake. Surely he was teasing. Taunting me to keep up. He'd done the same when we'd fled the Order—challenging me in ways that seemed harsh. But his intent had been to help us make ground. Maybe this was more of the same.

I hobbled after, but when he broke into a jog along the shore, I recognized the futility of trying to catch him. I stood and watched Brantley in his great rush to be rid of me. When I turned back, the number of villagers had shrunk. Others were eating last bits of breakfast, rinsing their hands at the water's edge, and gathering bundles. I hurried to Morra, who was closest to me. "Wait. Where is everyone going?"

"We be returning now," he said cheerfully. "Fare you well." And he strode up the hill, pausing at the top to look back at me. At least he offered that much acknowledgement, unlike Brantley. Then he turned and headed into the woods.

Sudden emptiness filled the hillsides around the basin of the convening. Last hints of smoke wafted upward from fires that had been extinguished. Masses of stray vines, moss, and other foliage withered along the edge of the lake. A bitter scent rose as they rotted and sank into the ground. I quickly moved away from the reminder of the night's events and the Gardener's threats.

I limped up to the pine tree where Brantley and I had slept and retrieved my cloak. From this vantage, I watched Brantley reach the far side of the lake and disappear from view. Disbelief held my ribs so they could scarcely open or contract. This couldn't be happening. The chatter of villagers' conversation faded into the distance. A few birds caroled a greeting to each other as the suns rose higher. Then silence fell around me.

I sank to my knees, my shoulders trembling under the weight of solitude.

What should I do? Why had the Maker led me to this place and abandoned me? Why had I danced with such effort to hold back the Gardener's vines? None of it had mattered. The villagers welcomed their renewed numbness. Brantley had been altered by whatever the Gardener had done to him. My struggle had been useless.

And now I was alone.

My other experiences of loneliness washed over me. I'd endured the early years at the Order after I was ripped from my mother's arms and lied to—convinced I'd been given away happily as an honor. I'd faced the terrifying solitude of performing my final novitiate test before the panel of saltars. I'd wept under the stars as my mother's breath left her in the woods near Undertow. And I'd confronted the High Saltar and all the dancers in the center ground, standing against their lies and the power of their patterns.

You forget so quickly.

The quiet voice in my heart was warm and compassionate, even as it offered a gentle chiding. Guilt swept through me, heating my face. In each of those times when I felt bereft, I hadn't been truly alone.

"Yes," I said aloud, startled by the sound of my voice. "I'm not forsaken. You are here. But I can't see You. I'm so confused. How can I decide what to do?"

Ask. Listen. Wait.

The idea of waiting and listening to Him felt more challenging than my hardest technique class at the Order. Why hadn't I brought a copy of the Maker's letter with me? How could I have overlooked the importance of His words? That decision only highlighted how little I'd considered Him.

"Forgive me." I lifted my palms. "Teach me to remember You. To walk with You. Not only when I dance but all the time. Show me what to do next."

My muscles cramped, my hands trembled. Fears gibbered at me like the insects darting on the surface of the lake below. I resisted the ripples and waited until my heart stilled.

I longed for a map with step-by-step directions, much like the methodical form of the Order's patterns. Yet this effort of waiting, of listening, drew me closer to my Herder and Tender. I strained to hear His voice.

Instead, a different voice called out to me.

12

"WHERE DID YOU GO?" A MALE VOICE CALLED FROM THE nearby trailhead. My heart leapt, then dropped. Not Brantley. Of course not. He had long since disappeared down the path on the far side of the lake.

Instead, Morra's cheerful face scanned the tree line, lake, and empty hillsides.

"Over here." I waved from where I knelt under the shade of a pine tree, and he jogged over to join me. Leaning heavily on my stick, I eased to my feet. "I thought you'd left for your village."

He shrugged. "Started. Then kept seeing that picture. You standing here all alone. Didn't seem right somehow. Besides, I been curious 'bout the red star rain village for years now. Never got 'round to visiting. It be the path your companion took. Want to join me?"

I could have hugged him but didn't want to startle the young man. To have a travel guide would be a gift. Still, I held up my hand. "A wonderful idea. But let me listen first. I was asking the Maker about His plan."

Morra scratched his head. "If it's your plan, or my plan, be it not the makers' plan?"

He had returned as a kindness to me, and I was only confusing him. I drew a slow breath for patience and framed an explanation. "The course we set may appear wise, but I trust *the* Maker's wisdom, not my own. Or at least I'm learning." *Help me never again think of myself as maker. Help me listen to You, Maker of my soul.*

The freckles across the bridge of his nose scrunched. "Sounds too complicated."

I laughed, growing even fonder of the youth. "Life is complicated. More so when we call ourselves the maker apart from Him." I turned aside, lowered my head, and prayed silently. *Thank You for this unexpected ally. Should I go with him?*

A gentle inner nudge prompted me to accept Morra's offer. I was willing to stand alone if that was what the Maker asked, but it truly seemed He had brought me Morra as an answer.

I lifted my gaze and smiled at Morra. "Let's go."

Morra squinted at the ground near my feet. "Your Maker be down there? I didn't hear Him say anything." Before I could respond, he shrugged in a display of disinterest and led the way down to the lake and around its shore. As my ankle loosened, my limp became less pronounced, and we made better time than I would have expected. My companion whistled a lilting melody.

When we reached the new trailhead leading away from the lake into the unknown, I hesitated at the threshold of shadows. Trees grew close together here, and rustling sounds hinted at animals in the underbrush. Or worse. Perhaps the limbs whispered secrets to the Gardener. Just how deeply had his power infected this land? Morra seemed unconcerned, but then he seemed unconcerned about everything. "Is it safe?" I asked.

"Be it safe or be it not, it's the only path to the red rain village."

Brantley had come this way. I squared my shoulders and followed. As I walked into the gloom, the tendrils reminded me too much of the convening. I distracted myself by praying for Brantley. *Please keep him safe.* Would the effects of the Gardener's sleep wear off? I stumbled over a root and caught myself before falling headlong. *Help me find him.* If Brantley came to himself, he'd certainly return for me. What if he looked for me by the lakeshore? But what if his true self remained clouded? *You wouldn't let that happen, would You?* Subtly, my prayers turned into a spiral of worry.

I paused and scanned in all directions. "Morra, you're sure this is the only trail?"

Morra crouched and unearthed a purple-striped tuber from a pile of fallen leaves. He brushed it off and bit into it. "Want some?"

"We had tubers on my world—I mean . . . my village. None so bright, though." I bent forward and found another. In my palm, the odd stripes wavered and pulsed. The tangy scent was enticing. Too enticing. I had little trust for the unknown plants on this island, especially after watching the Gardener use plants to change people. My appetite soured, and I handed the root to Morra. "Is this the only trail to the red rain village?" I asked again.

"So I've heard." He chewed thoughtfully. "You come not from the red village? I've visited the blue and knew you not. Be you from the yellow, then?"

We resumed walking. Weary of dodging his questions, I opted for the truth, gently told. "I'm not from any of those villages. I'm from a completely other world: Meriel. Until we saw your island, we believed we were the only people adrift on the wide ocean. Brantley is a herder, so he trained a stenella—a sea creature—to help him gather fish. We rode her here and found your village." I cast him a sideways glance.

Worry puckered his brow, an unfamiliar expression on his normally cheerful face. "These tales you tell. They be not what we all know." He frowned, and I could see his mind working. Then he did what he and others all seemed to do when confronted with anything challenging in this place. He shook off the effort to reason and tossed his head. "Matters not."

He resumed whistling and striding ahead. I wanted to shake him and insist that many things mattered. They mattered greatly. Loved ones and home and purpose beyond ourselves. Instead I sighed and followed. Even through my shoes, I felt the chorus of the island again. *Forgotten, forgetting, forsaking.*

AFTER SEVERAL HOURS OF TRAVELING, THE SUNS splotched new colors across the sky like dye on wet linen. Orange and pink blended into swirls of blue-tinged clouds. Around us, the trees cast wide shadows, and green leaves darkened in growing shade. As wind rustled branches, I heard echoes of the Gardener's hiss, *You'll pay for your interference.* I stopped, scanning the deepening woods that surrounded us.

"Almost there," Morra said.

A faint mewling rose from a bunch of ferns off the trail. I froze. All day as we'd walked, I'd been hypersensitive to unfamiliar sounds. Morra had laughed off my tension, but that wasn't reassuring. How could I trust his common sense when he had no care for anything—including our safety?

"Be your leg tired?" Morra came back to me.

"Listen." I cocked my head. Now a plaintive wail drifted out. "Is it an animal?"

"I know not. Warm shelter waits right beyond the bend."

The sound changed to a plaintive hiccupping cry. Whatever the creature was, it sounded small and wounded. I stepped off the path and pushed aside bracken with my walking stick. Edging around large ferns that grew almost to my shoulders, I stepped farther into the dark overgrowth. An incongruous flash of crimson caught my eye. Crouching, I bent aside another broad leaf.

A baby lay on the damp ground, two small fists flailing weakly. His red blanket had fallen open, and he shivered and mewled again.

Gasping, I scooped him up in one arm, bracing myself with my cane. "You poor thing. What are you doing out here?" I carried him back to the trail where a few fingers of sun offered warmth. Against my chest, he nuzzled weakly, lips rooting in hunger.

Morra tapped his foot. "Put him back. The village waits."

I gaped at him. "He's dying. We have to take care of him. How did a baby end up alone here?"

Morra leaned closer to peek at the newborn but only wrinkled his nose. "Who knows? Not our business."

My warmth toward Morra cooled sharply, and I wrapped my cloak around the infant. "We're taking him to somewhere safe. To someone who can care for him."

Morra's eyes widened at the steel in my voice. "Bring it if you must. I be going."

He tossed his hair and stomped away. I continued bouncing and shushing the baby in one arm, hobbling forward with my stick in the other hand. He needed milk . . . from the mother if we could find her, or a wet nurse, or at least a herd animal if the village had some.

I caught up to Morra and passed him. "Hurry! We need to find help for this baby."

He sighed and walked faster but didn't match my urgency. Heat boiled up from my core, and my skin burned. I hoped the added warmth would help the infant as I held him. "Who would leave a child to die? Have you heard of a baby being stolen from its parents?"

"Parents?"

Honestly, talking with Morra was often like shouting into a cavern full of echoes. "The baby's family."

"All are family."

"But the mother—someone gave birth to him. Where is she?" A new fear struck me. Perhaps the mother had died, leaving no one to care for the child. Yet that still didn't explain the abandonment.

Striding alongside me, Morra muttered under his breath. "You should camp back at the lake. You be needing more convening time."

My sense of horror built, not only at a baby left to die, but at how Morra brushed off an abandoned child as a common occurrence. I rounded on him. "More convening is the last thing I need. Or any of you need. You may lose a few cares, but apparently you've also lost your heart."

Morra wiped sweat from his forehead with the back of his hand as the path widened into a sun-dappled clearing. "Here we be." Relief was evident in his voice.

I felt immediate regret for taking out my frustrations on him. I tucked my cane under my arm and reached out to touch Morra's shoulder. "Thank you for coming back to the lake. Thank you for helping me find my way here. Will you stay near?"

He gave a heavy sigh that reminded me of a sixth-form novitiate sent on a shift to mortar walls. "Wherever you be from must be a strange place. You worry about small problems and be wanting no convening." But a hint of sympathy flickered in his eyes.

We emerged from the overgrown path to confront a tall pine trunk, stripped of branches. Above our heads, a cabin rested on wide boughs, tethered with ropes. A ladder fashioned from braided vines dangled from the other side. Bridges hung overhead, joining the little home to other cottages up in the trees. They swayed as the earth made familiar rocking movements.

"Hello?" I hurried under the first cabin and looked up at the open doorway, desperate to find help for the warm bundle in my arm.

No one answered. With Morra trailing me, I rushed farther into the village, peering up at the rough wood-and-vine cottages. All seemed empty, and none held the elegance of the green rain village. No ornate carvings or vibrant paint drew the eye. Yet their rustic forms created a simple beauty. Under other circumstances I would have loved exploring the swinging bridges and ladders and platforms scattered among the treetops.

Right now, I had more urgent matters. "Where is everyone?"

Morra grinned. "Suns be setting soon. Time to revel."

I groaned. More revels? I had appreciated the shared art forms at Morra's village but couldn't face another night of such festivities. Besides, a revel would be the last place Brantley would go. But at least I'd find help for the infant.

Morra slapped my back. "Stop your worries. Not time for their star rain yet, so it be a short revel." He led the way, and I urged him to move faster. The baby had stopped stirring and felt limp and weak in my arm. He needed help quickly.

As we neared the far side of the village, sounds rose from the huge field beyond. The roars of a large group of men and women rumbled and growled as if a pack of forest hounds fought nearby.

In the clearing a crowd surrounded an open area, cheering, shaking fists in the air. These villagers didn't wear ornate fabrics of fine weave. Instead, leather and coarse wool were the clothes of choice, with tufts of animal fur adorning shoulders or pockets or cuffs. I took a minute to absorb the strangeness of yet another unfamiliar group of people. I'd expected another scene like Morra's village. This snarling, shouting mob frightened me.

But Morra grinned and ambled forward, elbowing his way through the pack. "Excuse me," I said, following him, but no one heard me. I cradled the baby more closely to protect him from careless elbows and jostling.

We reached the front. In the center of the rowdy crowd, two men crouched and circled, swords glinting red as the setting subsun touched their steel. Blades met, the crowd cheered. The men shoved away from each other. A giant of a man, with a fierce beard and bits of bone woven into his braids, bellowed. He swung his sword downward toward his much-smaller opponent. A roar rose from the people watching.

I squeezed my eyes closed, unwilling to watch a man cleaved apart.

Another thunder of approval punched the air.

My eyes flew open against my will. The smaller man had rolled to the side and now sprang up, grinning and all too familiar.

I gasped. Brantley, flushed with exertion and with a new scrape on his chin, raised his borrowed sword, a feral grin on his face, ready to plunge back into the battle.

"No!" I cried.

But a roar from the throng smothered my scream.

13

I ELBOWED ASIDE TWO BURLY MEN IN THE WATCHING crowd, ready to dash into the middle of the duel. Morra tugged me back. "Be not interfering."

I froze. He was right. I didn't dare distract Brantley. If he didn't give his full attention to the man and his sword, the sharp tip could find his heart. Besides, I couldn't endanger the babe tucked in my arm. I bit the inside of my cheek until I tasted blood.

Brantley charged toward his opponent. The larger man made a clumsy swing—too soon. While the giant was off balance, Brantley spun in from the side. He slammed the man's sword arm with the flat of his blade. The weapon fell, and Brantley brandished his sword overhead.

Relief whooshed out of me in a breath. The spectators cheered. The bearded man rubbed his stinging arm but gave a wide grin, then pounded Brantley on his back. Brantley swung the sword a few times from his wrist in a lazy circle. Then he switched his grip, offering the hilt to one of the villagers, as if he were an attendant serving a platter of saltcakes.

"Well played," the man said, taking the sword. "Who's next?"

Brantley's eyes skimmed past me, pausing only a moment before he turned away, indifferent.

My heart contracted.

Two young women rushed forward with long branches and began a contest of aggressive swiping, jumping, and ducking. The crowd shouted encouragement and jeered mistakes.

Staring after Brantley, I rolled my shoulders, coaxing life into my tense muscles, and leaned into Morra. "What just happened?"

"They be playing." Morra bounced on his toes.

"Playing?"

Reluctantly, he pulled his gaze from the battlefield. "Your people don't play?"

I pictured the Order, where novitiates walked with careful steps and moved with precise posture. Some of our dances were fierce and powerful, but always in controlled patterns with focused purpose. The drills that the soldiers performed were no different. I shook my head. I'd never witnessed dangerous "play" like this. Weapons of battle had only ever brought violence, wounds, and death.

Now that I knew no one was about to be killed, I returned my attention to my first priority. I stroked the infant's head. "We need help for this baby. Don't forget—"

Too late. Morra bounded across the field to a man with a parchment and willow pen. He apparently planned to sign up for a turn at this "play."

I hurried along the edge of the circular field toward Brantley. He was blotting sheen from his forehead with the sleeve of his tunic and puffing up his chest as he received congratulations from bystanders.

If the heart-numbing effects of the Gardener's work were going to wear off, it hadn't happened yet. Brantley barely managed to raise one brow. "Carya? You followed me here?" His gaze took in the bundle in my arms, and his brow lifted a fraction higher; but his tone was still weighted with indifference. "What is that?"

I lifted back the corner of the blanket. "He was left in the woods. We have to get him help."

He made a wide gesture with his arm. "Plenty of folk here can give you aid. I have somewhere to be."

A woman with nut-brown hair sidled up beside Brantley, resting a possessive hand on his shoulder. "Well fought. A warm meal and warmer bed await."

He threw an arm around her and strolled off toward the village. My jaw gaped, my face burning as if I'd been slapped. What was he thinking?

Had he forgotten everything about our mission to bring aid to Meriel? Had he forgotten me? What we meant to each other? We'd talked about our vision of life together, and now he dismissed me without a thought.

Heat bubbled up from my core, purging my humiliation and pain until nothing remained but a white-hot blaze. I stomped after him, ready to pull him away from the woman who was still managing to twine around him like tangleroot as they walked away.

The baby sniffled weakly and managed one coughing cry. I paused. Confronting Brantley had to wait. The infant's needs came first. After scanning the bystanders ringing the field, I headed to a woman who looked promising. She was stout, with an ample chest, and reminded me of Ginerva. "I found this child in the woods. Do you know his mother?"

The woman pushed me aside because I was blocking her view of the games.

Not to be ignored, I dropped my cane and tugged her arm. "Please. Where does this child belong?"

She glared at me. "Most likely in the woods where you found it. Folks only keep around the strong ones that can be trained for the games. Leave it for the welfen beast."

My stomach lurched as if I'd missed a step on the marble stairs back at the Order. "No. You're wrong. This life is precious, and someone must miss him."

She stepped away, waving a fist and yelling advice to the women fighting on the field.

I tried another woman, and another, and then several men. Their disinterest turned to annoyance when I kept interrupting their fun. I even approached a few unkempt children who scrabbled about in the dirt and dashed between the legs of the adults. Their young bodies bore bruises and scars. No one wanted to bother with the problem of a forsaken baby. Brantley had been right all along. This island was a dark and dangerous place.

Holy Maker, why don't they care? What can I do?

Warm meal and warm bed. That's what the woman with Brantley had said. Well, that was what the baby needed. I squared my shoulders, gripped my walking stick, and stormed toward the village.

Although most of the houses among the trees still appeared deserted, lantern glow flickered from one of the cottages wedged on broad limbs above me. A rope ladder dangled beneath, but I couldn't navigate that, not with an infant and a cane. "Hello?"

When no one responded, I braced myself and shouted. "Hello! This baby needs care. I'm not leaving." For good measure, I tossed a stone in the direction of the doorway. It struck the lintel with a satisfying clack.

The brunette woman emerged, balancing on the jutting threshold above the ladder. "You again? Are you challenging me for the man?" Her gaze skimmed my cane and bandaged ankle, and she sneered. Another distant roar from the field behind me warned how these people enacted their challenges, but I wasn't about to back down.

"No, she's not." Brantley joined her on the landing. "I'll deal with this."

The woman flounced back inside. Brantley navigated the ladder with ease, jumping down from the halfway point. The thump of his landing punctuated the irritation in his face. "Carya, what are you doing here?"

I jutted my chin forward. "Help me find someone to care for this baby so we can resume our search for a way home."

He shook his head, his focus sliding to the bundle in my arms. Something in his expression softened. When his gaze lifted, I saw glimmers of affection—a familiar tenderness I used to find often in his eyes.

And then dullness fell back over him, like a mist blocking the view of the suns. "The child's not my concern. Not your problem either."

I glared at him. "Saying so doesn't make it true."

He rolled his eyes. "If I help you, will you give me peace?"

Not if he intended to set up camp with the woman in the tree cottage and forget our own world. But this wasn't the time to tell him that. Instead, I nodded. "Of course."

"Fine. I'll ask Reeya."

"No, that's not—" He clambered up the ladder before I could stop him. I eyed the ground for more rocks to throw if it became necessary, but after a few minutes, he returned.

"She said there's a tender on the lakeward side of the village."

"A tender? Of livestock?" What help would that be?

He shrugged. "Are you coming or not?"

I took a few steps, leaning awkwardly on my walking stick while hitching the infant more securely in my arm, which ached from his weight, tiny wisp though he was.

Brantley sighed. I had never tolerated pity from him, but he'd always offered concern or understanding. Now hints of disdain etched his face. My ankle throbbed with an ache that traveled to my heart. I saw myself through his eyes. Crippled. Broken. Annoying. He abruptly took the bundle from my arm, although certainly not out of kindness. He merely wanted to hasten this errand. Still, my arm tingled with relief when he carried the baby, and I was better able to keep up.

He led us through the maze of trees, ladders, and ropes. How had he gotten so comfortable here in the few hours he'd had before I arrived? His skill at navigating harsh environments was remarkable, another glimpse of the true Brantley, the man I admired so much. Would I ever get him back?

Not far from the trailhead where Morra and I had arrived from the lake, a cottage and paddock nestled under broad willows. At last, a building that wouldn't require climbing to reach. "I wonder why this home isn't up in the trees like all the rest."

Brantley snorted. "Perhaps because ponies can't climb trees?"

Ponies? I hurried forward. Sure enough, in the far corner of the paddock several sturdy ponies tore at tufts of hay, chewing thoughtfully. It was such a relief to find the familiar creatures on this strange island that ridiculous tears gathered in my eyes. I slipped open the gate and hugged one of their warm necks, drawing comfort from the gently pricked ears and snuffled greeting.

"Here, you!" a woman called from the cottage doorway, her hair pulled back into a tufted shape that resembled a mane, with the sides shaved close. Her tattered dress hung to just below her knees. "What be you doing?"

Brantley may have changed in many ways, but he still took charge before I could speak. "Reeya suggested we come to you. She"—he jabbed his chin my direction—"found this infant abandoned in the woods off the path."

I stepped away from the pony. "I don't know how long he was left there, but he's cold and weak." Pleading made my voice shake. I couldn't bear more indifference to this little one's suffering.

Brantley thrust the bundle at her. "Will you find his mother?"

She shook her head but gathered the baby into her arms. "The mother would only be leaving him again." She pulled back the corner of the blanket, and her eyes softened. "Ah, poor lamb. You be needing milk. Lucky for you my nanny goat has plenty to spare."

Her response was so warm and normal that something in my spine melted.

She turned a smile toward us. "May as well be coming in for a mite. The kettle just boiled."

We followed her into the cottage. She listed to one side, placing little weight on her right leg. A posture with which I was familiar. She waved us to stools beside a tiny table while she gathered a small linen scarf and a clay pitcher. The gamey scent of goat milk wafted as she settled in her chair and dipped the fabric into the liquid. She offered the corner of wet scarf to the listless babe. After she cooed at him and tickled his cheek, he made a small effort to suckle. As she continued soaking the scarf and offering it to him, I scanned the room.

A tidy pallet rested near a small hearth, whose fire shared generous warmth. Pegs held a cloak, a few bridles, and a large basket. Open shelves contained other necessities: jars with neat labels, bowls of herbs and tubers, one plate, one mug, and surprisingly, a stack of parchment and pile of willow pens. Where the first village had used elaborate ornamentation on any spare surface, this cottage was almost stark. I welcomed the clean simplicity.

"My name is Carya of Meriel. This is Brantley of Windswell."

"Strange names they be." But she spoke with a smile in her eyes. "I be Jalla, the tender." When she shifted her grip on the baby, her hem hitched up, and I could see her right knee. Angry purple swallowed the joint. No wonder her gait was uneven.

"What happened?" I asked, nodding toward her knee.

She tugged the dress lower and kept her attention on feeding the baby. "A rankled old nag kicked me."

"Do you have herbs? Compresses? Can I help?"

Brantley sighed heavily, and his gaze traced the path to the door.

I wanted to elbow him for his lack of compassion. This wasn't Brantley, though. I remembered the true man, the one I hoped was still inside. Maybe in time my love could draw him back out.

Jalla smiled. "You be kindly. Worry not. 'Tis healing. Though I've missed two convenings." She squeezed more drops of milk into the baby's mouth, tracing a finger along the tiny pursed lips. "Missing like that does funny things to one. Makes it seem everyone else is strange. But I know the problem be me."

"No." I spoke so sharply that Brantley straightened on his stool, eyes wide. I patted her arm. "Everyone *is* strange. You are finding the way you're meant to be. Caring about others. Being connected to others. I see it in the way you welcomed the babe. Please, whatever you do, do not go back to the lake."

Jalla clutched the baby closer and glanced around, as if fearing spies lurked outside her windows. "I must. We all must. Surely you know that." Her eyes narrowed, and she stared at the bandage on my leg. "Did you miss a convening? Is that why you be speaking mistakes?"

"I was there. With the green star rain village."

Jalla leaned forward, a spark of interest lighting her eyes.

Perhaps I'd finally found an ally who wasn't completely mesmerized by the Gardener. "A man . . . a creature . . . uses the plants and—"

"I'll be going now." Brantley's stool scraped back as he stood. He yawned, clearly bored with my efforts. I eyed the pitcher of goat's milk and contemplated flinging it in his face. Perhaps that would wake him from this apathy.

Jalla blinked and leaned back. "Yes. You should leave. That's best. I'll care for the little one. That is, I'll do all I can unless they . . ." She shivered.

Brantley's muscles tensed, some of his old instincts flaring. "Are you in danger?" His voice carried a hint of interest.

I hid a grin. That was definitely the Brantley I recognized—alert to threats and ready to protect the powerless.

Jalla's shoulders curved in protectively. "As you know, there be little mercy for those who miss convenings. Thankfully no one has paid attention yet. But if someone notices the next time I miss, I'll be staked out for the vines to consume. At the very least, I'll be forced to become a remnant."

"Next time you should ride one of your ponies," Brantley said, before I could recover from the image her words called up and ask her what she meant by "remnant."

I shot him a glare, then touched her arm. "Don't listen to him. Not about the convening."

The woman gave us both a quizzical frown. "I'd not be allowed to ride. Everyone knows the walk prepares us for the convening. And all be knowing we must attend."

"Everyone *thinks* they know. That doesn't make it true. The convening is harming people. This baby is proof. What evil makes a mother forget her child? And you're one of the few who can recognize that."

Jalla's forehead creased, and her hands shook as she dipped the fabric into the milk again. "You be speaking perilous words. You must go."

"Come on, Carya." Brantley crossed to the threshold. "You're upsetting her. You found someone to take the child. Now leave it be."

I stood. The woman had the right to ask me to leave her home. My arguing was only causing her agitation. "I won't trouble you anymore. Just think about what I've said."

She turned away as if my presence carried disease and death into her home.

I ached for her and the confusion she must be feeling. I ached for the baby—and how many other little ones? Snippets of comments returned to me: *pretty enough . . . only the strong ones . . .* I ached for the unloved children, neglected and forgotten, and for the entire island, suffering under the deception that made the people numb and isolated without them even realizing what their lives could be.

I followed Brantley outside. "I think we should borrow some ponies and go back to the lake. We must confront the Gardener. I'm sure he's the one that's preventing our escape."

"Escape? Why should I? I like this village just fine."

Of course he did. The people here would appreciate his reckless and aggressive side, and he had none of the burden of responsibility placed upon a leader on Meriel. "We don't belong here. We have to get home."

He tugged his leather vest down over the belt that held his longknife, his gaze traveling up the path toward Reeya's tree home. "Do what you wish. I have somewhere to be." Once again, he walked away from me.

This time I let my hurt and anger coil into fierce determination. He wasn't going to brush me off so easily.

14

"WAIT!" EVERY OUNCE OF MY DESPERATION FLEW ACROSS the air between us.

Brantley stopped, his weight still canted forward. All my hopes balanced between his stride. I reached out a hand he couldn't see, as if that could draw him toward me, and scrambled for a compelling idea.

"Navar." His purest and most uncomplicated bond. "If you stay, you'll never see Navar again. And Brianna and Orianna and your mother—all of Windswell. And I have a question."

He turned, forehead creased. At least I'd grabbed his attention. Now to keep him engaged. "How long can Navar dive? Could she make it to the lake?"

His frown deepened. "Why would you ask that?"

I limped a few steps closer to him. "I've seen you call her from the water. If you used your whistle in the lake, would she hear? Could she join you?"

His tousled bangs shifted upward, and he pursed his lips. Now he was definitely interested. "Maybe."

"I could write a letter and seal it . . . maybe in a jug? We can attach it to Navar's harness, and she could swim back to Meriel. If Teague sees it, he will let Saltar Kemp know we're alive."

Brantley had begun to lean forward, but now he crossed his arms. "And then?"

"Then . . ." My shoulders sank. "I don't know. I'm not sure what comes next, but if Saltar Kemp knows we're still alive, she will find a way to keep Meriel in reach. We can return home."

His smile was as patronizing as the highest high saltar, a sickening sight on his once-familiar face. "Carya, let it go. We're here now. I like this place. They appreciate my skills. You'd fit in well with the green village. Find your way back there. You need to accept facts. We'll never again see Meriel."

The man before me now was callous, distant. And because he spoke with Brantley's voice, the effect jarred me even more. Still, when he walked away, I followed him. He returned to Reeya's house and called up to her.

She stepped into the doorway, but a man appeared behind her. She shifted one shoulder. "You left. I'm busy now."

I breathed a sigh of relief that I wouldn't have to watch him disappear into her house. Brantley simply shrugged. A distant roar from the combat area pulled his attention. He sketched a careless wave and headed toward the sound.

If I let him walk away again, I'd never get him back to our world.

I limped after him as fast as I could, the pain in my ankle fueling my anger. "Stop!"

He ignored me, and I couldn't outpace him. Every muscle in my body tensed. Frantic, furious, I didn't know what to do. I raised my walking stick and flung it at him.

I gasped at the same moment it thudded into his back. What had I done? What had I become?

Brantley spun, every inch the alert warrior. The heat of battle blazed from his eyes, and his head moved sharply as he scanned all directions.

I lifted my arms in apology.

He blinked, then saw the object that had struck him: my walking stick lying benignly in the daygrass. He grabbed it and crossed the distance to me. The anger in his eyes didn't frighten me as much as the lack of the love that once shone from them. Would I never again see warmth and affection from him?

"You're lucky you're so frail." The curls that framed his face were no longer playful. They looked as wild and threatening as his expression. He thrust the cane at me with a snarl. "Go back to the lake. Maybe the Gardener can grant you some sense."

I took my stick, vowing never to use it as a weapon again. "Come with me. Please. I know you don't remember, but the convening changed you. Changed everyone. This isn't you."

The battle fury had shaken him from apathy, but already the pulse along his neck slowed, and the fog closed over his expression again. How could I hold his attention? How could I convince him to return to the lake and try to contact Navar?

In the distance, a woman shouted, "New challenge!" Jeers and applause floated through the air.

That was my answer. I stabbed my stick into the ground. "A new challenge. From me!"

Brantley backed away a few steps, squeezing his forehead as if it ached. "You want to fight me? You don't even know how to hold a longknife."

"I want to race you."

His gaze swept my weary form, settling on the bandage supporting my injured ankle.

"You're touched in the head. Look at yourself."

His disdain froze the core of my heart, but I raised my chin. *It's not really Brantley. The Maker still loves him. I still love him. He just can't receive that yet.*

"A riding race. We'll ask the tender for two ponies and race to the lake."

Interest lit his eyes to the shade of a fresh-washed sky. "And if I win, you'll stop following me around like a lost kit?"

"If I win, you'll try to summon Navar."

He perused the sky. Violet streaks lowered over the homes overhead, and our shadows stretched, one pale and the other dark. "It'll be dark soon."

He was right. As desperate as I was to try my plan, I didn't want to brave the island's unknown dangers at night. "First light?" I offered my hand.

He grabbed my forearm as if I were a soldier. "Deal." The distant crowd noise pulled his attention again, and his teeth flashed in a feral grin. "I think I'll try a few *real* matches first. See you at primary sunrise."

This time as he strode away, I stood my ground and squared my jaw. When I was fleeing the Order, we'd traveled together for months, faced cold, hunger, rough terrain, dangerous creatures. Yet he still had no idea how much determination dwelt in the heart of a dancer.

I trudged all the way back to the tender's home and leaned on the fence. One lively mare tossed her mane. The scent of hay and manure grounded me, reassured me of all things real and normal. Resting my head in my arms, a memory spun through my mind and fed my hope.

Saltar Kemp had taken our class to the village tender as a reward when we graduated from form six. Some of the other novitiates showed little interest in the mangy ponies, but I'd fallen in love. I rode a speckled bay who trotted around the corral. The rhythm of riding was not far different from learning to follow the patterns of the drums. With the saltar's encouragement, I braced my hands against the withers and pulled my legs under me in one smooth motion. The pony cantered in a fluid gait as I straightened from my crouch, balancing on my feet, absorbing the warmth of his back. Arms wide, I was a bird in flight or a gust of wind sailing past the blur of my classmates' faces—until a slight buckle of the earth made the pony lurch. I had tumbled off but sprang up laughing.

Now I studied the lines of a white mare. Strong, sound legs—unlike mine. Bright eyes. She'd do. My plan had to work. I limped to Jalla's door. I wouldn't be showing off my balance by standing on a pony's back tomorrow, but at least I could ride. And I would have to ride fast enough to win my wager with Brantley.

Jalla's eyes lit at my request for ponies for a race. "They be in need of a frolic."

I asked if I could sleep in the stable, but she hustled me into her cottage instead. "You'll be holding the babe while I fix us a bit of stew."

Tiny perfect fingers curled around mine as I emulated the tender's technique of soaking a cloth with milk and coaxing the baby to suckle. A wash of affection coated my heart, soothing the many wounds of the day. All my years in the Order, I'd foresworn family. Dancers were destined to an exclusive calling that left no room for husband or children. Or so we had been taught.

The baby's face blurred, and I blinked several times. The Maker had invited me into the freedom He'd always intended, even the freedom of attachments, of love. And I was trapped on an island that erased love.

"Be not worrying. I'll care for him." Jalla plunked a bowl in front of me and scooped up the child. "I be thinking I'll miss another convening. Just to be sure my caring remains."

"Aren't you worried that other villagers will hurt you?"

"They need my ponies for the games. And in recent months the creatures be better than ever before. Perhaps I be caring, but perhaps that benefits their mounts. That should be enough for the Every to blind their eyes to my absence. At least for a time." Her cheeky grin startled a laugh from me. When she settled at the table, I gratefully indulged in the stew to warm my belly while our conversation warmed my soul. She was so normal. Curious, clear-eyed, connecting. After dinner she gladly shared a few sheets of parchment. I wrote a letter to Saltar Kemp, rolled it, and coated it with wax before sealing it in a small jar. I also wrote out the opening pages of the Maker's letter, explaining His story to Jalla as I worked. His truth was one gift I could leave with her.

She listened, open-mouthed, until the baby whimpered and demanded her attention. When she pushed back from the table, she paused, staring out her door into the darkness. "Seems our world could be using these words," she said quietly. A tingle skittered across my spine. I'd grown so focused on helping Brantley and finding a way home, I'd forgotten that the Maker might have a larger plan, one that seemed to require far more courage than I had.

"And perhaps I be sharing something of value with you, as well." Jalla reached for a small container on a top shelf. "Liniment that eases injuries in my ponies. Made from a rare herb and hard to make. I only be having a bit, but may I tend you?"

I unwrapped the bandage around my ankle. The potion had an astringent scent mingled with the sweetness of yellow wildflowers. The instant it touched my skin, a tingling warmth spread over my oozing scar, erasing the pain. A sigh escaped me.

"Helping?" she asked.

"Very much so. Thank you."

She nodded, pleased, and tucked the remaining liniment into my pack. "Wish I had more to give you, so use it sparingly. Save it for when you be most in need of healing."

On a borrowed pallet near the hearth, as I drifted in and out of sleep, I tried not to think about where Brantley would shelter for the night. Perhaps he'd get so caught up in the play battles that he wouldn't seek out some woman's company. Perhaps he'd get hit on the head enough times that he wouldn't keep his seat tomorrow. On that satisfying thought, I finally fell into a deep slumber.

The next morning, I rose in the predawn darkness and took myself through a careful dancer warm-up, engaging each muscle, pleased that my ankle, though stiff, wasn't as inflamed. Jalla agreed to let me use the lively mare I'd admired, and winked as she saddled a heavier old gelding for Brantley. "They be knowing their way home. If you don't ride them back, just set them loose."

"Thank you for your help." I pressed the rolled parchment with the Maker's words into her hands. "Are you sure you can avoid punishment if you keep missing convenings?"

"Ah, they can't be bothered with a lowly tender. Worry not for me.

Now, you'll be needing a satchel." She scurried about gathering supplies for me, invested in my mission. "Her name is Windrider, and she be fleet. But you'll be wanting carrots and a few persea for her. Puts the pep right back in her stride. I'll water her light before you go. There be a well halfway to the lake."

"I remember. I'll stop there." Her enthusiasm coaxed a smile to my lips, but it faded quickly. Brantley might not show up. Even if he came, he might outrace me. Even if we contacted Meriel, he might insist on staying. The effects of the Gardener's spores might never wear off. When Jalla offered me a saltcake, I shook my head, stomach twisted in knots.

She pursed her lips. "I'll put them in your pouch. Takes strength to ride full out."

I slipped the satchel's strap across my body and tied my cane across the back of the saddle. Jalla led both ponies out of the corral. I pressed my face against Windrider's warm neck. "We have to win," I whispered to her.

The glow of the approaching primary sunrise streaked the sky, and I studied the path from the main cluster of tree homes. Would Brantley appear?

PREDAWN BREEZES TUGGED A STRAND OF MY HAIR, AND I
tucked it behind my ear while I waited by the stables with Jalla. I'd used
my headscarf to wrap Brantley's thorn-scraped hand our first day here.
Now my hair refused to stay in its braid. My leggings were stained, my
bandage was tattered again, and my tunic smelled of sweat and needed
a good washing. The last few days had taken a toll. At least the pony
wouldn't mind. I ran my fingers through Windrider's coarse mane
and checked the saddle's girth strap. The sound of footsteps pulled
my head up.

"Why be you racing so early?" Morra ambled toward me, tossing an
apple from hand to hand. "I'm all for challenge, but this be so early it's
still the backside of night."

His red-rimmed eyes testified to lack of sleep, and a bruise on one
cheek told me he'd tried a few contests. But his cheery smile was a
welcome sight. "What are you doing here?" I asked.

He leaned a pudgy arm on the corral fence. "Can't have a race without
a witness to the winner. Brantley told me your wager." He turned to Jalla.
"Can I be having a fast one? I'll start out now."

"So Brantley's coming?" I asked.

"If not, I be having a long ride for no purpose." Morra laughed, and
today his vacuous manner didn't irritate me. Whatever the outcome of the
race, it would help to have a friend of sorts at the finish. If Brantley even
followed through.

Jalla quickly selected a mount for Morra, and he took off down the
trail toward the lake. "Wait," I called. "When did you last see Brantley?"

But Morra was already out of earshot, his pony galloping with so much enthusiasm the ground sent out ripples that I felt underfoot.

The baby's plaintive cry rose from the cottage, and Jalla hurried inside. In spite of my worries about the race, I smiled. The infant would be cared for here—as long as Jalla stayed away from the next convenings. It was a wonder any child survived its parents' indifference. An instinct must draw adults to take over the feeding and shelter of at least some children after each trip to the lake, or none would survive. But to have the little ones shifting from home to home with no faithful parents? My smile drooped. *Maker, these people need to know Your love.*

A bird chirruped from a nest in a nearby willow, and a wave rolled underneath. The people of this world hadn't seen the ocean, but they could feel its effects each day. The angle of the sun changed as the island turned. The earth rocked as currents shifted. Tree homes swayed, and the tang of sweet, citrus sea air carried from beyond the barrier vines. Even their art carried images of waves and stenella. Their ancestors must have known the sea. How strange that no one believed me when I attempted to explain the ocean. Just as my world saw evidence of the Maker all around, but some still chose not to see.

I stroked Windrider's forehead. "Have you raced before? Or do you usually carry loads to other villages? We have to win. Today is your day to be fully the pony you were meant to be."

"Let's get this over with. I've signed up for another sword combat tonight. After I win this wager, I want to return in time." Brantley's voice was as rough as the scuffed leather of his vest. He couldn't spare a "Good morning?"

I bit back a sarcastic reply. His curls were slicked back and still damp. His trousers had been brushed clean, and he no longer wore the makeshift bandage on his scratched palm. He could have at least returned my scarf. "I'm ready. I've *been* ready."

His lopsided grin didn't charm me today. "Had to give Morra enough lead time," he said. "Do you accept him as our official judge?"

"And if I don't?"

"This wager was your idea. I have better things to be doing. So, if you'd rather concede—"

"Mount up." I waved to the stodgy gelding.

He frowned, walked around it a few times, but then shrugged and hefted himself into the saddle without using the stirrups. His legs dangled close to the ground. If he tried to use the stirrups, his knees would be forced up to his chin. And Brantley didn't bother dismounting to adjust the length. I hid a grin. Jalla was giving me every advantage she could think of.

"How long ago did Morra start out?" he asked.

I squinted at the position of the subsun, barely peeking above the tree line. "Just after primary sunrise. He's had a lengthy head start." I placed my good foot into a stirrup and settled onto Windrider, shifting my shoulder bag to hang behind me.

"See you at the lake." With that taunt, Brantley kicked his heels and urged his pony into a full-out run.

I lifted my reins and squeezed my thighs, leaning forward to signal Windrider. She trotted to the trailhead, then surged into a smooth canter. My fear tempted me to coax her into a harder pace immediately. But if Windrider was anything like a dancer, she would preserve her stamina better if we didn't spend all her energy in the first mile.

Even with occasional shifts when the path rode up and down from a wave beneath the island, my pony's gait was smooth as a windless sea. I kept her at the relaxed canter, watching the path unfold before us. Trees and fields blurred past, and a sheen formed on her neck, but her ears stayed forward and eager, and her hooves moved with the lightness of a novitiate in the first class of the day.

I kept my weight forward, my thighs cramping with the effort to become one with her and make her journey easier. Straining ahead, I still didn't see Brantley, although occasional hoof marks marred the boggy sections of the path.

Had he gotten so far ahead that I'd never catch up? After an hour, my physical strength was failing, even though Windrider was doing the true work. I lurched sideways, my bad ankle no longer supporting equal weight in its stirrup. Gritting against the pain, I pushed my heel down, regaining my center.

She stumbled at my awkward shift but didn't slow. I bent over her neck. "Thank you, brave creature."

Her ears pricked and swiveled, and her gliding gait increased a fraction.

The trail burst from a section of forest to a broad meadow. Finally, I caught a glimpse of Brantley. My heart sank. He was so far ahead. This was hopeless. But I had to keep riding.

Where the field of yellow grains transitioned to the pale green of daygrass, a stone well stood out against the softer colors. Jalla had told me to let Windrider rest there.

Brantley reached the well and looked over his shoulder. I drew closer. White foam flecked his pony's mouth, its eyes wide with strain. After his brief glance, Brantley turned forward and urged his mount onward. His pony ought to be exhausted by the clumsy and breakneck pace, but they ate up ground and disappeared into the trees.

When we neared the well, I reined in Windrider to a soft trot, and then to a walk. Jalla knew this route, and she knew her ponies. I slid off and walked Windrider in loops around the well, letting both of our heart rates slow. Then I pulled up a half bucket of water, drank a few sips, and offered it to her. She drank a small amount, then nuzzled my pack.

I laughed. "When we reach the lake," I promised. Jalla hadn't specified how long to rest, and my bones itched to keep moving. But I took the time to check the pony's hocks and fetlocks. No swelling. No tenderness. Her bright eyes proclaimed that she was enjoying this race. I tightened the girth and remounted.

We left the well and sprang into a gallop. I was tempted to give

Windrider her head and let her tear along at full speed, but we were only halfway to the lake. There were many miles ahead. "Shh. Easy now. Save a little for the end."

She settled back into her canter. Even moderating her gait, we still soon caught another sighting of Brantley. He jostled side to side as his pony's hooves dug into the turf. I pressed my lips together. Brantley showed none of the grace that was so evident when he rode Navar. Yet they stayed far ahead with no sign of slowing.

He would surely win. How close was the lake? I didn't recognize any landmarks, so I couldn't gauge our progress. But Windrider knew it was time to sprint. She strained against the bit, and her strides stretched as far as the canter would allow. I'd invested every ounce of self-control to pace our pursuit. Now it was time to fly.

"Haw!" I tapped my heels against her flanks. "Run free!"

Windrider almost unseated me as she bounded into a gallop. My spine jolted back, but I quickly tightened my core muscles and leaned forward into the exhilarating pace.

We gained on Brantley with each stride. His pony valiantly fought for the gallop, but then pulled up and reared as if annoyed with the unreasonable man on his back. To his credit, Brantley kept his seat, tugged his gelding around, and continued down the trail. He shook the reins, shouted, kicked his heels, yet still we gained.

The path was narrow, so as we caught up, I looked for a way to get around them. How close was the lake? Was there still time for me to pull ahead?

The blur of green parted, and we emerged into full sunlight. Windrider needed no direction from me. She bolted to the left side of the path and sailed past Brantley's pony, who snorted, frothed, and dug in with new vigor.

The other mount wasn't as weary as I'd hoped. Each time we pulled ahead, the other pony surged in again, as we ran neck and neck. I kept my focus on the rise ahead of us, where trees again rose against the blue of the sky. The hill marked the surrounding slopes of the lake.

"Almost there," I called over the sound of hooves, jangling tack, panting animals, and gasping humans.

As we ran up the hill and entered the last stretch of forest, Windrider never broke stride. Beneath my legs her mighty lungs swelled and fed her the breath she needed for the last bit of the race.

I didn't dare turn and risk losing my balance, but the pounding sound of pursuit seemed only inches behind us.

We crested the hill. Below, the lake spread in a deep, blue expanse with ripples displaying a broken impression of the sky and the far bank. Morra sat on the tangleroot near the edge but jumped up at our approach. I focused on his wide eyes, the circle of his astounded lips, and the way those lips pulled into a grin. I had no idea how to adjust the stride for the downhill slope, but again Windrider proved her name. Her posture shifted, and she carried me smoothly down the hill as I leaned back against the momentum.

When she pulled up near the lake's edge, I slid off, flushed, heart still racing. My pony couldn't step any closer to the lake's shore because the mat of tangleroot wouldn't support her weight. Would Brantley recklessly charge past us and declare himself the winner by technicality? How close was he?

I looked back.

Sweat matted my hair, and I pushed it out of my face. His gelding bucked and skittered in circles at the crest of the hill. Brantley flailed around trying to regain control. His pony reared one final time and unseated his rider, then sagged, sides heaving. From the bottom of the hill I could hear the creature's snorts and Brantley's curses.

Morra beamed at me and reached out a hand. "Come touch the water. Make it official." My legs felt permanently bowed, but I managed to hobble to the edge and sink to my knees. I splashed a handful of water into the air, celebration and relief sprinkling down over me. Then I indulged in a long drink. Morra filled his hat and offered water to Windrider, then walked her in a circle until her breath came smooth and even again.

As soon as I could convince my shaky legs to support me again, I stood and hugged my mare. "You were amazing. Thank you. You have no idea how important this was, but thank you."

"Glad I was being here to serve as witness." Morra grabbed a fistful of moss and rubbed down the sweating flanks of my pony. His efficient efforts reminded me of Ginerva massaging sore muscles for the dancers in her care. "When we be going back to the red village, they be cheering for you."

Back? No. We could never go back to the red village. I had to find a way to keep Brantley from returning there, else I'd surely lose him completely. The allure of their form of play would entice him to forget all about our world, our people.

Brantley stormed away from his pony and strode down the hill, a thunderstorm brewing on his brow. "Wretched animal decided to fight me in the last minute."

I hid my triumph and said mildly, "You were ahead most of the way. Great riding."

His pony now strolled toward the lake, and Brantley glared a sour look the creature's direction. Morra hurried to tend it. Brantley crouched by the water and splashed his face, then tossed back his wet hair. "My riding wasn't good enough."

"You'll honor our wager?"

"A futile gesture, but if you insist."

He yanked his whistle from a tunic pocket. Still glaring, he stretched onto his stomach, head hovering over the water. He played a slow pattern of notes, then lowered the end into the water and played again.

When he finished, he leapt up and walked a few house lengths away, settling on the ground like a pouting child. His anger at losing was an encouraging contrast to the uncaring disposition he'd adopted since the convening. Perhaps the effects *were* wearing off?

I debated approaching him, but he bristled like a thorn bush, so instead I helped Morra attend to the horses. Windrider was rewarded with an apple, but I also gave a carrot to Brantley's gelding and thanked him for rebelling against the man's breakneck pace with such fortuitous timing.

Morra's gaze kept lifting to one of the trailheads. Not the one where we'd emerged, but the one leading back to the green village. I smiled. "Do you remember the young woman who caught your fancy?"

He startled. "Of course I remember. But she be no longer special to me. The gift of the convening."

I snarled. "The convening is not a gift! Caring for someone isn't wrong."

He pulled his head back like a startled chicken. "You be needing time at this lake. You be so upset by things."

I drew a steadying breath. "Some things are worth being upset about."

He scratched his head, mussing the auburn tangles. "There be plenty of girls at the red village."

"Yet your heart is pulling you back home. I see it in your eyes. You miss her."

His fist rubbed over his chest as if to erase what stirred there. "That be an offense." Then he rolled his shoulders back, shook off the moment of worry, and laughed. "But what be your plan now?"

I looked at the calm surface of the lake. "Now I pray that Navar heard the whistle and can dive deep and long and find us here."

Morra dropped to the ground and leaned back on his elbows. "And if not?"

I glanced over at Brantley's sullen form, his prickles stabbing me even from a distance. "If not, our world may be lost to us forever."

Morra crossed his hands behind his head and laid back, squinting against the suns. "That be grand. You'll be staying here then."

Trapped among people who chose to numb their hearts. Forsaken on a world with the man I loved who cared nothing for me. Would the pain become too much? Would I eventually join them in the soothing emptiness of the convening?

I sat on the tangleroot and dangled my legs into the sweet, milky water. If I considered that fate, I'd go mad. Instead, I'd stare at the surface and wait for a ripple, a wave, a signal that the stenella would emerge. However long it took.

"TRY ONE MORE TIME. PLEASE." I STOOPED BESIDE BRANTLEY, where he sprawled on a slope of daygrass, and gestured toward the water's edge. "Or give me your whistle and let me try."

Brantley scoffed and turned away, so disinterested that he didn't even watch the lake for Navar's possible arrival. At least he wasn't insisting on returning to the red village. He was honoring the terms of our wager. And perhaps his longing to see Navar was at work on some level, if not obvious.

The primary sun slid past its zenith, the subsun's warmth joined overhead, and I grew anxious. We had to shelter elsewhere before nightfall. I couldn't risk another encounter with the Gardener. Morra had tied the horses up by the forest's edge in case we decided to ride them back to their village, or even use them to return to the green village. The youth seemed caught in an endless debate with himself about the best course. I sympathized. Should we camp in the woods near the lake, or would that be too dangerous? Should I venture back to the green village, and could I convince Brantley to come with me?

Meanwhile, Brantley remained surly. I pulled myself away from my vigil at the lake's edge long enough to gather apples, persea, and lenka. When I brought them to Brantley, he accepted grudgingly. But all of my attempts at conversation fell flat.

I stared at the water, praying, willing, longing for Navar, then marched over to Brantley once more. "She may have been too far away to hear the first time. It's worth trying again."

He yawned. "No. You got what you wanted, now go away."

I eyed the tunic pocket that held his whistle. "Morra wants to know if we're camping here tonight." I kept my voice casual and conversational, still measuring the distance to the whistle.

"Do what you like. I plan to head back to the red village when the ponies are rested enough." Brantley wadded up his cloak, placed it behind his head, and closed his eyes.

His dismissal made my hands clench, but I forced a smile into my tone. "Well, thank you for trying." I flexed my fingers, watched his even breathing, then reached for the whistle.

Quick as a darting harrier, his hand clenched around my wrist. I tried to pull away, but he sat up, his grip tightening. A sharp jerk yanked me closer to his face. His eyes changed from ocean to stone. Hard, cold, empty of life. "Until now I've tolerated your badgering because we traveled here together and because we once escaped the Order together."

Even while his fingers bruised my arm, a seed of hope sprouted in my heart. Talking about our past would surely bring him to his senses.

Then his gaze skimmed over me with scorn. "But I can't understand why. What did I ever see in you? Why would any man tie himself to a frail cripple?"

I gasped as if he'd slammed his fist into my chest.

"Leave me alone." He squeezed my arm for emphasis. "Do you understand?"

The pain drew a small whimper from my lips. This was more than just the numbing effect that I'd witnessed in the other people. He wasn't merely uncaring. He was hostile. Whatever the Gardener had planted in Brantley's mind was germinating into cruelty. Was such a thing possible? Most of the people at the convening had been coated with moss, entangled by vines, blanketed. Subdued. But I'd seen a thorn pierce Brantley as he had struggled and resisted the Gardener. What had that unleashed?

"You're hurting my arm." I choked out the words.

The snarl on his features dissolved into a wrinkle of confusion. He stared at his hand clenched around my wrist and released me as if my skin had burned him. He shook his head, rubbed his temples, then met my eyes. "What—"

"The lake be exploding. Every help us!" Morra's shout propelled us both to our feet.

Ripples surged outward from a spot not far from shore, sending a wave cascading over the tangleroot. Morra fell to his knees and covered his face.

A familiar head rose from the water, craning to take in the new surroundings. Her long ears flopped as she angled her neck, and her lashes fluttered as she blinked.

"Navar!" I limped to the water's edge. Her perpetual grin widened into joyful recognition, and she swam to me. I threw my arms around her neck, nuzzling the soft, leathery skin, not caring that my tunic got wet.

Brantley joined us slowly, as if sleepwalking. "It worked?" The stenella butted her long muzzle into his chest. As if that bump opened a lock, a chuckle emerged from the man's lungs. He threw back his head and whooped. In one smooth movement, he threw off his tunic and knife belt. Then he sprang onto Navar's back and waved his fist. Together they raced around the lake, water churning. For good measure, Brantley guided Navar into a brief dive. When they emerged, the sea creature used her muzzle to bat copper fish through the air and onto shore.

"Wha-what be that monster stirring the lake?" Morra still cowered on the ground, peeking out through the fingers of one hand.

I laughed. "She's not a monster. We rode her here to the island. The same way you ride ponies."

He dared another look at her. "'Tis the sea lord! I've seen her image in our books. But the Every say she be a myth. Has she always been in the lake? Why has she not been seen at convenings?"

"You wouldn't have seen her because she lives in the wide ocean. The ocean you don't believe exists." I found my cloak and used it to gather the fish. "Come help me get a fire started. We'll have a hearty meal."

Morra eyed the cavorting pair in the lake dubiously, then built a fire far from the shore. The scent of roasting fish eventually lured Brantley from the water.

I brought him the sealed jar with my message for Saltar Kemp. "Can you direct her to return to Meriel? Will she find your apprentice? Do you think they'll see this? Maybe we need something bright."

He actually quirked his lips at my breathless questions. "Yes, there's a whistle to direct her, though she may be confused if I give that signal when I'm not on her back." He brushed wet hair off his forehead. "Wait. I could strap myself to her back for the dive. Perhaps she'd carry me back to the ocean. What an adventure that would be!"

Still no mention of home, no qualms at leaving me behind. But at least in his zest for risk-taking I saw glimpses of the true Brantley. Not that I'd let him try something so foolish. "It may have taken her hours to travel under the island. You'd drown in minutes. She couldn't surface anywhere. Unless . . . could she fly out?"

He scoffed. "She doesn't fly. She can glide if she catches an updraft. You won't find that here. Certainly not enough for her to coast overland all the way to the sea."

This time his disdain didn't make me bristle. He was right. It had been a foolish thought. I tied our message to Navar's halter, right on top where the bump would be obvious to apprentice Teague.

"You best send her now. We have to find a safe place to camp in case the Gardener returns."

He picked up his knife belt, pulling out the blade and testing its sharpness against his thumb. "I'll get the answers from him that you could not."

I rolled my eyes. "That didn't work so well for you last time. Give Navar the indicator for home. If the saltars believe we're lost, they'll allow Meriel to continue on her way, and our mission will fail. They're counting on us to bring back provisions."

Brantley threw me a sour look but unearthed his whistle and blew a sequence of clear notes. Navar's neck stiffened, and she cast her wide-eyed gaze on me, as if to ask me to explain. I hugged the leathery coolness of her neck one more time and stroked her muzzle. "I know you don't want to leave us. But you need to get our message to Teague."

A new worry struck me. "What if Meriel is already so far away that Navar can't find it? What will she do?"

Brantley shrugged. "Return to her pod?" He stood beside me and scratched Navar under the chin. She closed her eyes and gave a low chortle. A wrinkle creased Brantley's brow, but the hint of concern fled so quickly I believed I'd imagined it. He turned and strode away without a backward glance.

Navar made a low, plaintive sound. "I know," I whispered. "He's not himself. I'm working on it." With a last hug, I stepped back. The stenella swam in a tight circle around the lake and then plunged into the depths and disappeared.

Morra, who had stayed well away from the water since her appearance, walked up beside me. "Too bad I'm not being a weaver of stories. Would be quite the tale to share at the revels."

"Do you know if the Gardener comes here each night, even when it's not time for a convening?"

He scratched his head. "Maybe. Folks be coming here between if they be needing more peace."

Peace? Not what I would call it. I looked up the slope to the horses. Brantley was heading their way. "Morra, stop him."

The youth tilted his head. "How?"

"Run. Tell him if he goes back to the red village, he'll be mocked for losing the race."

Morra puffed out his chest. "That be true. I'll be telling them all how the girl with the limp beat him by outriding him."

He galloped up the hill and stopped Brantley from untying one of the horses. While I watched their argument, a movement caught my eye from the green village trailhead. A large figure emerged, barrel chest slumping and heavy steps plodding. When he lifted his chin enough to stare at the lake, I recognized Harba. I waved a greeting, and he clomped down the hill toward me. His arrival must have stirred Brantley's curiosity, because he and Morra left the horses and approached as well.

Harba reached me first. I rose onto my toes and lowered. "I'm so glad to see you. How is Wimmo? And the baby?"

He offered a half-hearted flourish with his bow. "The babe did be arriving."

I caught my breath. Had they abandoned the infant somewhere? "Is the child safe?"

"Yes. It be a fine girl, and Wimmo be wanting to hold it all the time. But Wimmo be having no remembering of me—of how we were."

My heart squeezed. "And you still care."

He shook his head sadly and rubbed a spot on his barreled chest. "The ache. It be throbbing. I hear her laugh. I think of her smile. I be attached. 'Tis wrong. I be desperate for help from the lake tonight."

I grabbed his shoulders. "No. Harba, listen to me. Don't stay here. You don't want to deaden that love. Wimmo needs you. The baby needs you."

"This be hurting." He rubbed his chest with a meaty fist.

Brantley reached us, cutting a cold gaze my direction. The ache behind my own ribs throbbed each time I looked at the man who had once loved me. "I know," I told Harba. "But we mustn't give up. Some things are worth the pain."

"Speaking of pain," Brantley said, "have you figured out what you're doing next? So I can go the opposite way?"

I lifted my chin. Until now, I hadn't thought much beyond sending a message back to our home island. Since that was accomplished—at least that was my hope—my next goal was to find a way to get Brantley back to his right mind.

"You don't want to go back to the red village right now. You'll lose status when Morra tells them I won the race."

"Maybe you're right." He threw his cloak down on the shore near the water's edge. "You do what you want. I'll spend another night here."

"No!" My shout was so emphatic that Morra and Harba drew back in surprise. I crossed my arms. "We've got the ponies. We can reach the green village shortly after dark. Now that Wimmo had the baby, Harba needs help reminding her to care for it. And maybe we can help her remember she cares for Harba."

Morra brightened. "Can that work? Could someone's attachment reawaken?" Then he blushed and rubbed a hand over his mouth, clearly embarrassed to be speaking so openly about a taboo.

"I don't know," I said honestly. "But I know we can't stay here at the lake. If the Gardener returns tonight, he could numb your soul to nothing."

All three men stared at me blankly, and I wanted to knock their heads together. "Morra, think of the tale you could share among your people. They'll love hearing about the stenella."

The youth straightened and nodded toward Harba. "It be true. A creature with the body of a fish and the face of a pony did be swimming in the lake."

Harba shot him an incredulous look. Then he studied the lakeside. "I suppose . . ." he said slowly. "If you can help Wimmo, I can wait for my peace." He rubbed his breastbone again.

"Besides, there's always the Grand Convening. Should be soon." Morra grinned, obviously glad someone was making a decision that would take him back to the girl he admired.

"Thanks to the Every." Harba twirled his hands overhead.

Morra grinned. "Thanks to the Every." Then he ran up the hill to fetch the ponies.

A cloud passed over the primary sun, and a chill brushed my skin. "I don't like the sound of that."

Brantley shrugged. "I'm sure you'll have ample opportunity to learn about the Grand Convening. Enjoy your stay with these folk who have nothing between their ears. I'll return to the red village."

My hurt and fear coalesced into a hard ball behind my sternum, then burned until I could taste bile in my throat. I couldn't stand seeing this strange version of Brantley any longer.

"Fine. Leave. Go play games like a child. Forget your mother and

Brianna and Orianna. Forget Windswell and all the others in your village who rely on you. Go off alone. It's what you always do anyway."

Irritation drove away his disinterest for a moment. Then he shook his head and gave a dark-edged chuckle. "Safe journeys, dancer." Every bit of scorn with which he'd ever spoken that word filled his tone. He strode up the hill, mounted his pony, and rode off down the red village path.

Morra brought me my mount. "Harba and I will take turns on my pony. Shall we go?"

I held my pony's reins and stood, paralyzed. Should I follow Brantley? I couldn't give up on him. Watching him disappear was like feeling my grip slip from a last strand of tangleroot while ocean waves tugged me under. Morra settled onto his mount, and Harba trudged alongside as they headed to the green village trailhead. Wimmo's baby needed protection—from the disinterest of the villagers and probably from her own parents. If I could help Morra and Harba resist the effects of the convening, perhaps more people could break free.

I walked gingerly to the edge of the lake and scooped up a drink of water. I had a third choice. I could wait here and confront the Gardener.

Harba and Morra disappeared into the woods. I had to make a decision. The effort tore at my heart. *Loving Maker, what should I do?*

YOU CALL ON ME, BUT WILL YOU HEAR? THE VOICE CAME NOT from my own mind, yet not quite riding waves of sound in the air. Stronger than a thought, softer than a voice, woven within my heart, yet also beyond me.

Joy tingled throughout my body. I could bear anything with my Maker present. I sank to my knees, settled back on my heels, and scanned the lake, the slopes of daygrass, the forest's edge. Would He come as a pillar of light? Would he hover over the water? Awe and longing swirled together. "Where have You been? I'm so alone. Even Brantley can't help."

I am here.

I squeezed my eyes shut. "I see danger, I see choices that rip me apart, I see a barrier that traps me. But I can't see You."

A sigh rustled the upper branches in the trees at the top of the rise. *The people of this island can't see the ocean. Yet they are carried by it.*

I uncurled my fingers where they rested on my legs and lifted my palms. "Open my eyes." Like the scattered illumination of star rain, pictures tumbled through my mind: Windrider's smooth gait, Morra's youthful laughter, Wimmo's gentle smile, Trilia's herbs, Navar's chortle, Jalla's conversation. Blessings and allies. Gifts to ease my path.

"Thank You," I whispered. "You *are* here. Will You help me? I think I should go to the red village. I have to be with Brantley when the effects wear off. They will wear off, won't they?" I clenched my fists and looked up to the trailhead.

You've chosen a course and want Me to bless it.

I was glad He understood. Certainty built. There was really no other choice. Love was guiding me, and love was always the right course.

You call on Me, but will you hear? He asked again.

My certainty crumbled like a day-old salt cake. "I should go back to the red village, right?"

No.

"You want me to go to the green village instead?"

No.

A cold dread looped around my stomach. He truly wasn't remembering how frail I was. "You want me to stay here and fight the Gardener?"

No.

I pressed the heels of my hands against my forehead. This guessing game frustrated me. "Then what? Those are my only options."

Can the One who created all worlds also create a new path? But will you hear?

"Why do you keep asking me that? If You will guide me, of course I'll listen."

The blue village needs to hear truth. The path begins near the large pine on the opposite rise.

"The blue village?" I lurched to my feet. "Why would You want me to go there?"

The impression of a gentle smile wafted through my heart. *How eager you are to hear My guidance.*

My shoulders slumped. I longed to trust Him fully, yet my first reaction was to resist His path. "I'm sorry. If that is where You send me, I'll go. But Brantley isn't in his right mind. Shouldn't I help him first? If I go to the red village, he can work with me. This mission is more likely to succeed with the two of us." I realized I was bargaining, but surely He would understand.

Release him.

No, no, no, no, no! How could He ask that of me? Didn't He care? I had waited my whole life without even knowing it to be connected to someone like Brantley. And now ... "You can't want me to forget I love him—like the people here do after their convenings. That isn't Your way. You've only recently shown me it isn't wrong to care."

After a quiet moment, He spoke again. *I don't ask you to give ground but to give way. Release Brantley to My care. Trust that I love him—even more than you do.*

As gently as it had arrived, the sense of the Maker's tangible presence withdrew. He wouldn't force me. He gave me room to set my course.

I turned to face the trail that would lead me back to Brantley. Windrider perked up her head and sniffed the air.

I checked the saddle and mounted, then rode to the top of the rise. I reined her in to a stop, and she strained against the bridle. She had a mind of her own, just as I did. Gathering the fragments of my love and obedience, I turned her head and rode her slowly to the path the Maker had indicated.

"What will the blue village be like? What will I find there?" I whispered. "And will You promise me that Brantley will not be lost to me forever?"

Silence answered.

I guided Windrider past the tall pine and into the woods. Shadows reached their fingers toward us. I squeezed my heels against her sides, and we settled into a canter. If the blue village was a similar distance as the others from the lake, we'd have to hurry to reach it by nightfall.

FROM THE DAY I ENTERED THE ORDER AS A YOUNGLING, I followed a set course. My goal was clear, and every ounce of energy focused on that goal. I advanced through each form as a novitiate, longing for the day I would dance in the center ground as a true dancer of the Order. My drive allowed me to ignore the signs of darkness around me—the cruelty and lies that crept through the Order like cracks in the stone walls. From the time I fled those walls, that clear, direct course was lost to me. I'd run from soldiers, ridden the shore from village to village, and wandered through midrim towns. The Maker led me on a path that wound in inexplicable ways.

As a novitiate, I understood that each exercise, each class, each pattern had a purpose. Now the Maker asked me to trust Him when I couldn't unravel a purpose. Why had He allowed me to be hobbled, yet still asked me to dance for Him? Why had this island drifted into view? Why hadn't He stopped the Gardener from tangling Brantley in the numbing vines? And why was He now sending me to the opposite side of the island from the man who needed me so much?

As the primary sun lowered, Windrider slowed to a walk. With each clop of her hooves, the questions pounded into my heart. The Maker's love had opened doors in my soul that I'd never dreamed possible. But could I follow Him now, when nothing made sense? I wanted to. I wanted to give back a fragment of the huge love He'd given me. My trust could be my gift to Him. But offering that faith was so hard.

"Help me," I whispered, realizing the irony. I needed to ask His help even to love Him.

A cool breeze tugged my hair, and I tasted the citrus tang of the ocean. We were nearing the rim. Perhaps this village wasn't blocked from the shore by barrier trees. My heart quickened. Maybe that was why the Maker had sent me here. To show me the way of escape.

I squeezed my legs and leaned forward, and Windrider bounced into a trot. We emerged from the wooded trail on a slight rise that gave me an instant view of the town.

Cottages and shops, platforms and stairs, all connected into a mass of shapes and forms with moving parts. I slid from my pony, shook my legs to ease the stiffness of a day of riding, and blinked several times.

My eyes traced a windmill that clacked as it spun, pulling up well water that traveled through wooden pipes and into a trough on the opposite side of the town. How strange. Why hadn't they simply dug a well at the far end of the village if they wanted water in that location?

I draped Windrider's reins over my shoulder, clutched my cane, and walked slowly into town. Whirring, tapping, and clicking sounds assaulted me, and the scent of burning oil hovered in the air. The primary sun's rays faded, but torches lit the circular paths and bolstered the pale light of the subsun. A woman stood behind a table in an open-sided store, her shirt puckering with plackets and pleats. I wandered closer, trying to gauge her mood. "Greetings. I'm Carya of Meriel."

She looked up, and her eyes flashed white. She clutched the collar of her tunic, pinching the row of buttons and a second row of hooks and eyes that seemed to serve no purpose. "How dare you!"

I took a step back. Was she upset by Windrider's presence? I should have tied her outside the village. "I mean no offense. I'm a visitor—"

"Hush!" She pointed to the table and a carved shape burnished with the copper coloring of a fish. The object looked like a hollow sheep's horn, attached with thin wires to a matching one. She picked up one end and glared at me.

When I didn't move, she grabbed the other horn and shoved it at me. With the open side of the horn over her mouth, she stepped away, stretching the wires. "The Every would never speak apart from our talking tool." I barely caught the words as she whispered them into the carved shape.

She gestured sharply, and I cautiously lifted my horn to my ear. "What be your ailment, that you can't use a talking tool?" Her voice now carried loudly.

I jerked in surprise. Somehow her speech traveled clearly through the instrument.

"I truly meant no offense. I've never seen a talking tool."

She rolled her eyes and shook her head, then pointed to my mouth. I quickly copied her, repeating the words into the horn, as she moved her end over her ear. What a confusing way to communicate!

She waved a hand, and we switched positions of the tool again so I could listen to her. "My name be Plexia. I've never ventured past the lake to other villages, but they must be as backwards as I've heard."

A repeating theme. Each village believed they were superior, and as far as I was concerned, they were all troubled. I smiled at her, hoping that wasn't forbidden as well. Learning the rhythm of the tool, I shifted it from my ear to my mouth. "From what I've seen, each village has different skills."

She puffed out her chest. "And ours be the best." Her brow furrowed. "Though since we haven't convened in a long time, some can't work as well."

Continuing to use the horns and wires and trying to ignore how ridiculous they felt, I invited her to show me more of her village. At her instruction, I tied Windrider to a post supporting her store's porch roof. Then I followed closely—linked to her by the wires between us—as she led me deeper along streets that wove a complex pattern between shingled buildings that seemed to cant inward like leaning trees.

Curving between the rear of two buildings, we emerged at a patio. An old man moved energetically about a bench that held what looked like a strange sculpture. Yet pieces of the sculpture moved. He twisted a knob, tinkered with a blade, and scurried to one end of the bench. With a sharp crank, he set the whole sculpture into motion again, as I puzzled out its purpose. A wheel spun and knocked a lever, which pulled down a thread that reached several feet up from the bench to a weight. As the weight lowered, a knife pulled across a persea fruit that had been pierced by a stick and held in place.

A few swipes of skin came free. The man leaned forward and stared hard at the effect, then hurried back to the starting point and turned the crank again. Then he pulled his attention away from the contraption and smiled at us.

"See?" Plexia said into her talking tool, worry shading her tone. "He notices us. He becomes distracted. He cares for people around him. He may need to be staying extra at the lake. He does much better work after a convening."

Still trying to understand the purpose of his machine, I moved to a full basket of persea, picked one up, and peeled it. A few easy movements, and the fruit was ready to eat. I handed it to the man. A rueful smile tugged the corner of his mouth, but he didn't offer one end of his talking tool to me.

Plexia pulled me away. As we walked to the next building, she spoke into the horn. "Did you mean to mock his skill?"

"Not at all. I just don't understand. Why make things so complicated?"

"With his machine, there is no need to touch the fruit."

And that was important? I loved the texture of the bumpy persea skin, even the taste of my fingers after peeling the creamy fruit. Before I could question her further, we reached a tall tower constructed with flexible branches and vines. A young woman balanced on a platform higher than any nearby buildings. A fragile railing surrounded her, and as a wave rolled beneath us, I caught my breath. The movement could make her topple from the high perch.

She didn't seem alarmed, even as the tower swayed. Both her hands held a glinting telescope. She scanned the sky, angled away from the setting subsun.

"Does your village study the sky?" Plexia asked.

A huge mounted telescope rested atop the Order's tower but was used to spy on the villages or study weather patterns out to sea. "Can she see over the barrier trees from up there?"

"The what?"

Conversation this way was tedious, so I waved toward the side of the village furthest from the lake trail. Her mouth puckered, but she nodded and led me onward.

Deep in the town, more torches lit the streets and plazas. Devices mounted on the buildings held three or even five torches, and glinting metal panels reflected and amplified the light. As the sky darkened, the village still glowed and buzzed with activity.

I wanted to hurry to the rim and see if I could finally find a path to the sea, but my steps slowed often as I passed more curiosities. Some of the inventions seemed useful, and I wished I had time to draw diagrams of their lighting devices, the lens for telescopes, the vat that churned laundry. Ginerva would love that.

Most of the people wore trousers and tunics covered with pouches and pockets, straps and buckles. Most also wore a talking tool draped around their necks. Two young men seated at a table didn't even glance up as we brushed past them. I stopped. Their feverish eyes stared, unblinking, at the surface of the table where springs and gears and tubes passed a colored liquid back and forth between them. One man snatched up a carved channel, added a few drops from a mug in front of him, then replaced it. Liquid swirled through, and the color altered subtly. He sat back and crossed his arms, nodding to the man across from him.

A frown of concentration puckered the other man's brow, and he shook his head. I wanted to keep watching and figure out the purpose of their efforts. They both looked as if they hadn't slept in days. When I asked Plexia, she beamed. "A complex game. When we design or play or build, our focus is true. Sleep be a waste of time."

I limped along behind Plexia with a coil of tension winding up my spine. The spinning, whirling motion on all sides made my head throb. Frenzied and absorbed expressions strained everyone's faces. They were so driven, so lost. I hadn't wanted to come here, but now I prayed I could offer this people a breath of truth and peace.

We reached the last few cottages on the seaward side of town. As with the other towns, a wide field provided room for village gatherings, although tonight the fire pits were cold and bare. Plexia stopped. "What did you mean to see here?"

Hope sped my pulse as I let go of the talking tool and limped more quickly across the field and whispered to myself. "A way home."

PLEXIA CROSSED HER ARMS AND SETTLED ON A BENCH NEAR one of the cottages at the edge of the village. I hurried across the daygrass meadow toward the barrier trees, glad to leave behind the smoky air trapped between buildings and the incessant grinding and buzzing of machines in perpetual motion.

I broke into a loping gait and quickly reached the barrier trees. As with everywhere else along the island's rim, the foliage towered many stories above. Supple trees wove together, and vines bound them to create a tight cage. I traced the edge, pushing aside bracken, poking my head into small gaps, searching for a path toward the sea.

Nothing.

What should I do next? The Maker must have a purpose for guiding me to this village. But how could I help the people here? The familiar throb pulsed through my tendon again. Jalla's liniment had helped for a while, but now every limping step took huge effort. I could use more of the balm, but there was such a small amount, it was probably wise to save it for my most dire need.

Don't delay. The multicolored star rain comes soon. The powerful yet nearly imperceptible voice of the Maker resonated through my being. I turned from the rim to study the strange village. People scurried about, so involved in their projects that I had no idea how to even get anyone's attention. Another woman approached Plexia, whose head tilted as she listened on her talking tool. The woman gestured, although her face was hidden by the carved horn. The two women didn't even face each other, more concerned about keeping the wire between them taut.

I crossed the open field toward them, noting again the empty fire pits. When I reached Plexia, she offered me one end of her talking tool. "Do your people gather here after the work of the day?" I asked. Plexia relayed my question to her friend. They both laughed. The other woman said something to Plexia, then handed the free end of the tool to me and walked away.

Plexia lifted her chin. "The work of the day never truly ends, does it? We only gather for the revel before the convening."

I blinked against the blazing torches that lined the nearest alley. "But the land is full of tubers and fruit and easy bounty. You have sturdy shelters. Why work so hard?"

"The Every knows we must." It was hard to tell with the tool over her mouth, but Plexia seemed annoyed at my questions.

My eyes stung from smoke, my ankle throbbed, and my stomach growled and reminded me of my long day of riding. "Have you considered that the Every can be in error?"

She drew back, gaping, then tugged the tool away from me. She slung it around her neck and stalked up the path into town. I'd become as undiplomatic as Brantley, but I wouldn't berate myself.

I caught up to Plexia and touched her shoulder. She bristled but stopped walking and allowed me to pick up the mouthpiece.

"I'm sorry. I meant no offense. I'm from a different land where the voice of the Every was spoken through the Order. Yet that Order damaged our people."

She sighed. "It's clear you have no understanding of how the world works. Perhaps you're addled from your journey. Do you have a place to rest tonight?"

I shook my head, relieved that she actually looked at me to see the movement, so I didn't need to speak into the infernal tool. She beckoned, and I followed. We returned to the lakeward edge of town and moved Windrider. We tethered her where she could nibble tender daygrass and reach a low water trough. Then Plexia led me into her home.

The entryway was a closed box surrounded by doors. She hung her talking tool on a peg and opened the left door. I followed her, fighting to shake off the claustrophobia that the segmented space—and the entire cluttered village—evoked. The room held a tiny hearth with a small fire. When she stirred it, the flames pushed back the room's shadows and revealed walls lined with shelves. The shelves held small cupboards and drawers with a variety of handles. Tools whose purpose I couldn't discern hung from hooks, filling one wall.

"Have a seat. I'll heat water for tsalla." Unamplified, her voice sounded more gentle and sweet than when it carried through the wire.

"We don't need to use the speaking tool?" I perched on a stool near the hearth.

She rolled her eyes. "Not indoors, strange girl. How far away *is* this land you claim to come from?"

My ribs contracted around an empty longing inside my chest. A good question. How far was Meriel right now? Had it followed the currents and traveled far across the expanse of the sea? If Navar had safely reached Meriel, and if Teague found the message, and if Saltar Kemp found a way to move the island toward this one, my land may be just on the other side of the barrier trees. But if any link in that chain had broken, my land could be lost to me forever.

Lost like Brantley. The insidious whisper in my thoughts was as different from the Maker's guidance as shadow from firelight, and I reached my hands out to the warmth of Plexia's flame as I fought back that dread. That was not the voice I wanted to listen to. "Our island floats on the currents, just as yours does. When we saw you in the distance, my companion and I traveled here, seeking help for our people."

She cast her gaze around me, and her eyes narrowed, gauging if I was addled enough to imagine a friend that no one else could see. "And your companion? Be he invisible?"

"He is visiting the red village."

Her expression relaxed. She lifted a pitcher, poured water through a tube, and watched as it dripped into a kettle, which pivoted on an ingenious holder to rest over the flames. Then she opened a ceramic jar and pulled out a handful of herbs. Instead of crumbling them and sprinkling them into the kettle, she placed them in a box on the table that held round stones suspended by string. After the herbs were in place, she vigorously shook the box, sending the rocks into a clacking frenzy. Once she was satisfied, she shook the shredded herbs into the kettle.

I stretched my ankle out toward the fire. "What's the purpose of that tool?"

"Don't you smash your herbs when you make tsalla?"

I picked up some stray leaves from the table and rubbed them in my palm. "Like this? Does your tool do so much better?"

Plexia frowned. "Perhaps not, but it saves time."

I still didn't understand. "And why do you need that time?"

A log popped, and sparks flew upward. Plexia's eyes reflected their glint. "There is so much more to be done." Her words jammed together with pressure behind them.

She was every bit as trapped as I had been at the Order, when a saltar would make us jump over and over until our muscles screamed for mercy. Little difference that these villagers held the whip to their own backs, they were still trapped.

Plexia served me a mug of tsalla. Homesickness washed over me at the flavor of sweet seawater and citrus herbs, and I pushed aside the melancholy, preparing for a fruitful conversation. If the Maker wanted me to help these people, this was the place to start.

My hostess had other plans, though. She took only a few sips before setting down her cup and opening a nearby cabinet. A desk-like surface folded down from inside the cabinet, and rows of compartments glittered with metal gears and rods and bits. She hustled across the room and grabbed parchment and a willow pen. Soon she was lost in scribbling and assembling the metal bits.

If I waited for her to finish her work, I might be waiting a long time. "What are you working on? Can I help in some way?"

She jerked and looked back at me, blinking a few times. "Oh."

Clearly, she'd forgotten I was even there. I sighed and passed her the cup she'd left on the table. She managed a sheepish smile and rolled her shoulders. "We all be getting lost in our work."

Maybe that could be a point of connection. I nodded. "I was a dancer, and when I was memorizing a new pattern, nothing could distract me."

She rubbed the bridge of her nose. "But this close to the convening, I do get distracted. Our people be needing this, and I'm getting behind."

"What is it?" I asked again.

"A way to measure fractions of the hours between primary sunrise and subsunset. We be needing to mark time."

My people marked time by days passing. And the gradual movement of the suns throughout the day. "I never thought of measuring time in smaller pieces." I took another drink, rolling the thought around in my mind. "Although at the Order the bells declared midday and first sunset."

Her eyes gleamed. "Yes, yes. You see, don't you? We have so much to do, and if people feel the time beating past, they will work harder." She set down her mug and turned back to her work. "I almost have the first part figured." With a squinted adjustment, she lifted her hands away, and a metal rod swung side to side with a loud tick as it bounced off each side of a triangular box.

I stood and leaned over her shoulder. As much as I worried about the strange obsessions of Plexia and her people, I couldn't help but admire the shining machine. "It's like the drums I used to dance to . . . or like a heartbeat."

She rubbed her eyes, bags from sleeplessness darkening beneath them. "Next I be calculating how many beats in a day. Then I be making this larger." Another flare of energy surged through her, and she picked up the pen. "Imagine the whole village hearing the measure of time all day!"

The frenzy was taking hold again. I didn't want to lose her in her frantic work again. "Plexia?"

"Hmm?"

"Have you eaten? You've accomplished something amazing, but maybe now would be a good time for a meal?"

"No time." She scrawled another diagram on a scrap of parchment.

"But you told me you saved time with the herb smasher. You've probably used other contraptions today that have saved you time. So why not take some of what you've saved and eat?"

Her hands stilled. "Where does the time go that we have saved?" A thread of weariness wove through her quiet question.

"I don't know. But I do know your village will endure even if you pause to eat and sleep."

Persistent coaxing finally wooed her away from her project. I helped make a rich soup full of tubers and mushrooms. Much as I loved the abundant fruit always available for the picking, I appreciated the warmth in my belly and new flavors that the soup provided. The lunch of roasted fish had been many hours ago.

"How's your soup?" I asked, ladling another helping into Plexia's bowl.

She leaned her chair back against the wall and rested her feet on a stool. "You were right. The lenka pit added a nice bite to the broth."

"I'd like to return your hospitality with a gift. A better gift than a new soup recipe."

By the firelight, while Plexia was in a warm, receptive mood, I shared my story. The years in the Order, the darkness hidden behind perfection, the discovery of the Maker's letter, and how He offered us freedom.

Her gaze drifted to the invention and her parchments. When she rubbed her eyes, I felt her exhaustion. Endless studying, designing, improving, and altering must be a heavy burden. For a moment a wistful longing wafted across her face.

This was my chance to convince her. "The Gardener does something to each village when they arrive at the convening."

She focused on me again. "Of course. The convening unites us. Protects us. Puts our attention back on what is important."

I shook my head. "No. He changes people. Think about it. It's nearing time for the next star rain. How are people acting?"

"Terrible. They linger in conversations. They slow their efforts."

"They are human. They remember connections and . . . and love. That's not a terrible thing. If you can help me convince your village to stay away from the lake, you'll see."

She pushed back her chair and slammed her empty bowl onto the table between us. "How dare you?"

I lengthened my spine, refusing to recoil from her anger. "I've been there. I've seen it. And there is a better way. A Maker who—"

"Get out!"

"Please, let me explain what—"

"I've been hearing these dangerous lies before. Chanic spoke such things at past revels."

My pulse quickened. "Chanic?"

Her lip curled. "Outcast. Useless. I'll be having naught to do with such talk." She grabbed a broom and brandished it. "You be leaving now."

I stood and eased toward the door. "I didn't mean to upset you. But please hear me out—"

She slammed the broomstick against the wall, causing all her tools and mechanisms to rattle. "Not another word."

I opened the door to her entryway and backed away to reassure her that I was following her instructions. "Just tell me where to find Chanic."

As I stumbled out her front door, she relented enough to say, "The path beyond the skywatch tower. Past the orchard in the bracken wood."

She slammed the door in my face. Regret pierced me like a broken rib. I thought I'd made a connection, found a possible ally. Once again

I confronted disdain and rejection.

As had the Maker. I drew in a sharp breath. However much I longed to help these people, He longed for it even more. Did their disdain wound Him as it did me? Another puzzle. He was the Maker, how could He allow Himself to be wounded?

I limped past the tower, out of the noise and haze of the village, onto the orchard path. There I knelt and placed my palms against the earth. As when we'd first arrived here, the ground echoed the Maker's call. *Forgotten, forgetting, forsaking.*

I didn't understand this mystery of the One who formed everything taking on the pain of love. But new resolve filled me. I stood, squared my shoulders, and set off to find Chanic.

AWAY FROM THE VILLAGE, THE PATH FELL INTO DARKNESS.
Overhanging branches of willow, persea, and lenka all blocked the
starlight. I moved cautiously, startling at every rustling sound in the
underbrush. I'd witnessed the way the Gardener controlled the plants
by the lake. Did his influence extend to the rim villages? Was he stirring
the underbrush to snag me, or the trees to loom against me? My cloak
should have provided ample warmth against the evening chill, yet fear
found its way through the seams and made me shiver.

At last a muted glow appeared. As I drew closer, the silhouette of a
humble cottage revealed itself, pale light outlining the windows and
gaps around the door. "Hello?" I called softly, leery to approach the
door. I had no idea what this outcast would be like.

When no one answered, I gathered my nerve and limped to the
door. My timid tap was answered by an equally timid voice, crackling
with age. "Please be letting yourself in."

I eased the door open. A tiny low table to my left held one fat candle
that valiantly chased shadows from the corner. To my right, a warm
hearth lit the rest of the room. A woman hunched in a bent-willow
rocker near the fire.

"I'm Carya. Are you Chanic?"

A wheezy chuckle answered me. "Who else would be so far from
the village? Come away in." She gestured with a hand that was as bent
as her chair. Gnarled fingers curled in the grip of disease. The poor
woman must be in horrible pain. She still hadn't lifted her head, and I
realized she couldn't.

To allow me to look up into her eyes, I drew close and eased to the floor in front of her. "I'm a visitor. Sent to convince your people to stay away from the convening."

Her eyes were bright as a bird's, younger than the rest of her body. Her smile was more a wince, as if even that movement hurt. "Ah. That would be a feat." Her wince deepened, all humor fleeing. "I tried. Oh, how often I tried."

"Until they drove you out?"

"When the disease of fire took my joints, I could no longer walk to the convening. And a strange thing happened."

"You remembered your true self." I gently rested a hand on hers, hoping the warmth of my touch could soothe.

Her chin bobbed a tiny motion, and the bones in her neck creaked a warning. "But my hands"—she turned them—"could no longer shape my inventions. I had no value to my village."

How had this poor woman endured, waiting out her days, rejected by her people, with no one to help her? "You have value to your Maker."

She focused her quizzical gaze on my face. "If a Maker formed me, He used some faulty parts." She gave a wheezing laugh.

My giggle joined hers. "I've accused Him of the same." I rubbed the skin above my bandage, and the astringent scent of Jalla's liniment lingered on my fingers. "Perhaps I can help."

I rummaged through my pack and unearthed the small container. The rare and potent ointment had soothed my wound for several blissful hours. I pushed aside my longing for relief, scooped out the balm, and worked it gently into Chanic's hands. The stiff and twisted joints softened. She moved her fingers, wonder lifting her eyebrows. Next I rubbed her neck and shoulders.

She gasped, and I froze. "Does it hurt?"

"No, no." Her head lifted to a near-normal alignment on her neck. "I hadn't remembered what it could be like to not feel the pain."

I pressed the little jar into her hand. "Keep this. I know there isn't much left, but Jalla at the red village knows how to make it. Maybe she can supply you."

She pressed the container to her chest. "If I be keeping my hands nimble, my place in the village can be restored."

I drew in a sharp breath. "But don't go along with them. Even if you are strong enough to walk to the convening. Don't lose what you've found. You can help me convince the village to stay away."

"You don't understand. The bargain goes deep. There be no changing it."

"What bargain?"

She lifted her chin an inch more and studied me, lips pursed. "My words can't sway the village. And you be an outsider who doesn't understand. But there may be a way I can help you."

She rubbed a dab of liniment into her knees, then rocked forward and used the chair's arms to stand. "There is a place of remembering not far from here."

The last thing I wanted to do was venture back out into the night. The day had already taxed me beyond my limit. "Maybe tomorrow?"

"I haven't been able to visit it for years. Only your potion be giving me hope my legs will carry me. But for how long?"

A good question. The pulsing burn in my tendon reminded me that the effects of the ointment were temporary. "Just tell me where this place is. I'll find it tomorrow."

"You won't be finding it without help. Come." She took her candle and handed it to me. Then she grabbed two walking sticks propped against the wall and opened the door. I caught her urgency and followed, promising my aching body it would have rest soon.

Impossibly, the night had grown even darker. We stood for a few moments until our eyes adjusted, then she shuffled forward into the bracken. Lifting the candle, I followed her, carrying a pack of worries with me. She was barely able to walk. What if she collapsed and couldn't make it back to her home? What if this "place of remembering" was another evil work of the Gardener? Or what if she meant to lure me out in the darkness and leave me?

Dearest Maker, am I following or wandering? How can I know? Guide me. If going with Chanic is a mistake, show me and protect me.

"There," she said.

Before us, a strange tree loomed in the flicker of my candle. Fronds draped down like branches of a willow, but when I pushed some aside, I could see a trunk so wide it could nearly house Chanic's cottage.

A deeper shadow indicated an entry.

She rested a gnarled hand on my shoulder. "In there. I'd join you, but if I wait much longer, my legs may not carry me home."

"Wait. How will I find my way back to you? To the trails?"

"I'll use the ointment again in the morning and come for you."

The earth rolled gently. I swayed, wavering with indecision. "The morning?" I didn't want to spend the night in the hollow of a tree that was likely infested with creeping insects or perhaps more dangerous creatures. "Do predators dwell near your village?"

But she had already shuffled past several trees, and the darkness swallowed her. She must have the night vision of a forest hound to navigate. I could still try to follow, but what would that achieve? When I first stepped on this land, I'd heard the sorrowful cry of forgetting. Maybe a place of remembering was what this world needed. Or what I needed to learn how to help them. Maybe it could even be a place to bring Brantley, where he could be restored to himself.

I propped my cane against the trunk, cupping a hand to protect my feeble candle from any errant gust of wind. Leaning into the opening, I lifted the light. Mossy daygrass coated the ground. The inner surface of the trunk wasn't rough as I'd expected, but smooth as a bowl polished by loving hands. I limped inside and raised the light. A quick scan of the space revealed little else. No letter to discover, no parchments to offer clues or guide me. No tool to investigate.

Disappointed, I eased to the ground. At least the interior was a dry and comfortable place to rest. The scent of liniment lingered on my fingers, so I removed my bandage and rubbed the residue onto my scar. Then, with my pack as a pillow, I curled up and felt my weary bones sink into the spongy earth. The thick trunk muted any sounds from the forest. No rustling, no strange calls, no voices of the night. My heavy eyelids closed, and I smiled at the sense of peace that cradled me.

"COME AND SEE." A MIGHTY, LOVING, AND EVEN PLAYFUL voice woke me. I recognized the Maker and bolted upright. Without thinking, I sprang to my feet. Light streamed into the hollow. Morning already? I raced outside and looked around. Trees sparkled with dew, their branches bobbing a cheery dance with the rolling earth. The primary sun warmed the air, and birds chirruped their approval. Giddy at the beauty, I spun a few times, arms open to gather up the dawn.

I stopped suddenly. I'd forgotten my injury. When I stretched my bad leg to the front, the bandage was gone. The skin was whole. No scar, no pain. My heart swelled with wonder. *Thank You, thank You! I'm me again.*

A current pulsed beneath the ground, and the earth rose on a small crest. I caught the timing and catapulted into a leap higher than even years of dancer training could produce. When I landed, I sprang up again and again, until breathless.

"Come and see!" the Maker called again. Where was He? I peered around the trees. In the morning light, the undergrowth no longer menaced. Roots tucked themselves demurely out of the way, and ferns parted for me as I padded deeper into the forest.

Laughter spun through the air. Mine? His? The island's? I couldn't be sure. "I'm here." I lifted my arms like a flower seeking warmth.

The trees and shrubs around me shrank and fell away. No, they hadn't changed. It only appeared that way because I was being lifted. As when

I'd first encountered the Maker, He bore me up above the treetops. A swirl of clouds cushioned me—or perhaps that was His arms. "Look." His word rang like a joyous bell or bounding music.

Beneath us, the island was a tiny shape, with plants covering a floating area only a few yards in all directions from the remembering tree. I gasped. "What happened to all the villages? To the rest of the island?" *All those people? Brantley!*

"I've brought you to the time before."

I cautiously turned, angling to get a better look downward. The tangleroot grew and spread from the shoreline in all directions. Soon dirt appeared and coated it, then daygrass, then more plants. From this position I watched as creatures emerged from the bracken around the tree and explored outward. Shy bunnies, regal forest hounds, ambling ponies, vibrant songbirds.

Surely I was dreaming, but I wanted to live in this dream forever. "It's beautiful," I whispered. But the word was inadequate.

He drew me higher as the island grew. Wider, richer with life, it spun along a current and partnered with the sea in a carefree journey. The Maker breathed across the land. Treetops bobbed, leaves stirred, and as the wind swirled in small tempests, people appeared. They tested their limbs, greeted each other, and bounded across the island in riotous, irresistible glee. I cast my focus to the rim. No tall vines blocked the people's view of the ocean. No lithe trees wound together to create a barrier.

I grappled to understand. "What happened?"

Movements sped. The island blossomed and exploded in growth. From this vantage I watched the green village spring up, and the people develop artistry of all sorts. Their creations celebrated the beauty of their world and their Maker. The people of the red village organized their play, training their bodies to great strength and agility, reveling in the skills they'd been given. Nearest to the place we hovered, the blue village buildings sprawled outward, and people scurried about. Even with years compressed into seconds, I could sense the villagers' fulfillment as they created their new machines as if it was joyous play. People visited other villages, and all the island's paths were well traveled. Couples met and married. Families raised children, served each other in love. Everyone intermingled, rejoicing in each other's interests and gifts. How had it all changed?

As if in answer to my unspoken question, the whirl of passing time slowed. Now I watched as people from every village made the trek to the lake in the island's center. It seemed every single person made the pilgrimage. My muscles tensed. Was I going to witness another convening? I squeezed my eyes closed, not wanting to relive that horror. Then curiosity got the best of me, and I peeked.

Instead of what I feared, a beautiful celebration began. Various individuals and groups from each village shared their gifts as multicolored star rain exploded across the sky.

"The true gathering." Tenderness resonated in the mighty Voice that breathed life into my soul. "Until . . ."

The Maker lowered me closer to the island. Time sped past again. Star rains. Gatherings. Celebrations. Families. Fellowship. Days and nights flickered by as if I were fluttering my eyelids. Then, like landing hard from a jump, time crashed to a stop.

From my vantage point, hovering above the lake, I watched as another joyful gathering commenced. In the midst of their loving, jubilant spirits, a figure walking among them stood out like a demented shadow.

The Gardener! Even safely wrapped in clouds and far above the scene, my hand moved to my throat. I watched the painfully vivid activity as he spoke to person after person.

Heads nodded in assent. "No! Stop! Don't listen!" I shouted, but the sound floated away. Instead, my ears were opened. I was able to hear his next conversation.

A young man was singing to the group—a tender lyric of thanks to the Maker for the beauty surrounding them. But the Gardener whispered in the ear of a different young man, one who wore the rugged clothes of the red village. "Useless. And look how the watchers adore him. They didn't offer that much praise when you showed your speed in the race. And now look. That girl from your village. See how she approaches him? She should be yours."

Like dye dripped into a vat, a color bled and spread across the people. A color of envy and pride and selfishness. An ugly stain. The youth from the red village accosted the singer and girl, and a fight erupted. I winced, hearing too clearly the rage, the thuds of fists, and the crashing of stone against bone.

Oh, Maker, no!

But my horror didn't stop this unfolding. Evil had entered. Many of the villagers' faces reflected the same shock that I felt. Amidst their worried conversations about how to deal with this new and frightening occurrence, the Gardener stepped to the rim of the lake.

"The Maker didn't protect you from yourselves. But I will. I can erase this pain and confusion you feel. I can prevent this from ever happening again. And I can take your gifts and help you develop them beyond your wildest dreams."

People flocked toward him, begging him for his aid. I pressed my hands over my ears. I wanted to scream to everyone below that they were fools. But the words stuck in my throat, because I knew I'd pursued a similar path, surrendering my life to the Order in an effort to reach my dreams.

The Maker's arms held me tighter, His warmth surrounding me. "He is promising them more of what they most cherish. He persuades them to give up their love toward Me and toward each other and offers them their desires instead."

I squirmed in His grip. "Stop him! If this is the time before, You can stop him from ever damaging this world."

Instead, we watched as the Gardener directed everyone. People settled along the rim of the lake. Tears burned down my cheeks as vines crept over men, women, and children, encircling their heads, erasing their ability to love. I turned away, not wanting to witness this first convening. I'd already seen the results.

A gentle touch brushed away my tears. "You see." He spoke with a sorrow that could make the stars weep. "The Gardener has the right because they invited him. And each convening, they continue to choose him. I set limits on his destruction until the fullness of time, but when the harbinger comes, only a sacrifice will halt the Gardener's reach from spreading across this world." As I watched, the barrier along the rim sprang up, taller and taller. Not to imprison, but to keep others from stumbling into this place of danger, rejection, and forsaking. I watched as the Gardener sought to travel to the villages but crumpled into a pile of vegetation each time he tried to leave the lake basin. A ravening hound on a short chain. Yet since the people came to him, he was still horribly dangerous.

"What will You do?" I asked.

"I could let them finish the course they have set for themselves." Images swirled through my mind. Red villagers lost in the chaos of ever-fiercer battles. Blue villagers obsessed with their inventions and puzzles until they forgot to eat. Green villagers adoring nothing but their own creations. Other villages under yellow, purple, and orange star rains also sleepwalking with numb disregard for each other. Fewer and fewer children, and those who were born neglected and forsaken.

"No." I breathed the word, half argument, half prayer. Clouds thickened around me, and I found myself standing outside the massive tree again. Daygrass tickled my bare feet. A kernel of hope, of realization, sprouted in my heart. "You love them too much. I know that. You won't forsake them. You have a plan."

I felt a smile as large as the ocean as His love rolled over me. "When the time is best, I will walk among them again and free them from their lies."

My hope bloomed. He would banish the Gardener. He would rescue His people. "Thank You for showing me. But I still don't understand why You brought me here."

"Will you prepare the way? When the harbinger arrives, the Gardener's evil can be squelched instead of given free rein, but there will be a cost."

Every part of my being that loved Him, loved His tenderness, His power, His justice, every open-eyed fragment of my soul swelled to answer, "Yes!" I longed to give Him some small gift to thank Him for making me, freeing me, loving me. No matter the cost, I embraced this request.

"But how? What do You want me to do?"

Even as I asked, I sensed the deep quiet. As He had before, He offered silence to my chittering questions.

The weight of the calling pressed against my shoulders. Even the air grew heavy and still. I squinted at the forest. The light was no longer fresh and dappled. Shadows lurked once again, opposing the dawn. Even the birdsong rang flat and sour. I was no longer in the beautiful time before, but squarely back in the present moment of the troubled world.

I turned to reenter the hollow tree and reclaim my pack. My first step drew a gasp from my lungs. My ankle buckled, and I fell. I stretched my leg out and stared in disbelief. The tattered bandage once again bound my wound. Each beat of my heart pressed a line of flame deeply through my tendon, as if the High Saltar had sliced it only moments ago. I gritted my teeth to hold back a moan, but my soul screamed.

No! He'd shown me the beauty and perfection of what this world could be . . . of what I could be. Having seen that, I didn't want to come back. I didn't want to limp through this broken place with my broken body.

A breath of compassion swirled around me. He understood. And one day, all the beauty and healing I'd glimpsed would be permanent. In the meantime, He was faithful. He was with me. That was enough. I brushed away a tear and drew a deep, determined breath.

"Did you be learning more understanding?" Chanic's voice warbled from where she hunched near a huddle of reeds. "I never could be convincing others to remember. Most aren't recollecting the tree is here."

I looked up at her and nodded. She'd indeed given me a gift by leading me to this place. I crawled a few paces until I could reach my staff, then used it to ease to my feet. "Yes, thank you."

"So you'll be going back to where you came from then?"

I lifted my chin. "Not yet."

CHANIC LED ME THROUGH UNDERBRUSH. THE THICK, FETID air squeezed my lungs. Branches scratched my arms as if they knew my purpose and wished to stop me. The glimpse of this world in the time before had exhilarated me. The reminder of who I was made to be had filled me like a deep, contented sigh. Yet it had all been some sort of vision, and here I was back in the reality of tangled woods, lost people, and a wounded body. I almost welcomed the sting of thorns for the distraction it provided.

Distraction. I shook my head. No, I couldn't hide there. In some way, each village on this island had embraced a life of distraction, of obsession, of anything that would disconnect them from the Maker and each other. A corrupted version of His original intent for their interests and gifts.

Chanic's cottage came into view. In the daylight, the shingled walls flaked like peeling skin, and the roof sagged to one side. Chanic was already struggling for each step, leaning heavily on her two canes. What a pair we were.

"I wish I had more liniment for you."

Her head drooped forward again, but she twisted her chin to the side to show me a faint smile. "Not to worry. Mayhap I be finding a young one to journey to the red village for me. Though I be having little to trade."

"On my way through your village, I'll look for someone to come visit you."

She snorted. "As if any can be bothered. Especially with the Grand Convening so close at hand."

There it was again. The Grand Convening that Morra had mentioned. What made this one special beyond a normal convening?

Before I could ask, she waved away the bitterness in her voice. "Even if 'tis hopeless, 'tis kind of you to be trying to find someone to help me. Where will you go next?"

Where, indeed? How could I fulfill the Maker's call to prepare the way for Him? Did He want me to wander the entire island? How was I to reach all the scattered villages? So many questions, but one begged for an answer more than the others. "What happens at the Grand Convening?"

She shuffled to her doorway. "Surely you be knowing. The Every gather." As she lifted her twisted hands, sorrow threaded her words. "All but the unable."

"You mean all the villages go to the lake at the same time?"

"Once per year." She drew a wheezing breath. "It be a marvelous sight."

I helped her into her cottage and tended her fire. "What will your village do if you become too weak to care for yourself?"

Her whole face puckered with sourness. "They be skilled at forgetting. I only be desiring that the vines are gentle as they consume me and draw me into the earth."

I shuddered. If that was the best she could hope for, this was a dark land, indeed. I took her hands between mine. "When that time comes, I know One who has not forgotten you. He will gather you into His arms."

Even though my commission was urgent, I took time to tell her about the Maker and some of the vision He'd just shown me. Her eyes lit with wonder and gratitude, and I hoped my future conversations would be as welcome.

After leaving Chanic, I headed up the path toward the village as fast as my bad leg would allow. If the Grand Convening gathered all the peoples of this world, it would give me a place to recount what I'd seen in the tree of remembering. A means to prepare the way, as the Maker asked. And a place to find Brantley once again. He'd surely come with the red village folk. I'd ride my pony to—

My steps quickened. What if Plexia had set the pony free and it had wandered back to the red village? How would I make the journey to the lake then?

Emerging from the woods, I drew a steadying breath. Windrider grazed leisurely behind Plexia's home. I hurried to the pony and hugged her neck, breathing in the reassuring scent of dusty mane and sweaty flanks. My rabbiting pulse slowed, worries abated—at least on that score.

I found Plexia and politely used her talking tool to thank her for directing me to Chanic. I tried to relay my experiences at the tree, but she brushed me aside, still angry with me for raising disruptive ideas. I encountered similar responses as I moved through the village. I did find one youth who was willing to visit Chanic and bring her supplies. Perhaps Chanic would be able to convince him to barter for liniment from the red village. I longed to ease her pain. But the best way to help her was to help the entire island. To do exactly what the Maker had asked of me.

I spoke to each man or woman who would listen and told them what He'd revealed. Stiff backs, cold shoulders, and gruff rejections answered my efforts. By the end of the day, discouragement pulsed through me as sharply as the ache in my damaged tendon. By the time the subsun lowered behind the trees, I'd offended everyone in the village and couldn't find a place to rest for the night. Dejected, I returned to Windrider and led her into the cover of the woods. The overgrowth made me nervous. Even though the Gardener might be leashed, I'd felt the tangle of darkness that sometimes flowed through the plants on parts of the island beyond the lake. But I was exhausted and needed to rest. With a few well-placed branches and my cloak, I built a small shelter and kindled a campfire. I roasted several persea and chewed handfuls of berries from the prolific local bushes. Warming my hands in the glow stirred memories of traveling with Brantley back on Meriel. Only here I didn't have his capable company. Instead, I drew comfort from Windrider's gentle snuffles and her occasional stomps or shudders to flick an insect from her skin.

My time in the village today had proven I was inadequate to the Maker's task. Not one person listened to me. I didn't expect my rhetorical skills to improve in a matter of days. And there was the Gardener. He possessed powers to stop me I didn't yet know how to oppose.

As my tiny fire shrank to crackling embers, I hugged my arms and shivered.

"Make me strong. But if You won't make me strong, make me faithful."
I crawled under my shelter and slept.

A BREAKFAST OF FRUIT AND A FEW TUBERS PULLED FROM THE
soft earth near my campsite fueled my enthusiasm for the new day. I
tethered Windrider in a grassy patch with a clear stream and limped back
into town. This time I didn't try to convince anyone of the wrongness of
the convenings. I didn't attempt to explain the world's history. I simply
admired their contraptions, watched them work, and sometimes handed a
gear or lever to a preoccupied inventor. My reward was a subtle softening of
attitude, even a few smiles of acknowledgement. Feeling that I'd built a few
bridges, at midday I returned to my campsite to seek the Maker's guidance.

His gentle stirring prompted me to travel to the lake. If I waited
until the night before the Grand Convening, I'd be forced into an
exhausting revel with the village and would offend others with my
need to ride instead of walk to the lake. Better to use my pony while I
could and wait at the lake. With relations at least moderately restored
with some of the blue villagers, I mounted Windrider and rode.

Eager to find a safe place to camp before dark, I urged my pony
into a smooth canter. She tossed her mane and pricked her ears
forward, enjoying the chance to stretch her legs as much as I once
enjoyed challenging my muscles with a vigorous pattern. Her rolling
gait reminded me of my childhood ride in Middlemost.

Bracing my hands against her withers, I pulled both feet under me
to crouch on her back. I had to shift my balance to let my good leg take
all my weight but then was able to straighten and stand. With arms
wide, the breeze of our passing washed across my body. I stretched
my bad leg out behind me, holding the most beautiful line I could
create. Our ride was a moment of worship, a time of celebrating the
pure joy of movement, of life. The passing wind blew away my fear,

my loneliness, my dread. My hair flew out behind, my tunic rippled, my muscles held strong and lithe. I'd faced the threat of death before. I would give myself to the Maker's purpose, whatever the cost.

The resolve carried me through the afternoon. But once the area of convening came into view, I hurried to build a small shelter to hide me from the lake. I'd be in place for the convening, ready to speak out—to shout if needed. I'd proclaim the truth. But there was no sense blundering into danger before it was necessary.

I chose to forego a fire, since I didn't want to draw attention to my hiding place on the edge of the woods. From behind boughs, I peered down the grassy crater toward the lake, watching for the skeletal figure who had caused so much damage to this world. When there was no sign of him, I felt a strange mix of disappointment and relief. Perhaps I'd traveled with Brantley too long, because a part of me itched for confrontation. Waiting—with the dread of the unknown outcome—seemed far worse than a rapid and decisive battle. No other villagers approached the lake, and eventually I slept.

The next morning, I wandered to the trailhead leading to the red village. I'd been told that only a short time remained before the Grand Convening, but perhaps there was time to ride back and search out Brantley. I'd run the risk of being caught in their pre-convening activities, but anything would be better than this solitary waiting.

After caring for Windrider, I prepared to mount. Just then, a voice spoke in my heart like a hand pressing against my chest. *Stay.*

I looked heavenward. "Is that You?" Perhaps the word was just my own indecisiveness speaking. If I rode to the red village, I could ask Jalla how to make more liniment. My efforts would help Chanic. Helping a woman bent with a crippling illness was indeed a good reason to go.

Stay.

Surely the Maker didn't want me to waste time lingering here when I could be useful elsewhere. Besides, I needed to learn how Brantley was faring. The Maker cared about him and would want me to look after him.

Stay.

This time, I breathed out in resignation. I could no longer deny the truth. This was the Maker's voice. Every bit of my self-will clamored for action. "I don't want to listen," I whispered. If I were still caught up in His arms in the beautiful vision of this world's creation, it would be easy to heed His voice. But I was back in the dust and thorns and confusion of the day. "Help me want to obey You."

I clung to the pony's neck. It would be so easy to swing onto her back. Just one quick check of the situation in the red village. The temptation built. In my mind's eye, I saw Brantley's joyful recognition when he saw me, the ideas we would share. He'd worry about what the Maker had asked of me, but he'd be there to support me. I gazed down the path. Was it really so wrong to want a human ally?

My conscience answered swiftly. Was it ever right to forsake the Maker to seek human aid instead? More simply, was it ever right to forsake the Maker?

Before I could give in to the longing to set my own course, I stepped back, patted Windrider, and sent her trotting down the path toward her home without me.

I hung on the sound of her hoofbeats until they faded into the distance. Part of me traveled with her. I dusted off my hands and plucked fruit for my breakfast, for the moment crowding out my doubts with busy activity.

Because of the bounty of food in easy reach, my foraging didn't use up much of the day. I set about weaving a mat for my small shelter and added more boughs to the slanted roof. As the subsun followed the primary into the sky, I limped to the lake and dared to dangle my feet in the rich, milky water. I missed Navar. Had she reached Meriel safely? Would she return? I spent the afternoon cutting reeds and trying to duplicate the whistle that Brantley used to call his stenella. Despite my efforts, I never managed to make a sound. As the sky darkened toward evening, so did my mood. I could have ridden to the red village and back by now. Where would the harm have been?

Two more days and nights passed, and my attitude grew more sour. The third day, a squall blew in from over the rim trees. Rain pelted my shelter and revealed how unskilled I was at building. Water dripped onto my head and trickled down my hair. I emerged from the shelter, glaring up at the sky. I eased into the early steps of the leeward wind pattern, wincing as my damaged leg took weight. Eventually, the pain subsided enough for me to continue. The clouds scudded outward from above the lake, and the suns warmed my face again. Breathing hard, sweat coating my skin, I finished the pattern and closed my eyes. When I opened them again, not only had the rain blown far out to sea, but tiny flowers dotted the daygrass on the slope down to the lake. Blue, gold, coral. The blossoms winked at me, opening and closing as if breathing. I eased to my knees and watched. Soon the petals moved in and out more swiftly, until the hillside seemed to be covered in gossamer butterflies. Transfixed, I touched one of the fragile flowers. A comforting scent rose from the blossom, like the smell of freshly baked bresh, or a clean blanket pulled up to my chin at the end of a hard day of classes.

As suddenly as they had appeared, the flowers vanished. Yet I knew I would carry the wonder of the experience for the rest of my days. The tiny blossoms, with an existence even briefer than daygrass, had spoken to me with more truth than any teacher of the Order ever had.

This time of waiting no longer felt like a punishment or test of obedience, but a gracious gift. He was granting me time to know Him better, to rest, to prepare.

As shadows lengthened, I limped back to my shelter. I'd had no glimpse of the Gardener. No other villagers had journeyed to the lake. I no longer startled at every sound in the woods.

As I settled, the thump of pounding hooves drew near. "Haw!" A shout carried across the valley. Branches rattled as a pony and rider crashed through underbrush and burst from one of the trailheads.

21

AT THE SIGHT OF THE PONY AND RIDER, I SPRANG TO MY feet and peered out from behind one of the trees beside my shelter. I'd learned enough to stay hidden until I knew whether a friend or foe was arriving.

Energy rode through the man's strong back. Both suns glinted off fair, tousled hair. I recognized him by the reckless gallop of his mount.

Brantley.

My heart swelled, and a grin spread across my face. He'd returned. No doubt looking for me. The days of loneliness and my fears about the task ahead all fell away. Help had arrived.

He charged his pony down toward the water, then leapt from his back.

"I'm here!" I waved my arms as I stepped from the woods to the edge of the grassy hill overlooking the lake.

Shielding his eyes, he peered in my direction. I waited for a smile to light his face, for his feet to race to me, for him to scold me with warnings—revealing his concern.

I limped down the incline, but he didn't smile. He didn't race toward me. He didn't scold.

He scowled. "Still around?"

I locked my gaze on him and swallowed my disappointment as I joined him at the lakeshore. His leather vest held a ragged gash. A strip of cloth bound his upper leg over dark stains. Blood? I pressed my lips together. The competitions at the red village were more violent than I'd realized.

Then I met his eyes. Still distant, still cold, but something more swirled in the sea-blue depths. Pain flickered there, the sort of confused pain of a youngling who burns his hand on a boiling kettle. His eyes cried out, what happened? How can this be?

Rescue him, dear Maker!

I gently touched his cheek. He hadn't bothered to shave since we'd arrived on this island. His beard had passed the point of being bristly and was a light velvet coating on his jaw. I caressed his face once, then lowered my hand.

His rigid shoulders softened.

Only then did I speak. "Yes, I'm still here. We're in this together, remember?"

He rubbed the back of his neck as if trying to push off thick cords of tangleroot. "I threw myself into the games. And I won most of them. But something . . ." His ribs contracted, the confusion swirling again. A boy sitting among the broken pieces of a favorite toy.

My heart ached for his loss. I had to find a way to call him back. Perhaps his confusion showed a crack in the Gardener's control. Perhaps I'd finally be able to reach him.

I'd once tamed a forest hound simply by joining his movements, creating a new dance that soothed the dangerous beast. Drawing from that experience, I copied Brantley's posture. He sighed, and I echoed the sigh. He took a few steps toward the lake, and I mirrored him. When he cocked his head toward me, I offered my hands. Frowning, he slowly took them. We'd danced together at the green village revels. I stepped closer into that comfortable posture. I hummed one of the melodies I'd heard many weeks ago in Windswell. Music had been forbidden to novitiates of the Order, so my throat rasped as I struggled to find the notes.

The corner of Brantley's lips quirked upward. His rich baritone took over, singing a lilting story of sea and herders and families and broad horizons. When he repeated the chorus, I joined in shyly. We began to circle each other. We pulled in and away, slid several steps to one side and then the other. He'd looked clumsy astride his pony, but now he moved with grace and confidence. Soon he scooped an arm behind my back and spun me off the ground in a wide circle that left me laughing. We abandoned the dances we'd performed at the revel. He guided me in movements that spoke of his village, his family, the years of striving, of celebrating, of community. The song he sang came from deep memories, rich with connections to all those he loved.

As we danced, the tightness of his back softened. The light in his eyes grew more natural and familiar. Our movements built a new connection between us. Our hands linked. Our gazes joined.

The song finished, and I leaned toward him, peering into his eyes, scarcely daring to breathe. *Who are you now, my love?*

He shook his head, bemused, and released my hands. "Something has been . . . wrong."

I bit my lip. The coldness had left him. Did I dare hope? "Yes. Ever since the Gardener—"

"The spores. The thorn." He pressed the heels of his hands against his forehead. "I fought it, but it swallowed me. As if I were drifting in the sea and there were no currents to draw me home."

Every minute of his inner conflict and suffering played across his face. My heart constricted for his pain. "And now?"

He touched my face. His eyes brimmed with life again. A rueful smile tugged his lips. "You still have remarkable power in your feet, dancer."

I laughed. "And never a better reason to dance a change into being."

His eyebrows slid together. "Much is still foggy. Why did I leave you here? I remember someone saying cold and horrible things. Did I—?"

I placed my hand over his and leaned into his palm that cupped the side of my face. "It matters not. Let it go. We have plans to make."

He gave me one, long searching look. "It does matter. I hurt you. The last thing I ever wanted to do. I'm sorry."

"It wasn't your fault. The Gardener—"

"Forgive me. Please." Gravel rasped in his voice. He held me as if he couldn't move until he had my absolution. I wanted to brush aside all the hurt without truly confronting it. How much of his indifference and coldness had come from some core inside him?

I swallowed. "Yes. Of course. You're forgiven."

He paused, measuring my sincerity. Then in that practical way he had, he nodded, completely trusting the matter was past. "You've learned how to get through the barrier trees?"

I shook my head. "No, but the Maker wants me to prepare the way for Him to walk among the people of this world."

He scowled, and for a moment I feared he'd slipped back into the disdain he'd shown for me while under the Gardener's influence. But when he rubbed his chin thoughtfully, I realized the scowl came from worry, not disdain. "Let me guess," he said. "This will involve danger and sacrifice."

My lips twitched. "Your favorite things."

"Not when I have to watch you face them. What are you supposed to do?"

"I don't know yet."

"Better and better," he grumbled.

"We can trust the Maker." I stepped closer, resting my head against his chest, and welcomed the way his arms circled me. "If nothing is done, the people of this world will destroy themselves."

He squeezed me protectively. "Sounds like a problem for the Maker to solve. Why does He need you?"

I smiled, drawing warmth from Brantley's embrace. "He doesn't *need* me. He offers me the gift of serving Him."

"He could pick someone else once in a while." But there was no heat in the words. He gave me one more squeeze, then stepped back and scanned me. "This world has been hard on you."

I shrugged, hiding how warm his concern made me. I probably looked a mess, with twigs in my hair, dirt on my bandaged ankle, scratches on my arms from time in the underbrush. But he looked far worse—bruised, torn, and seeping blood. "You should talk. What brought you here? Did they run out of bandages in the red village?"

He barked a laugh. "Something like that. They didn't like a stranger winning contests. And a longing drew me."

"To be close to the only glimpse of sea we have here?"

"That. And perhaps a deep part of me remembered the person I want by my side when everything goes wrong."

I blushed. "It's good to have you back."

"What's our next step?" His gaze skimmed our surroundings.

"From what I've learned, all the villages will gather here at the next star rain. It's called the Grand Convening."

"More of the same? Odd people doing odd things, but in greater number?"

"Something like that," I parroted him.

He laughed again.

I would happily spend the rest of my days making him laugh—however many days I was granted. "I made a camp just inside the forest's edge. Hungry?"

He rubbed his stomach. "Always."

I led the way, newly self-conscious of my heavy limp. I had managed to forget my bad leg when Brantley and I danced, but now my awkwardness shamed me again. His arm slid around my waist, subtly supporting me as we climbed the hill.

The lean-to branches covered the nest I'd made with my cloak and pack. He immediately jiggled one of the supports, causing dried leaves and pine needles to shower down. "Carya, how did you expect to defend your position with this flimsy shelter?"

I bristled. "I was trying to stay out of sight."

"This wouldn't even protect you from rain."

I raised my chin. "I didn't need protection from rain." A careful spin and a flourish of my arm showed him I had my own way of dealing with problems.

He grinned. "I forgot. And I didn't mean to criticize."

"Oh, yes you did. You can't help yourself. But I don't mind."

And I truly didn't. He could fuss all he wanted. Every tiny thing he did that once irritated me had become sweet as seawater and welcome as the morning suns.

Instead of grabbing fruit, he immediately gathered more branches and shaved them with his longknife. As the suns heated the ridge, he tossed aside his vest and kept working. I sat in the shade and stitched the worst tear in the leather vest for him, while he built a sturdier campsite for us.

When he was satisfied, he flopped down and accepted a juicy lenka from me. Staring out at the lake, he leaned forward. "How long have you been here?"

"About three days, why?"

"Any sign of Navar?"

"No. I tried to make a whistle but failed."

"I'll go to the water's edge and call her." He grabbed his whistle from his pack, then hesitated. "If you think that's a good idea?"

I smiled. "Absolutely. We'll be able to see if the people of Meriel got our message." A sobering thought hit me. "What if the jar and message are still tied to her? Would that mean our island is too far out of reach? That we'll never get back?"

"One step at a time," he said.

I nodded. As he set off toward the shoreline, I grabbed my walking stick and followed. After losing him for so long, I couldn't bear to allow any distance between us. I joined him on the tangleroot, settling beside him and once again dangling my feet in the water. He stretched onto his belly and blew a call into the water.

When he sat up, he pulled off his tunic. "Care for a swim?"

He knew I feared the water, but here the vastness was contained. This part of the sea didn't spread into the horizon. The border of tangleroot all the way around gave me a sense of safety. Until I thought of the unending depths beneath this lake. A shudder rippled through me. Still, he was a man of the ocean. To fully join him, I wanted to share his affection for the water. Or at least try. I wanted to show Brantley my love while I had the chance, because I suspected I might not have much time left with him.

Back on Meriel, I'd given my life to the Maker's purposes. Although I still wasn't clear how to prepare the people of this world for His visit, the Maker had warned there would be a cost. I suspected it would take sacrifice—an ultimate sacrifice. I wouldn't speak of that to Brantley. Not yet.

"I'd love a swim," I declared, enjoying the surprised lift to Brantley's brow.

We frolicked like two copper fish. The water welcomed and supported me. When a surge of current rose from the depths, I rode it with laughter rather than screams of terror. Although our swim was lighthearted, Brantley kept a careful watch on me. Once, when I choked on a swallow of water, he was beside me in an instant, guiding me to the tangleroot edge and pounding my back.

Besides helping us feel clean and refreshed, the swim had an added benefit. The healing water washed blood from Brantley's leg bandage, and no more seeped through. The persistent throbbing in my tendon also eased. We shared more fruit and lingered at the side of the lake, watching for a ripple to announce Navar's arrival.

When the primary sun sank behind the ridge, we retreated to our camp. Brantley stoked a small fire, even though we didn't need the warmth. "How long before this Grand Convening you're waiting for?"

I bit my lip. "I'm not sure. Back at Meriel, I never noticed a pattern to the star rains' arrivals or kept count of days. I'd know it was nearing time when stars swelled in the night sky. Sometimes I'd taste it in the air."

"The tang." He wrapped an arm around my shoulders, bracing his back against a tree. "Once I was a day's journey out on Navar when star rain fell. The taste in the air is even stronger out at sea."

My spine melted into Brantley. I could stay here forever in this warmth, sitting by his side, studying the tiny flames and watching the subsun settle toward its bed. "One day when this is all over, I want to watch a star rain out at sea, with you by my side. Do you think such a thing is still possible?" Or would my assignment on this world rob us of that chance?

He angled his head toward me. "Before we met, I'd have said the odds against us are stacked too high."

"And now?" I searched his gaze, so near. So confident.

"Now I know better than to underestimate your ability to leap over all the stacked-up odds in your way." Brantley's lips found mine, gently speaking his love through his touch. When our lips parted, his breathing was ragged. "Oh, dancer . . . how could I ever have forgotten loving you?"

I wrapped my hands around the back of his neck and answered with an enthusiastic kiss of my own, but he jerked away. Had I done something wrong? Was I supposed to feign reluctance?

"Hear that?" He sprang to his feet.

Still muzzy from our embrace, all I heard was blood rushing through my ears. I reached a hand toward him, wishing to coax him back to my side. The air felt suddenly cold without him. But he misunderstood my intent and pulled me to my feet. Frowning, I wobbled. "What are you—?"

He clamped his palm over my mouth.

Over the rustle of a rodent deep in the underbrush, a rapid pounding sounded nearby. Brantley silently smothered our small flame and drew me deeper into the shadows.

22

EVERY MUSCLE CLENCHED AS I BRACED MY HAND AGAINST
a tree and squinted toward the sound of pounding feet. Brantley
squeezed my shoulder—whether in comfort or as a reminder to stay still,
I couldn't tell. Not that a warning was needed. This world had deepened
my instinct for caution. If we stayed here much longer, I'd be as alert
as Brantley.

A wave rolled beneath the island, stirring the trees. At the trailhead a
short distance from our camp, a man stumbled as the hillside bobbed. He
caught himself and continued his awkward jog toward the lake.

"It's Morra," I whispered.

"What's he doing?"

The young man who had once welcomed us amiably to his village now
paced the shoreline, tugging at his hair, beating his chest, and muttering
to himself.

I sighed. "Looks like his quest failed."

"What quest?"

"He went back to the green village to win the heart of a girl. Not an
easy task here."

Brantley cocked an eyebrow. "I can relate."

I tucked a strand of hair behind my ear. "You won my heart long ago.
It's not my fault you forgot."

Morra plopped down at the shore and stared toward the last rays of
the subsun as it brushed the treetops. Sitting cross-legged, he began to
sway in the strange movements his people had used in the convening.

I grabbed my walking stick and hurried down the slope. Brantley dogged my heels. "What are you doing? Don't get close to the lake now. It's almost dark."

Brantley had every reason to fear the Gardener and the damage he could cause, but we had enough time to coax Morra away from the shore. I couldn't leave the youth there to conjure an extra dose of the Gardener's "gift."

"Don't call him!" I shouted to the young man.

Morra sprang to his feet and delivered a formal bow, one leg stretched in front of the other. I rose to my toes and lowered. He offered a friendly smile, until he remembered his purpose. Then a scowl scudded across his brow. "Don't interrupt. I need the Gardener's help."

"That's just it. You don't. The Gardener is only here because people traded away their ability to love long ago. The Maker gave me a vision and showed me the time before."

Morra snarled. "You don't understand." None of the friendly greeter remained in his visage. Rage hardened the pudgy lines of his face, just as it had before he'd attacked a man at the revels.

"Carya, back away." Brantley stepped closer, hand to his weapon.

I blew out a sharp breath. "No. Give me space." I eased closer to Morra, copying his posture. Dance had cleared Brantley's mind. Could it work again with Morra—at least to deter him from his purpose? His shoulders hunched forward, his lips formed a tight line. His arms wrapped his stomach as if he'd eaten spoiled meat. The youth's suffering was easy to read. Gently, slowly, I lifted my shoulders and watched as his moved a fraction. I reached out to him, and he loosened his grip around his middle to take my hand. Cloudy eyes met mine, and I swayed with soft waves tickling the earth beneath us. As if I were teaching a second-form novitiate, I coaxed him to mirror my movements. Inch by inch, I eased him from the water's edge where the Gardener's vines had enmeshed the people who called for him.

Brantley's posture was less soothing. He snapped his head side to side and glared at the tangleroot. As Morra and I moved up the slope, Brantley backed away from the lake, protecting us. "Hurry," he urged.

Morra stopped, our connection wavering. "What are you doing?"

I threw a frown toward Brantley for interrupting us, then gave a comforting squeeze to Morra's hand. "I've learned so much about your world. Come up to our campsite so we can talk."

I'd once watched my friend Starfire coax a honeybird to her finger. Any flinch would startle the creature to flee in a frantic flutter of feathers. I sensed the same tension now. One wrong word or move could send Morra back to his original purpose. I kept our progress careful and deliberate. Violet tinted the sky. A forest hound howled. From across the lake, the throaty cackle of a welfen beast threatened all in hearing. Thankfully, Brantley didn't interrupt our slow process again.

When we reached our campsite, I coaxed Morra to sit, his back to the lake. He pulled his hand free and rubbed his eyes. "It's dark."

"It's all right." I settled across from him, relief turning my body limp as blood rushed back into knotted muscles.

"But the Gardener . . ."

"You decided not to call him tonight. He's not there." I glanced at Brantley.

He leaned out and scanned the entire shoreline, then nodded. "No sign of him. Thank the Maker," he added under his breath.

I blinked. Had my companion actually invoked the Maker's name in gratitude instead of irritation or accusation? I tucked the moment away to think about later.

"Morra, why were you so upset when you arrived?"

His fist clenched over his heart. "I tried to remind Crillo of our pact, but she no longer cares. I need the Gardener to erase the pain."

I shook my head. "It's the convening that makes her unable to love. I don't know her true feelings for you, but I know that erasing your ability to care is not the answer." I explained every detail of my vision outside the blue village, and also the hints the Maker had given me about my purpose here. For once Morra didn't automatically dismiss my words. He scrunched his forehead into tight puckers.

Eventually his eyes lit with hope. "If I keep her from the lake, she'll remember she cares about me?"

I nodded. "There are others who aren't firmly in the Gardener's grasp. A pony tender in the red village was injured and missed a few convenings. Now she's begun to care for others. She even took in the abandoned baby we found. And there's Chanic, an elderly woman outside the blue village. She knows the truth."

Morra rubbed the back of his neck and looked at Brantley. "And you? What be you saying of this?"

Brantley's crooked grin in my direction warmed me to my toes. "She always speaks the truth. Even to her own cost. You can trust her."

The young man glanced back to the darkening void of the lake. "If the two of you don't seek the Gardener, why are you remaining here?"

Brantley pulled out his whistle and trilled a quick melody. "I was calling my stenella."

Morra bounced like a youngling. "Will she return?"

"That's our hope."

My eyelids dragged downward, and I stifled a yawn.

"I'll take first watch," Brantley said quietly. I longed to be the unselfish and heroic sort who would volunteer, but exhaustion won out. I gratefully agreed, then burrowed into my cloak and let sleep capture me.

THE NEXT MORNING, MORRA JOINED US IN OUR VIGIL AT the shore. I sat a little distance from the edge, while Morra whittled a branch and dangled his feet in the milky blue lake. Brantley whistled his call into the water several more times. As the subsun chased its bigger companion across the sky, dread began to chase my hope away. If Navar didn't return, it meant our world had drifted too far from this one. Would I ever again see the beloved people of Windswell, or the familiar shops of Middlemost, or the unified dancers creating beauty in the center ground? My chest contracted, and I suppressed a whimper.

"What's wrong?" Brantley left the shoreline and settled next to me. He was far too alert to my shifting moods. I wanted to remain strong for his sake. Still, the offer to unburden my heavy thoughts was too alluring.

"If Navar doesn't return, we'll probably never see our world again." My voice tightened with the despair I attempted to squeeze back into my throat.

He pressed his lips together, worry etching his brow. Then he leaned back on his elbows. "Oh, I wouldn't worry about that. With the task the Maker gave you, I was guessing we'd both die soon anyway."

My jaw gaped, until I saw the twinkle in his eye. A nervous chuckle rose from my chest, then a deeper laugh welled up. Soon we were both laughing, rolling on the soft daygrass. I clutched my stomach, gasping for breath. "You're right."

Nearby, Morra stood and stared down at us. "And you be claiming that the Gardener addles our minds? Mayhap you be the addled ones."

Somehow that struck me as funny, and I collapsed into more peals of laughter. When I caught my breath, I patted the earth beside me. "I'm sorry. When everything is uncertain, sometimes it helps to laugh."

Morra sank down and showed me the results of his woodwork. He'd shaped the thick branch and hollowed it into a bowl. The lip carried precise scallops, and the outside was decorated with a carving of a man and a woman.

My fingers traced the images. "This is beautiful."

He shrugged one shoulder. "A pledging bowl. One of the elders be telling us they once used these in the village. But that was in the time before—long before my remembering. Even before the Gardener."

I passed the bowl to Brantley, who examined the handiwork with a raised brow. "I've never seen the like. You have a gift, youngling."

Morra shrugged again, but color rose on his face. "Needs oil from a persea skin to give it polish." He retrieved his bowl and strode up the hill to the trees.

"I'll be right back," Brantley said. He sprang to his feet and followed Morra. The men talked earnestly for a few minutes, then Brantley returned and played his signal into the water again.

I continued staring at the surface, willing something to happen. A splash sounded, but it was only a curious copper fish that quickly submerged again. Across from where we sat, a ripple stirred the surface, but as reeds near the shore bent, I realized it was only the wind.

My somber mood returned.

When Brantley settled beside me again, I swallowed back my worried sigh and forced a smile. "I'm sure she'll be here soon."

He stared hard at my face, then narrowed his eyes. "You're worrying."

"Aren't you?"

"Sure, but with you, I don't understand it."

What was he thinking? That I didn't have a right to be worried?

He tapped my nose with one light finger. "After what I saw you do when you confronted the Order, I'm surprised you'd have any room for doubts. If the Maker can conquer the High Saltar and cleave the island, He can certainly get us back home."

Shame heated my cheeks. How quickly I forgot. "You're right. He's shown Himself faithful so many times. If I could stay in His presence, maybe the fear and doubt wouldn't return."

Brantley drew a slow breath, and his gaze took in the forest, the smooth hillside, the lake, the suns above. "Isn't He present here?"

"Of course. It's just—" I straightened my spine. "Wait. I thought you doubted."

He took my hand and drew aimless circles on my palm. "I've been angry at the Maker. Confused by the turns life has taken. But Carya, I'm a herder."

I tilted my head. What did that have to do with the Maker? "I know that."

He smiled. "Not really. Not what it fully means. I've spent days alone at sea. Do you think I haven't had to grapple with One who is big enough to set the currents in motion? I didn't doubt He rode the skies and the waves. I only doubted He cared for me."

Squeezing his hand, I leaned closer. "He does."

"Maybe. I've seen Him care for you, so that's something. I do have a question, though."

"About the Maker?" I wished again I had the Maker's letter with me. I longed to offer Brantley reassurance, but felt little qualified to explain anything about lofty truths.

He shook his head. "About the Gardener. I've been thinking about what you saw in your vision. You said that the people here made a bargain with the Gardener."

I nodded, warmed to know he'd been listening. "That's how he's had the right to control them."

"But I didn't. I didn't give him permission to numb me or change me."

I sank back, reliving the night of the convening. A flurry of fighting, of fear, of desperate dancing. The horror of Brantley's cold and still body.

"He meant to kill you," I said, forming tentative thoughts. "But the Maker limited the damage."

Brantley's lips swished side to side as if tasting the notion. "Then why didn't the Maker stop the Gardener from doing any harm?"

I blinked. "I don't know." At first my voice was small and apologetic, but then a giddy realization flooded through me. "I don't know. There is so much my little dancer brain doesn't understand about the Maker. But He's let me know Him enough to know He's good. He's wise. He's powerful. So I think"—I met Brantley's searching gaze—"I can be at peace not knowing."

Brantley's eyes narrowed, but he didn't look away. He seemed to see into my soul. Then his lips quirked. "You're almost making sense, dancer."

I snorted. "Go catch us some fish."

He sobered. "Would be easier with Navar's help."

As shadows darkened under his eyes, I regretted mentioning fishing. Brantley and Navar had been trusted partners for much of his life. I squinted at the water where the two suns shot glare into my eyes. Something stirred. My breath caught in my throat. "Look!"

23

THE DISTURBANCE ON THE LAKE'S SURFACE MADE MY insides churn as much as the water. Friend or foe?

I lurched to my feet, gripping my cane like a weapon. Brantley didn't indulge in my level of caution. He raced to the shoreline.

"Wait!" That man was far too eager to race into danger. And he knew I wasn't fast enough to pull him back.

He ignored my call and kept running.

A long neck stretched out of the water and scanned in all directions. I'd know those floppy ears and limpid eyes anywhere. Navar! My lungs filled, and I let out a whoop as she surged into full view, splashing her fins in a joyful welcome. A school of copper fish shaded the water around her as if she wore a sparkling cape.

Brantley dove cleanly from the tangleroot and swam with strong strokes. In seconds, he clambered onto her back. She chirped and chittered and spun in happy circles. Morra heard the commotion and ran closer but hesitated just behind me. He rocked forward and back like a toddler seeing a puppy for the first time, unsure whether to give in to fear or delight, and hovering somewhere between both impulses.

I squeezed his arm. "She won't hurt you. Come on."

We walked to the shore, and I dropped onto the edge, dangling my feet in the water. Navar swam giddy dashes across the lake, while Brantley stood astride, glorying in her speed. As they turned our direction, I waved. Navar chirruped and zoomed toward us. She butted a few fish as she approached, tossing them over our heads and onto the land.

The youth squeaked and stumbled back. When Navar pulled to a stop inches away, her wake splashed me, and I tasted the sweet citrus of the sea. I laughed. "It's good to see you too."

She lowered her muzzle, pressing her leathery skin against my chest. I hugged her neck, breathing in the clean scent of vast ocean currents, running my hands over her wet hide. The frayed leather harness still surrounded her chest, but I couldn't see the jar we had carefully attached days—or was it years?—ago. My heartbeat caught and fluttered. Had our message made it to Meriel? Was the missing jar a sign they'd noticed it and taken it?

Brantley crouched and ran his fingers along the leather strap, then plunged into the lake and swam under Navar. He stayed beneath the surface too long for my comfort. When he emerged, he shook his hair back and lifted the jar.

My pulse caught again. Oh no! No one had seen our letter. Even though I had braced myself for that possibility, I really hadn't believed we'd be trapped here for the rest of our lives. The fear had been too huge to fully confront.

Dearest Maker, please tell me we'll see our world again one day. The pain of loss twisted so hard in my gut that I couldn't breathe.

Brantley tossed me the jar and levered himself onto the shore. "I'll need to redo the harness, it's tangled and chafing her skin." But he waited, watching me.

I turned the clay vessel in my hands. Fine cracks scored the sides.

"I wonder how far away Meriel is now. If Navar couldn't reach it—" I pressed my lips together, pushing back words of doubt that crashed against my teeth.

Brantley snatched the jar from my hands and pried open the lid. "You're mighty quick to jump to conclusions." He upended the jar. Water poured out.

Perhaps the jar was empty after all, and an empty jar meant hope. Someone had read our message. Even now, the dancers could be hard at work, their bare feet guiding our world with their patterns and keeping this island in view. If we ever found a way through the barrier trees at the rim, our home might be in reach.

Then a soggy parchment fell to the tangleroot. I stifled a gasp before picking up the paper.

"Is it *our* message?" Brantley asked.

I hated hearing the low note of despair in his normally determined voice. When I unrolled the parchment, ink smeared across the page, but a few words stood out. ". . . hurry . . . can't . . . farewell."

My pulse thundered in my ears, and vertigo made me sway. "It's not our message to the saltars. They received our note. They answered."

"What do they say?" Brantley blotted seawater from his face and torso with his woven tunic, muscles coiled as if ready for action.

I spread the page in my lap, then my shoulders sagged. "I don't know. Water ruined the ink. I think they answered that we should hurry home, that they can't fight the currents any longer."

"What?" Brantley snatched the paper from me and glared at it, demanding it offer up its mysteries. One callused finger traced the few legible words. His jaw flexed, and he turned away. "Well, then. At least we know."

My fingers crept into his hand, and he squeezed. Our message to Meriel had been the last fragile tether to our old world, to our hope. Now even that was lost. Brantley's response was matter-of-fact and calm—at least outwardly. I couldn't allow my spirit to shatter. He would not be the only strong person in our partnership. I leaned my head against his shoulder. "We still have each other. And the Maker."

A low growl rumbled in his chest. "Seems He sends us on some odd paths." But there was no real hostility in the statement.

I managed a watery smile. "You told me once that the less traveled trails lead to the most interesting treasures."

"I believe I was referring to hidden berry bushes or undiscovered flint deposits. Not new worlds and murky quests."

I patted his arm. "I know."

Morra strolled along the shoreline, watching Navar glide around the lake. In spite of her glee in seeing us again, she seemed agitated. A breeze stirred overhead and made its way down toward the water. The stenella spread her side fins and leapt, but the wind was too weak to hold her airborne. Still, the sight of her full graceful body above the surface made Morra fall to his knees and clasp a hand over his mouth. As the light hit her fins, they shimmered with iridescent shades of pink.

Beside me, Brantley stared hard at the tangleroot rimming the lake, his whole body bent like an old man's. Our world was gone. Our families and villages and everything familiar. Emptiness gnawed like hunger, and even Brantley's warmth beside me couldn't soothe. "All right," I said. "Let's get it out of our systems. What will you miss the most?"

He pulled away and frowned at me. "Is this a good idea?"

"One time only. We need to grieve so we can move forward." I thrust my chin forward in challenge.

His gaze moved upward, unfocused, as he gathered memories. "The low bush berries that grow by the river. Orianna, Bri, my mother. The meeting house at my village. Riding in after a successful day of herding and watching the children laugh as they gather copper fish." His throat clogged. "The cottage I planned to build us on the creek under the willows." He squeezed my hand. "And you?"

My breath hitched. I should never have suggested this stupid memorial to all we had lost. But now that he'd shared, I would too. "I know it's crazy, but I'll miss the smooth white floors of the Order. The rhythm of the drums. But I'll also miss the sea. Standing on the edge of the world and seeing the ocean stretch into forever as the suns rise." My eyes stung. How could I possibly cope with losing my friends, my village, my entire world? "You're right, this was a bad idea."

He gently held my chin and turned my face toward him. "You had the courage to leave everything you knew in the Order and start a new life. This is our world now, and we'll build a life here. We can do this."

I blinked back my tears, determined to match his bravery. "Whatever happens, I'm glad you're here. That we're together. You're right. We will build a new life here."

He pressed his forehead against mine. "Now and forever."

Our forever might not last very long. But it existed in this precious moment, and I savored the warmth of Brantley's skin, the strength of his arms, the wet curls at his temples.

"What's she doing?" Morra called from a short distance away on the shoreline, pointing to Navar.

We pulled apart. The stenella was diving and reemerging, bobbing and making anxious chittering sounds.

"I don't know." Brantley stood and whistled to her. "She does this when a storm is near, but the sky is clear. Some other danger approaching?"

She surfaced near us, her head weaving a subtle dance even as she floated beside the tangleroot.

"I'll fix the harness." Brantley plunged into the water again. It took several minutes to struggle with wet knots in the leather harness. He also ran his hands over every part of her hide, checking for injuries. From what I could see, her smooth skin was unmarred, except for the scar from an old wound inflicted by a soldier of the Order.

Brantley climbed onto her back and leaned into her neck, whispering something to her.

I bit my lip. "Is she all right?"

She flipped a fin and eased along the shore. Brantley stepped off, his forehead wrinkled. "I don't know. I've never seen her like this."

The mat of tangleroot bobbed, and I stretched my arms out for balance. As we watched, Navar strained her neck as tall as she could, her floppy ears dangling above our heads. She gave another squeaky call, then dove.

The splash of her tail fin was the last thing we saw.

"Where is she going?"

Brantley rubbed the back of his neck. "I have no idea."

"Are you going to call her back?"

He glanced at the sky where the primary sun had already lowered past the tree line. "Not right now. Let's head back to our campsite before nightfall. Unless you plan to confront the Gardener."

I shivered. "We have to keep Morra away from him." And I didn't want Brantley anywhere near that danger again. If I had to see his eyes vacant and hear cold and uncaring rejection from his lips again, I would never survive.

Morra sat cross-legged close to the water, chin resting on his fists. He focused on the water, gaze darting toward any bubble caused by an insect's passage. "Will she be returning?"

Brantley sat beside Morra and clapped him on the back. He pulled on his tunic and boots. "She'll come if I signal her, but I don't plan to for now. Let's go cook the fish she gave us."

The promise of a roasted dinner made coaxing Morra away from the lake much easier. We settled into camp again and watched the subsun brush its last strokes of color throughout the basin of the hills and lake.

We crouched by the fire, picking flakey meat from the skewers, drawing comfort from flame, food, and fellowship.

Morra wiped his mouth with the back of his hand and eyed the last piece of fish I'd placed on a broad leaf.

I smiled. "Take it."

"You be knowing good ways to make food." He picked out a bone and chomped happily on the flesh.

"I suppose you don't get fish very often."

"Only if we be coming to the convening a day early." Morra tilted his head back, examining the carpet of lights in the sky. "Can't always be sure, but I'm thinking the big star rain will be falling tomorrow night."

My forehead pinched, and I studied the sky. Sure enough, some of the stars swelled and pulsed like clouds heavy with impending rain. Back on Meriel, my friend Starfire and I had eagerly awaited each star rain and found ways to slip outside to enjoy it. But now . . .

Brantley split a branch with his longknife and added kindling to our fire. He was frowning too. "So, it's time for the Grand Convening?"

Morra tossed the remnants of his fish tail on the flame, where it spit and crackled. His teeth flashed. "We be seeing them all gathering on the morrow." He snickered. "Oh, they be staggering in wearing the look of the revels. But arrive they will. I be recalling small villages be nearer. They get here first, no matter how early our folk be setting out." His chest puffed. "This time I be the first to arrive."

"The red village, the blue, the green . . . and others?" I asked.

He shrugged. "Yellow, purple, orange. And I heard tell the remnant sometimes come between the star rains. Suppose that's true. Who can recollect? All I be knowing is that at the Grand Convening, the whole rim of the lake be full."

There would be no way for me to keep this eager youth from joining his people for another dose of the Gardener's soul numbing. And what did the Maker expect me to do at the Grand Convening? I'd had little success so far when meeting with individuals.

Brantley poked a log with unnecessary force. It broke in a cascade of color and embers like . . .

Star rain. Overhead, the stars began to burst, pouring down glittering light like salt sprinkled from a cook's hand. I stood and stepped out of the shelter of trees, face cast upward. So many colors. So much brilliance scattered across the sky.

Brantley came up beside me. "I can see why you love to dance with the star rains. Don't hesitate on my account."

I shook my head. Would I ever feel the same about star rain? The beautiful event had become a marker for the horrible bondage these people embraced willingly. I wanted to dance under the generous night sky again, kicking up glitter, spinning and catching bits of light in my palms as the stars birthed new lights to paint the darkness. But my love for those past moments was now tempered with dread.

Brantley seemed to understand my mood. He wrapped an arm around my shoulders and leaned his head against mine. "Star rain always reminds me how small we all are."

I smiled. "It reminds me how loved we all are."

His chuckle rumbled beside me. "We do see things differently."

"Come on." I led him back to our campfire and the youth who was stuffing his face with the last of the copper fish. "Morra, tomorrow we must stop the people from inviting the Gardener."

He blinked my direction, and for a moment I thought I saw a flicker of comprehension. Then he threw back his head and laughed. "You do be telling odd jokes, you do."

Brantley examined the blade of his longknife. In the firelight, it flickered with shades of flame and blood. He stared at it as if seeing past skirmishes, as if tasting the flavor of ruthless battles, as if the steel could reveal our destiny. He frowned and slid the weapon into its sheath before turning to me. "Get some sleep. Sounds like tomorrow will be . . . eventful." He tried for a playful grin, but his lips curled in a feral snarl as if eager for violence. His shadowed eyes reminded me of the emptiness I'd seen there after the Gardener invaded him with vines and spores.

I curled near the fire but felt no warmth, even when I drew my cloak over me. *Trusted Maker, I've lost my entire world. Please, please, please, I can't lose Brantley too.*

"THIS IS MY WORLD." THE MENACING VOICE HISSED FROM behind me, and spores rose in a cloud of grayish green, choking me.

I tried to run, but vines twined around my legs, captured my arms. The Gardener stepped into sight, one gnarled finger pointing at me. "They need no Maker. They are mine."

"You've lied to them." I barely managed to speak, and I loathed the tremble in my voice. "You've stolen from them."

Rage flashed in his eyes, his long face distorting further, stretching, mouth gaping like an abyss. "Dare to oppose me, and I will destroy you." Green dust stung my eyes. His voice echoed through my entire being. "Destroy you . . . destroy . . ."

I woke with a start, sweat sheening my skin. I brushed my arms, still feeling the spores and vines. Pale light tinged the predawn sky. With each shaky breath, I gradually returned to reality. Only a nightmare. Had I cried out? Disturbed the others?

Under the deep shadows of tree limbs, Brantley and Morra slept as if sewn into the earth.

I sat up quietly. My muscles ached, reminding me I had been sporadic in my stretches and dance practices since we'd arrived. I welcomed the soreness, because it drew me further out of the remnants of dream and into wakefulness. I massaged the small of my back, stifling a groan.

Even though I was no longer a dancer of the Order, I needed to be more diligent with my daily training. Not that I'd ever again dance with the dreamed-of beauty and perfection. The former High Saltar had seen to that. I rewrapped the bandage around my severed tendon. It still seeped, refusing to fully heal, as if her blade had held a poison. Perhaps when Trilia arrived for the Grand Convening she'd have her soothing herbs. Or perhaps one of the people from the red village would carry the precious salve their tender used on ponies.

A rueful smile tugged my lips. Why was I worrying about my ankle? I had much more dire concerns with the approach of the Grand Convening and a confrontation with the Gardener. If his appearance in my dreams made me crumble, what would happen when I truly had to face him?

Across from me, Morra sprawled on his back, snuffling and muttering in his sleep. His bright auburn hair glinted in the early rays of the primary sun. Nearby, Brantley curled on his side, longknife in hand. I rarely saw him asleep. It seemed he was always on guard and protecting me. I took advantage of the rare opportunity to savor the sight of him. Fair curls scattered across his forehead, some dampened by sweat and clinging to his temples. Dark circles hinted at the depth of his exhaustion, and the pucker between his brows had deepened, as if worries had taken up permanent residence.

And they had. Ever since I'd crossed his path. In the quirk of his lips I could still find the daring and often playful man I'd come to know. There was the man who scaled the walls of the Order to rescue Orianna. Or who somersaulted from Navar's back while she glided a house's height above the water. Or who teased and cajoled me. He'd brought me so much affection and challenge that I wanted to coax the music of his laugh and kindle the special brightness in his eyes. Yet the days ahead likely wouldn't foster fulfillment of those longings.

I eased away from our campsite. After my morning ablutions, I took the time to work through my dancer stretches on the open hillside. At first my muscles resisted, but soon their suppleness returned. My dance would never achieve perfection, but the Maker had still used it to help us understand this world, and to protect others. If He could make use of my broken body, I'd offer it with no regret.

Drawing a deep breath, I rose from my warm-ups. By now the primary sun splattered shimmering colors across the lake. I performed the opening steps of the calara pattern. For a while, my bare feet caressed the daygrass under my toes. Then I moved on to other patterns, focusing only on the shapes I created in space, the precise steps, the intricate designs. When I tried a rain pattern, I couldn't do the required jumps, so I adapted the steps. As I finished, flashes of color caught my eye.

On the sloping hillside, tiny flowers appeared again. First one color, then another, until the slopes were a riot of shades. Were they responding to my dance?

Brantley's footsteps sounded behind me, and I turned. His lids were sleep-heavy, and his mouth held a grim line. "There you are."

I smiled and waved my arm over the sight spread out beneath us. "Look! Aren't they beautiful?"

He squinted at our surroundings as if trying to see what I saw before shrugging a shoulder. "Sure." Then he frowned at me. "But you shouldn't go wandering off."

I huffed and turned away. One day I'd get him to appreciate beauty for the sake of beauty. As quickly as they'd appeared, the tiny flowers bloomed wider, then shrank to nothing. At their departure, my body sagged, suddenly weary.

His hand rested on my shoulder. "Sorry." His voice was gruff, as if that was a word his throat had trouble forming.

I spun and hugged him. I would never tire of the sweet tang of ocean on his skin, the broad expanse of rough tunic across his chest, the warmth of his arms around me.

He stiffened, suddenly alert, focused on a spot a quarter of the way around the lake. A woman emerged from a trailhead we hadn't yet explored.

Morra lumbered past us. "I were being here first," he bellowed to her, then raced to the lakeshore. The woman startled and paused, then bobbed up and down on her toes, acknowledging our presence, and resumed strolling toward the water.

"Now what?" Brantley pressed his forehead to mine.

I stepped back and picked up my cane. "Now I let them know the Maker is coming soon."

"And if they don't want to hear?"

Squaring off against him, I stretched my spine to its full length. "Then I'll keep trying." I waited for him to try to dissuade me, to remind me of the impossibility of the task.

Instead he gripped my upper arms and grabbed me with his clear-eyed gaze. "If that's what you have to do, then I'll stand beside you."

My heart blossomed like the tiny flowers, swelling until it threatened to burst. "Thank you. But when evening comes, you have to leave. The Gardener attacked you once, and I couldn't face that again. Promise me."

"He won't affect me again." Brantley tightened his grip on my shoulders. "Let's get to work."

It was only as we walked toward the new arrival that I realized he hadn't actually promised to withdraw when the Gardener arrived. I shook my head. *Maker, protect him. My life is Yours, and if it serves You, I'll lay it down. But don't let Brantley's soul be strangled again. That's the one thing I couldn't bear.*

The young woman—barely more than a girl—bobbed up and down again as we approached. Long, uncombed hair framed delicate features, and dirt smudged her nose. "I be glimpsing you when I drew near," she said to me in a chirping voice. "That dancing you be doing. You must be coming from the green village." Her chin drooped. "I be wishing to make beauty too, but they not be having me."

On impulse, my arms reached out and gathered her in a gentle hug. "I'm Carya and this is Brantley. What's your name?"

"I be Noolee," she whispered, shyness and longing tangling in her expression.

"Where do you live?"

"Not far."

"Which village?"

"We be wanderers." Color dusted her cheeks. "Outcast. No village will have us." Then she brightened. "But I found a few others, and we be camping not far from here."

"So you don't come to a star rain convening?"

She tilted her head, clearly puzzled by my question. "I'm remnant. We be those that aren't welcome to any of the single-color star rains. They be only allowing us to come in between. And to the Grand Convening of course."

I pulled back, my breath quickening. Her eyes held a clearness, an alertness I had struggled to find in most of the other inhabitants I'd met. *Thank You, Maker!*

"We're a bit of a remnant ourselves," Brantley said cheerfully. "I'll go gather some breakfast. Lenka and persea sound all right?"

I nodded, and he set off, giving me time to get acquainted. "Noolee, it's good that you haven't been to frequent convenings."

Her eyes widened, then she rubbed her sternum. "But the longing. It hurts all the time."

"I know. I've felt it too. But the convening doesn't fill the ache. Using your gifts doesn't fill it. I tried that most of my life. There is One we are longing for, and He is coming."

As the suns rose, I told her what I knew about the Maker, about the time before on her world, about the damage the Gardener was causing. Brantley quietly slipped in beside me and offered her food as we talked. I urged Noolee to go back to the nearby enclave from which she'd come, but although she listened eagerly to everything I shared, she refused to leave.

More of the remnant people arrived as the morning progressed. Their journey was briefer than those of the main villages, since many apparently camped in the woods, so they were quicker to reach the

Grand Convening. One young woman carried a toddler on her hip. The little boy's face was dirty but rosy with health. A young man hovered protectively, and when the boy squirmed, he took the child and hefted him onto his shoulders. I approached them, admiring their little boy. The man swelled with pride. "He be a fine one. And she be ours too." He waved, and a girl of Orianna's age raced toward us, giggling.

I smiled. They had the sort of connection that Morra couldn't find and Harba and Wimmo were doomed to forget—that everyone on this island was doomed to forget if I couldn't interrupt the Grand Convening. "I take it you haven't been to a convening in a while?"

The woman shook her head and lowered her voice. "After the last Grand Convening, we recollected each other, and we wandered far to seek a village that be having us. None would."

I took her hands. "What you have—the love for each other and your children—is a precious gift. Those from villages who convene regularly have lost that. Take your little ones and leave. You don't want what this convening offers."

The man and woman both frowned. "The Every must convene." They chanted the words together, and after a little more pleading, I gave up and let them be. But when I glanced back, they were talking to each other, holding their children in their laps, whispering and agitated. Perhaps they would still reconsider. Hope fueled me.

All morning I moved from person to person. Talking, sharing, pleading. I couldn't convince anyone to leave, but many agreed not to sleep when evening came. I challenged them to watch and see what the Gardener did so they could decide for themselves. Surely if they saw what really occurred during a convening—the treacherous captivity, the insidious vines, the stupor—they would flee, and at least some of this world would begin to walk in freedom again.

When the subsun reached its zenith, louder voices sounded from one of the trailheads. Boisterous men and women strode into view from the red village, still tilting jugs of punch, laughing and staggering from the effects of their all-night revel. The knotted braids and bits of stick and bone in their hair were even more chaotic and threatening than I'd remembered. Their leather greaves and tunics were smudged with dirt and blood.

Brantley stayed close to my side as I wove among them and spoke to any who would listen. His presence smoothed the way, since they remembered his visit and joked about his scrapes and bruises, recounting various contests and duels. He slapped backs and laughed, but his hand never strayed far from his longknife. Thankfully, no one was in the mood for mock battles this morning. Unfortunately, no one was interested in my earnest message, either.

Music floated upward from the woods, voices in tight harmony accompanied by strumming from a small stringed instrument. At the top of the hill, people from the green village emerged from their trail. Their vibrant robes floated behind them as if they were a pod of gliding stenellas with fins unfurled. My spirit lifted. Harba and Wimmo walked beside each other, and Wimmo wore her baby against her chest, tied securely with an azure scarf. Trilia's jagged white hair stood out like whitecaps on a dark sea, and her eyes lit with recognition when she saw me. I'd certainly connected with more people from that first village than any others. Here was my best hope for willing ears.

Morra noticed them as well, and raced up the hill, not waiting for the arrivals to take their place at the lakeshore. Crillo emerged from the woods on the arm of a young man. She laughed up at him, leaning closer. Midway up the hill, Morra stopped short as if he'd crashed against an invisible wall. Even from where I stood, I felt the impact as his longing collided with reality.

Tossing aside a persea rind, Brantley jogged toward the young man and turned him away from the crushing sight. I could well imagine the earnest advice Brantley shared—he would be a wonderful father one day. My uncertain future pierced me again as I watched Morra stare straight ahead, shoulders slumped. The young man's expression didn't indicate if any of Brantley's words had taken hold, but at least he hadn't launched into a fistfight with Crillo's new beau.

I aimed for Harba and Wimmo. Harba bowed over one leg, nearly toppling when a wave rolled under our feet. "How you be?"

"It's lovely to see you. So much has happened. How is the baby?"

"She be well." Cheeks pink, Wimmo lifted her infant from the scarf so I could see her. Her eyes twinkled like stars, clear and bright. Her tiny lips pursed, then relaxed.

"She be always hungry," Wimmo said with a smile.

Harba wrapped a beefy arm around her and stared at his daughter. "Like me." Then he drew us into a tighter knot and whispered, "Wimmo be recollecting. We be giving tokens."

Wimmo tugged on a cord around her neck and drew out a carved-wood emblem that had been hidden by her tunic: an artful silhouette of a man, woman, and child. She glanced around nervously, then tucked it away.

Harba fingered a similar cord around his neck and nodded. "Our babe isn't being forgotten."

I hissed in a breath. "Tokens aren't enough. To protect your family, you need to stay away from the convening." Once again, I shared all I'd seen, begging them to turn back before the Gardener arrived.

Now Harba shot a worried glance around us to be sure no one overheard me. "The Every says we must be here."

My temples throbbed. "The Every isn't always right." The baby pulled one tiny fist free from her swaddling, and I touched it, marveling as perfect little fingers flexed and then encircled my thumb. Longing pulsed with each beat of my heart. Longing to protect my friends and their fragile family. And longing for something more . . .

Brantley joined me. At the sight of the infant, light sparked in his eyes, and he reached forward. Wimmo surrendered her trustingly. And why not? Brantley accepted the infant with the easy confidence of a man who had treasured his niece since her birth. He blew teasingly into the baby's face, and when the tiny face puckered, Brantley chuckled. "A fine child, this one. Congratulations."

Wimmo and Harba beamed. They could create a beautiful, long-lasting family if not for the Gardener's harm. The space between my ribs contracted and ached. I wanted that joy for them. For everyone on this world.

Buzzing rose from the trail that led to the blue village. A few men emerged carrying tall poles with spinning paddles mounted to the top. They caught the wind and spun, causing the strange sound. More people followed, most wearing the ridiculous talking tools I'd learned about in their village.

Trilia aimed for them and spoke through one of the speaking tools to another woman. It was clear she'd interacted with their culture before. As I cast my gaze around the lakeside, people from different villages as well as the outcasts called remnants all mingled. Morra had pointed out the yellow, purple, and orange villages as they arrived, and, though somewhat smaller than the other groups, each village had added its unique cultural flavor to the mix. Some folk pulled items from packs and traded for goods from other towns.

In the midst of the party atmosphere, I wandered slowly around the lake, speaking to any who would listen. Brantley stayed by my side but said little. Most people were dazed from lack of sleep and massive amounts of punch. Some laughed at me, others shoved me aside. As the primary sun arced toward the treetops, casting long shadows across the daygrass on the hill, I limped partway up the hill and looked at the mass of people. Creative, gifted, energetic. We each contained the touch of the Maker. Yet without Him, we fell apart.

"You're whistling into the wind," Brantley said, wrapping an arm over my shoulder.

I offered a sad smile. "I think the more they insist on not caring for others, the more I care about them. It's like I can feel the pulse of the

Maker's heart. And I wonder how long it will be before these convenings wipe out every bit of their humanity."

"Sit for a minute." Brantley helped lower me, and I stretched out my legs, too weary to argue. "And explain something."

I tilted my head his direction.

He rubbed the back of his neck, and the clench of his jaw drew hard lines across his face. His gaze skimmed the people around the lake and then cast upward, as if seeking answers in scattered clouds.

After a long pause, he finally met my eyes. "Why are you so desperate to earn His love?"

I blinked. "Is that what you think?"

"Look at you. He let the High Saltar cripple you. He trapped us on this miserable world. Yet you're willing to throw your life away because He told you to prepare the way for Him. You must be desperate to earn His love. Why else would you do it?"

My chest squeezed, and I wrapped my arms around my stomach. "No. Oh, Brantley. That's not it at all."

His clear eyes continued to pierce me, waiting.

I struggled to find words. "No sacrifice I could make would earn me His love."

Gaze still locked on me, his eyebrows drew together. "Then why?"

My fists clenched against my breast. *Maker, help him see.* I drew a breath. "He already loves me. So much that it's . . . well, it's everything. Sky, sea, life, breath. Nothing I can do will make Him love me more. Or could cause Him to love me less."

"If you believe that, then why can't we leave? You tried. You warned people. Let's go. We can try to break through the barrier again. And if that doesn't work, we'll find a safe place to build a home."

I reached for his hands. The soft scrape of his calluses provided a distraction from the temptation to agree with him. To flee. Daygrass tickled my ankles. A breeze brushed hair across my eyes. Currents deep beneath us lifted and lowered the earth the slightest fraction, every moment of reality a gift from the One who loved me completely. I absorbed each sensation, drawing strength, searching for a way to explain.

"When I served the Order, I was willing to give my entire life. I was willing to spend every moment in training. To forego family, friends, rest. And the Order wasn't even serving the truth. I was chasing the approval of the saltars, and their demands were never satisfied.

"After I felt the touch of truth, my new longing was to love Him. Not to earn His favor, like I'd once tried to win the approval of my saltars, but simply because my whole spirit filled with joy to know Him. If I once gave the Order my whole being, how could I give the Maker of my soul any less?"

Brantley drew a deep breath. Conflict churned in his eyes like opposing currents, and a tendon flexed along his neck. With one finger, I rubbed away the frown lines on his forehead. That coaxed a crooked grin from him. "Pity they aren't listening. You do have a way with words, dancer." Then he sobered. "What next?"

25

WHILE BRANTLEY AND I REGROUPED PARTWAY UP THE SLOPE, a smattering of men and women staked their places at the water's edge. With the suns lower in the sky, their shadows stretched and danced like ghouls as the tangleroot rippled. I shuddered, then pushed to my feet. "We're running out of time. I have to do something so they'll hear me." But what?

Their backs were turned, ready to begin the ritual to welcome the Gardener and once again surrender their spirits. Later, Wimmo would wake with a baby in her arms that she wouldn't remember loving. Perhaps she'd carry her back to their village, or perhaps she'd cast her aside. Harba would stare at Wimmo vacantly. Their carved tokens would be no more than a curiosity.

Not far from them, Morra tussled with a man from the red village who threw him down with a force that wavered the ground. The youth sprawled, the wind knocked out of him. What would happen to Morra after the Grand Convening? He'd stop pining after the girl he loved, and perhaps this time his longing for Crillo would be eradicated for good. He might try to catch the attention of another, which would only last until the next convening, and so on. He'd continue to visit the other villages, searching for a place to fit. His restless roaming would never be satisfied.

Now those of the remnant stood separated from the others. Disdained for some long-forgotten reason, they glanced nervously around and edged into a place by the lake. They could still think, still care, yet were scorned by the majority of this world. And soon that would cease to matter to them.

Maker, do something!

A copper fish splashed in the middle of the lake, sending ripples across the surface. A new idea sparked into my mind. I gasped and gripped Brantley's arm. "Call Navar."

He frowned. "That's not a good—"

"Hurry! While there's still time. I need her."

"*You* need her?" Caution filled his tone, protective of his bond with her, their years of working as a team.

I dragged him toward a spot by the lake that was still unoccupied. "No one is listening to me, and they're all staring at the lake. Don't you see? Please. You have to signal her."

Brantley's frown deepened as he worked out my plan. He squinted at the subsun. "There's not much time."

"That's why I asked you to hurry!"

His sigh was heavy, but he pulled out his whistle and blew the calling signal. The sound barely carried over the hubbub of the crowd. He also flung himself down on the tangleroot and sent the notes into the water.

"If she's near, she'll come. But we can't wait long."

Already, a few people settled cross-legged, swaying slightly. More and more of those still milling about pulled away from conversations, tossed aside lenka pits and jugs, stuffed new possessions into packs, and found a spot near the lake. Soon all places on the water's edge were filled, and men and women formed a line two deep in places. In my vision by Chanic's tree, I'd seen the early convenings, where villagers formed concentric circles four or five deep. The Gardener's interference hadn't only corrupted the hearts of this island, it had cut a swath through their population. A few children were held on laps. Others wandered, noticed their isolation, and toddled toward the crowd. But there were so few little ones. How could children survive when no one committed to caring for them?

A precious handful of people on our side of the lake stood back. Harba and Wimmo and their baby. Morra, who was still sulking and scarring the daygrass with his kicks. Several remnant people, looking uncertain.

I spotted Trilia sitting close to the water. She seemed to be respected by most in the green village. If I could get her to agree to stay away from the lake, more would follow her. I edged around a few people and tapped her shoulder. "Thank you for the assistance you've given us."

She looked up at me, one black eyebrow arching under the white fringe of her bangs. "I have no herbs with me if that be what you seek."

I shook my head. "I only want to give you a gift in return. The Maker of this world loves you. He is coming to walk among you and free you. Everything the Gardener offers is a bondage."

She held up a hand and turned away, directing her gaze at the water. "Cease. The Every must prepare."

Although Brantley kept an eye on me and continued to check the lake for signs of Navar, he also jogged between clusters of those standing apart from the lakeshore. Some nodded, others moved further up the slope to the woods.

I left Trilia and continued limping along the edge, speaking to any who would listen. With each rejection, the wound above my heel burned more deeply. I refused to look at the bandage, but I felt as if all the blood in my body were draining away.

A hum rose from the throats of the gathered villagers. They began to rock in unison. A few raised their arms, twirling their hands in small circles. Brantley's touch on my shoulder made me jump. "We should head up to the forest now," he said.

"Navar might still come."

"Or she could be miles away with her pod."

"I don't believe that. She'd stay close to you. She seemed worried when she was here before."

Brantley stared out at the water. "She wasn't herself. Almost as if she sensed . . ."

A gasp rose from someone near us. Then a scream carried from across the lake. Some people skittered back from the edge, colliding with those behind them. Most, deep into their ritual, continued to sway with eyes closed, ignoring the rising hubbub.

Navar's head poked up from the surface, shyly peeping at the faces lining the shore. She remained mostly submerged, searching for us.

Brantley shoved through the crowd and whistled. Her head snapped around so quickly, her dangling ears wobbled. I waved, and she swam our direction. By now, most of the people had backed away from the edge. Some fell on their faces, trembling.

"That got a reaction," Brantley said dryly.

He guided me through a gap in the villagers, right to the tangleroot that rocked gently up and down. Navar glided toward us, stretching her long neck fully, tilting her head to gaze at the strange sight of the crowd ringing the lake. I wondered if she was calculating how long it would take to scoop and toss enough fish for this crowd.

Her broad leathery back slid close. Brantley leaped aboard and reached for my hand. I stepped beside him, and with his arm to support me, I remained standing. A wave lapped over my bare feet. Like a caretaker's hands working a poultice into my wound, the water welcomed me and comforted me. I glanced down at the murky depths, and the sense of comfort faded. The sea—even this small inland portion of it—continued to unsettle me with nightmares of the endless deep that could pull me down toward whatever lurked beneath.

A breathless hush surrounded us. We floated outward from the shore, Navar as steady as a village street. Even when a hint of current shifted, she seemed to adjust her body to compensate, making it extra easy for me.

Brantley squeezed my arm and bent toward my ear. "Whatever you plan to say, do it now," he whispered.

I looked out at the people, some clutching each other, many with hands over their mouths, most wide-eyed. Overlaying their faces, I saw the vision of this world as it was meant to be. Joyous creating, playing, serving, loving. In harmony with the Maker and each other.

The longing that had kindled in me several times before now flared like a blacksmith's forge. My chest could hardly hold the swelling ache.

"This is Navar. A stenella. You've seen her image." My words burst out. In the bowl-shaped hills surrounding the lake, my voice carried clear as birdsong.

Trilia stepped forward. "The harbinger has come! The legends tell us the Gardener will now roam free, able to help us everywhere. We be awaiting this day. Imagine the Gardener in our villages!"

Excited murmurs responded to her. Faces lit with eagerness, then turned toward me again. I shook my head. "In the time before, your people saw these creatures often. Before the barrier trees blocked your view of the wide sea. Before you sold your souls to the Gardener."

A man lurched to his feet, fists clenched. A burly woman sprang up nearby. "She be defying the Every." The mood shifted, but their awe of Navar restrained the rising anger.

"You believe the Gardener eases your pain, but your people are dying. Try to remember. Your villages were once larger. Your children filled your homes with love and laughter. You faced the future with hope and longing."

I spotted Wimmo and Harba partway up the hillside. Their babe offered a mewling cry as if in agreement.

"The Maker gave you life so you could live in freedom, using your gifts with Him. Your bargain with the Gardener has destroyed that."

One imposing giant from the red village drew an axe and raised it over his head. "Lies! The Gardener made us stronger."

I shook my head. "Test my words. Leave this convening. Let your minds clear. The Maker plans to walk among you. How will you know Him if you let the Gardener dull your heart?"

Harba nodded and guided Wimmo and his baby up toward the forest. My heart lifted. One family saved. And I could count more. The tender at the red village whose injuries kept her from the lake. The isolated woman outside the blue village. The young remnant couple with two children, who even now were pulling back, talking to each other, casting worried glances toward those assembled at the lake. A handful of others from the remnant.

"Your art carries reminders of the sea that you've never seen and no longer believe in. Pictures of stenella." I stroked Navar's long neck. "She is a sign that what I'm telling you is true. There is a wide ocean beyond the rim. And a Maker who set the currents in motion."

A few more backed away from the edge. Trilia stood and faced those from her village. Perhaps we'd found a strong ally.

She tossed her head, the white fringe of her hair flying back like feathers of an angry hen. "Don't be deceived. She disrupts the convening. Not just any convening but the Grand Convening."

One of the men from the red village shook a spear over his head. "Shall we destroy them?"

Brantley's grip on me tightened. Others along the shore gasped. "But the creature!" one shouted. "Don't harm the harbinger of legend!"

"At least they don't want to hurt Navar," Brantley breathed against my ear. "But how am I going to get you to safety from here?"

I leaned against him, my bare toes gripping Navar's hide as she traced a circle around the center of the lake. Her side fins stretched partially open, then closed again rapidly, showing her nerves. "Don't be afraid." I was speaking to myself as much as to Navar and Brantley.

Trilia raised her arms and twirled her hands overhead. "Call the Gardener and let him deal with this!"

Only a handful had left the lake. The rest settled and began to sway and hum. Hands circled overhead.

"Wait!" I shouted. But the hum built to a crescendo.

"Now." Brantley pointed to a small gap along the shoreline. "Time for us to leave." Navar responded to his movement and eased that direction.

The swaying bodies shifted to a forward and backward movement. The humming grew frantic, the groaning buzz of a thousand insects. I had to find a way to shake them out of their trance. "Can you signal Navar to splash them?"

Brantley shifted his stance to face me. "Splash them? Have you lost your senses?"

"To wake them."

"Carya, you've told them what you wanted to tell them. A few people listened to you. Time for us to go."

"We have to try. The Gardener didn't come until the middle of the night at the other convening." I scanned the dusky sky where thin stars had begun to appear.

Navar twisted her neck and nuzzled Brantley. She probably didn't like to hear us argue. Or perhaps she hated the humming voices and hypnotic movement as much as I did.

In unison, the people around reached upward one more inch, then collapsed and fell into the deep, unnatural sleep I'd observed at the last convening.

Quirking an eyebrow, Brantley whistled a code of notes. Navar chirped a complaint, then nearly upended us into the lake as her body rippled. But she dipped her head and tossed water over the nearest bodies. No one moved.

"Satisfied?" Brantley sounded like I had stretched his patience to the frayed edge.

No. I wasn't satisfied. I'd done all I could to prepare the people for the Maker's promised arrival, but it hadn't been enough. The Maker had told me He would deal with the Gardener. But what better way could I serve Him than to chase away His enemy? I wouldn't tell Brantley, but I had every intention of remaining until the Gardener appeared. Hiding in the forest wouldn't help these people. In the meantime, perhaps I could still do more.

I stepped ashore and lifted a tiny, battered child from the red village in my arms, carrying her away from the edge of the water. Even if that wasn't enough to protect her from the Gardener's vines, at least it would keep her from tumbling into the water and drowning. No one else seemed to care for the little ones.

I scanned for another child and hurried toward a boy, expecting Brantley to protest. When I glanced back at him, he saw my intent and grabbed Trilia under the arms and pulled her some distance away from the pile of bodies.

Even in the cool of the evening, sweat soon ran down my back as I limped along the rows of bodies, moving anyone I could to what I hoped would be a safe distance. Why wouldn't the Maker heal my injury? My dancer body was lithe and strong, and I could have carried more people to safety if I had both good legs. Frustration seeped from my pores along with the sweat. The mound of people seemed endless. Despite Brantley's help, we had made only a small dent before our strength gave out. Navar chittered unhappily, and he waved a signal to her. She sank beneath the surface. I hoped he'd somehow asked her to stay near.

"This isn't working." Brantley doubled over near me, hands resting on his thighs, panting.

"I know. I need to wake them somehow."

He waited, watching me, willing to let me determine our next plan. A warm flush touched my skin in spite of the cool night air. He respected my ideas. Brantley—the impulsive, the confident, the leader—had begun to treat me with patience. With trust. Like a true partner. For a moment the dire sight of bodies sprawled along the lake lost the power to bring me to despair. I limped into his arms and hugged him.

He squeezed, but then held me at arm's length and furrowed his brow at me. "What was that for?"

My lips twitched at his confusion. "Thank you. For helping me even when my ideas seem ridiculous."

"If I only helped you when your ideas made sense, I'd never join you."

I didn't know whether to punch him or kiss him, so instead I looked back at the child closest to us. Drawing up the memory of drums and patterns and fellow dancers, I set a rhythm in my head. Brantley eased back to give me room and I began a sunrise pattern. Perhaps it could stir wakefulness in one or more of the sleepers.

My eyes closed as I lost myself in the movement. *Maker, wake them. Save them, please.*

"Stop!"

My eyes opened. Standing out against the dark background of the hillside, an even darker shadow loomed far too close. The voice was creaky with unnatural age, yet deep as a crack of thunder. A voice I'd hoped never to hear again. "Do not wake the sleepers."

26

THERE HAVE BEEN TIMES I'VE LONGED WITH EVERY FIBER of my being to turn back time, even if only by a fraction. If only I could have hidden the day the soldiers tore me from my family's arms and took me to the Order. If only I could have stopped the High Saltar's blade before it sliced my tendon. And now, if only I could go back a few precious hours and retreat to the forest.

In a flash of recognition, I understood my hubris. The Maker had given me a message to share. When the results weren't as grand and complete as I'd hoped, I'd decided for myself to do more. Instead of trusting His purposes, I had determined to fight the Gardener in my own power—through the physical effort of dragging bodies away from the lake's edge, through the tools of my dance, through any means.

"Offworlder, it is time for your interference to end." His words grated like two heavy branches rubbing together. He moved closer, not quite floating, not quite walking. He was just suddenly closer to me. Close enough that I smelled decay like rotting leaves.

"Brantley, run!" I tried to shout but barely gasped. And of course, he ignored my plea.

He drew his longknife and stepped beside me. "I won't leave you."

Even as my lungs quaked, even as I needed him to listen to me and flee, the reminder of Brantley's love gave strength to my bones. And the Maker loved me even more. That truth firmed my spine.

Help us, Maker! Help Your people! I stretched my arms out, blocking Brantley from advancing, trying to protect him. I glared into the murky eyes of the Gardener. "Leave us alone."

The Gardener laughed. Brantley and I edged back a few steps, moving closer to the lake. The evil before us stretched taller, his talon-like fingers weaving strange patterns in the air. "Those who convene are mine."

"No! We are the Maker's children. You have no right."

"This island is mine. These people gave me the right." Malice burned in the green-gray eyes set deep in his bark-like face.

Balancing on the tangleroot, Brantley let out a sharp whistle.

The Gardener's arms froze in place. He bent his head to one side. Then he chuckled again, a sound that made the daygrass wither beneath him. "Everything on this island does my bidding."

"We made no bargain with you. We don't belong to you." Brantley crouched, brandishing his longknife and ready to fight. The Gardener flicked one hand, and vines shot from the rim, wrapped the blade, and yanked it from Brantley's hand. Spores rose around our ankles. Putrid dust as in my nightmare.

I held my breath, desperation squeezing my lungs. We had nowhere to run. I couldn't bear to see Brantley's soul numbed again. Or would the Gardener's curse take us both this time? I would lose Brantley and not even care.

"The water!" I gasped.

Brantley squeezed my shoulder, then turned and dove cleanly into the lake. His head broke the surface, and he beckoned. "Carya! Hurry!"

I wavered. I had no raft to hold, no stenella to carry me. Under the night sky, the water was black, and the reflected stars held no comfort for me. My fears roared back. My leg throbbed.

The Gardener loomed over me. His gaze traveled to the tattered bandage on my ankle. "Serve me, and the pain will be gone."

His taunt had the opposite effect than he'd hoped. I squared my jaw. "There is only One that I will serve. With my last breath."

One bony shoulder hitched upward in a shrug. "So be it. Take your last breath." The Gardener reached for my throat.

I flung myself backward into space.

I HIT THE WATER AS IF I'D TAKEN A BAD FALL IN A LEAPING pattern drill. The wind left my lungs. Darkness surrounded me, and I sank and sank and sank. I flailed, but every direction held only blackness with pinpricks of stars. I didn't know where the surface was. I couldn't find Brantley.

The sweetness of the ocean flavored my lips, but soon it would invade my lungs. *Oh, Brantley, I'm so sorry for all my mistakes. For holding you away for so long. For insisting on my own plans.*

The darkness swallowed me. *Oh, Maker, carry me to Your arms. Save the people here in spite of my failures.*

My lips parted, ready to draw in the water that would take my life.

Something bumped against my spine. I fought back a gasp, squeezing my mouth tight. Terror warred with hope. Then I was propelled—whether toward precious air or toward the bottomless depths, I didn't know. My ears ached. My lungs burned.

"Carya!" The muffled cry reached my ears, and my face broke the surface. My scrambling hands found the soft hide of Navar beneath me. Air exploded into my lungs. I choked, coughed, collapsed across Navar.

Warm hands rubbed my back. Brantley treaded water beside the stenella. "Don't scare me like that."

His scolding made me laugh along with my wheezing cough. "Sorry."

"I tried to catch you, but you sank like a stone. I taught you better than that."

I let his ire lap over me, then pulled myself up to straddle Navar's back. I patted the stenella. Her neck stretched fully, she twisted her head to look at me, her eyes glistening in the starlight. She chirped and whistled a scolding every bit as fierce as Brantley's.

"I said I was sorry." We were still close to the shore. Vines and moss had begun to carpet the bodies sleeping on the tangleroot. But something had changed.

The Gardener stood stock still, facing us, mouth open. Even in the darkness, his surprise was evident. Was that because of our escape? I hoped his vines couldn't reach us in the water. I squinted at him and realized his focus zeroed in on Navar.

"You brought the harbinger!" His roar seemed exultant. "While the harbinger lives, I will be free to traverse the whole world."

Except I knew the Maker had another plan—a way He hadn't yet revealed to me—to rescue His people. I drew a shaking breath, praying the creature's glee would be short lived. Surely the Maker would stop the Gardener from being fully loosed. Otherwise even deeper darkness would consume this island before the Maker walked the land as promised.

Brantley traced a tight shape in the air, and Navar spun and raced to the far side of the lake. He leapt to the shore, nearly stepping on one of the men curled unconscious at the edge. "Come on. This is our chance."

I clambered after him, picking my way around the bodies two layers deep. If only I could run, perhaps we'd reach the safety of the forest. Or did the Gardener already have the right to pursue us away from the lake?

But after only a few steps on the tangleroot, as we reached the daygrass, the Gardener rose before us like a weed sprouting from runners. He blocked our path toward the hill. "You brought the creature! The sign that my power is at hand."

When he snarled, he exposed teeth like sharp chips of bark. A cloud of fetid rot burned my eyes, but I squared my shoulders and confronted him. After all, we could always retreat to Navar again. "Leave these people alone. You've done enough harm."

"What do you foolish mortals understand of my work?"

"I know the Maker is coming. Your time on this world is ending."

The Gardener raised his head and howled an unearthly cry. The earth rumbled and tore near his feet. A narrow sapling sprang from the ground.

Brantley reacted before I could make sense of our enemy's plan. "Retreat!" He barked the order.

The Gardener grabbed the sapling and hefted it like a spear.

I stumbled back across the tangleroot and leapt onto the stenella with Brantley a whisper's space behind me. Navar spun, and her powerful tail fin propelled us toward the middle of the lake. Brantley's arms surrounded me as the frantic speed nearly cast me off. The spear flew past us and disappeared into the depths. In her urgency, Navar had stretched out just below the surface, leaving water lapping our feet. But now she rose to her normal riding position, and I gratefully sank to her back, shaking.

Navar twisted her head quizzically toward Brantley. He reached past me and patted her neck. "Clever girl." Then he scanned the shoreline in all directions before settling beside me. "Are you all right?"

The stars glistened on the black surface, reminding me how fragile our lives were. One tumble into the darkness, and he would lose me. One aim of the spear, and I could lose him.

"I'm fine," I lied. "Where did he go? Do you think he can swim?"

"He didn't follow us into the water before. He seems to lurk along the edge." Navar spun in a tight, nervous circle, chittering. "Sorry, girl. We need to wait him out." Brantley's hand moved to his belt, but his longknife had been snatched from him earlier. We had no weapons.

I searched the sky, but dawn was an eternity away. I drew my feet up, suddenly cold. What slimy tangles could the Gardener conjure beneath us? "He just appears out of nowhere."

Brantley squeezed my shoulder. "Can you hide us?"

Weariness cramped my muscles, and I couldn't dance very effectively teetering on Navar's back. But at least it was a way I could contribute.

I crouched, afraid to rise all the way. But after waiting several cautious minutes, I stood, toes gripping Navar's hide. The swirling rhythm of fog played through my memory. My arms moved side to side. Then I circled, my feet finding tentative purchase on the wet surface beneath me. Balanced on my good foot, my other leg rose in front of me, stretching to eye level. I ignored the dangling edges of my bandage and continued the dance, carrying my leg around to the side and then forward again. Bending my standing leg, I pushed off and spun in a smooth rotation, my free leg drawing a low circle around me. I had to adjust the movements so I wouldn't knock Brantley into the water as my leg flung outward. My hands painted the air around us.

Brantley eased as far away on Navar's spine as he could, giving me room. "It's working."

A soft cloud of mist stirred around us, coalescing and rising. I continued the movements, the memory of drums beating with my pulse. Gently, softly, the fog glowed in the darkness and covered us. We could no longer see the shoreline. The reflection of stars disappeared beneath us. Then the pinpoints of light above vanished, coated by a blanket of pale mist. We were so cocooned I could almost believe the sky no longer existed; but the stars gave a comforting light to the fog, reassuring us of their presence.

I finished the pattern, sweat beading my skin. Strength fled my bones, and I sank onto Navar, letting Brantley's arms catch me. He smoothed hair back from my face, then rested his chin on my head. "You did it," he whispered.

"For now." The fog muffled our voices and every other sound—the lapping of water, the cooing of night birds, the whir of insects on the hillsides. The stillness didn't calm me. My ears strained for a warning of the Gardener's approach. "Is he coming for us?" While the bank of fog hid us from his sight, it also made it impossible for us to know what he was doing. All we could do was huddle in the white darkness.

The sound of a small splash penetrated our hiding place. I pulled my feet up and hugged my shins. Brantley's warm breath brushed my ear. "We'll be fine. Hope for the morning, Carya."

My tight muscles loosened, and a slow breath calmed me. As a child newly brought to the Order, I'd huddled in a storage closet, locked in, lonely, afraid. But morning eventually came. As a renegade dancer I'd endured many nights curled by a tiny campfire listening for the heavy step of soldiers. But we'd survived. I found Brantley's hand and squeezed it. We would endure this night as well, bobbing on the lake. The Maker had given me a call, and I'd done what I could to prepare the way for Him. Tomorrow we'd begin our new life on this world and hope for His arrival. Hope for the morning.

Behind me, Brantley's chest rose and fell with enviable steadiness. I longed to talk with him more but didn't dare draw the Gardener's attention. For now the fog covered the entire lake, and Navar drifted aimlessly.

A tendril crept across my foot and I flinched, stifling a gasp. Had the tangleroot spread toward us? I brushed at it and realized it was only a trickle of water running from my soggy tunic. Still, the sensation triggered trembling that I couldn't stop.

A louder splash sounded nearby. I chewed my lower lip, shivers wracking my frame. "He's throwing more spears."

"I've spent many a night on the sea with Navar." Brantley's murmur against my ear was softer than a whisper. "Much better with company."

If he'd meant to distract me, it worked. Heat blushed across my skin and stopped the shakes. "Does Navar understand not to go near shore? Can she see where the shore is?"

"Trust her. Better yet, trust our Maker."

His quiet faith shamed me. I'd dragged Brantley all over Meriel as I told villages about the lost letter from the Maker. He'd had no tangible encounter like mine. Yet he helped me, supported me. And now he was showing more trust in One whom he'd never seen than I was. I nodded, then rested my head against his chest. His arms cocooned me like the fog. *Hope for the morning.* But the Gardener was out there. I feared morning would bring a dire reckoning.

INHUMAN HOWLS PUNCTUATED THE LONG NIGHT. NAVAR shifted away from the sounds and occasional splashes. Each time, I tensed, my heart pounding out of my chest. Each time the threat came to nothing. There was nothing more draining on the human spirit than these surges of danger and then long stretches of waiting. I began to pray silently, asking the Maker if there was more He wanted me to do, reminding Him of the precious handful of people who were not in the Gardener's thrall, asking Him to come soon to free everyone. I prayed for the man sitting behind me, recounting all his virtues as if the Maker didn't already know them. The pattern repeated again and again. Sounds. Terror. Tension. Gradual realization that we were still safe. Prayer. Sounds. Terror. Tension . . .

And all the while, another fear throbbed through me. I hadn't managed to stop the Grand Convening. I'd gathered that, according to the legends, the appearance of Navar marked a new era wherein the Gardener's power over this island would be loosed more completely. What would that mean for the people of this island? How much pain would he cause before the Maker walked among the people and rescued them? And since Brantley and I were trapped on this world, what would our lives become now?

The silhouettes of treetops at the crest of the hill were the first image to pierce the murky air. I straightened and tapped Brantley's arm. His chin came up. "Do I need to dance more fog?" I whispered.

He pointed toward the other side of the lake. "Look." Threads of color unspooled over the clouds. The primary sun was waking.

I shifted position so I could see Brantley's face, my muscles stiff from the long night.

Even in the dim early light, his eyes were alive and bright, and his teeth flashed a smile. "G'morn."

I clasped his hand, grateful for our survival. After this dire night, I promised myself that I'd never again take for granted all the simple blessings of life. The tart flavor of lenka. The patter of rain on a cottage roof. A beloved's smile. "We made it."

His grin widened. "Stay here."

As if I had anywhere to go. The shore was distant in all directions. Navar's instincts had kept her near the center of the lake.

Brantley sprang up, scanned in all directions, then crouched. "I don't see him. None of the villagers are moving."

I feared the Gardener had taken out his frustration on the people along the shore. Instead of numbing them, had he decided to end their lives? I shuddered. "He said he isn't allowed to give them death. At least not yet." But uncertainty wavered in my throat. The harbinger had arrived. And I was the one who had asked Brantley to call her. What worse powers did the Gardener now possess?

"Let's check on them." Brantley gave a low whistle, and Navar craned her neck, then glided toward the edge. We eased in slowly, scouting for any sign of our enemy. At the rim, Navar chirruped nervously. Brantley frowned, stroking her neck. "She hasn't been acting like herself. The presence of the Gardener upset her."

"Good instincts." I patted her withers. "It's all right, girl. He's gone now." I couldn't stand the sight of all the unmoving bodies another moment. I slid from the stenella onto the tangleroot, then found my footing and shook the closest moss-covered shoulder.

Brantley sprang to the land as well, sending ripples through the tangleroot.

I stumbled, but then limped to another still shape. "Wake up. The convening is over."

No response.

Brantley poked at a few people with his foot. "Carya, there's nothing we can do here. I think we should—"

Woosh. A swirl of loose daygrass spiraled upward and coalesced into an angular shape. In the dawn light, the Gardener's features were even more harsh than in the darkness. Sharp brows, jagged chin, bony arms, long gnarled fingers, tattered green-and-brown clothes that looked like a diseased tree with flaking bark.

I drew in a sharp breath, throat too tight to speak. Brantley and I both backed to the very edge of the shore.

Oddly, the Gardener's focus skimmed past me, zeroing in on Navar. "The harbinger," he said, repeating what he'd said the night before. His bony shoulders hunched, and he chuckled darkly. "The light yet burns me, but her presence means it is time for me to do my work in every place. Night and day. Here and everywhere."

I didn't want Navar's presence to be a symbol for him. Perhaps that legend was simply another lie, like those that pulled villages to the convenings. Yet the Gardener stood before us in the light of the rising suns and didn't retreat.

He turned his gaze toward us and snarled. "My time to rule this island completely may be brief, but there is yet time to repair you interferers."

A tree limb sprang up from the earth, which he lifted and aimed at Brantley. Under the brightening sky, there was no place to hide.

Time slowed.

Each heartbeat burned vivid as lightning.

The spear flew.

Navar squealed a high-pitched sound I'd never heard before. With her body against the tangleroot, her neck lunged forward. She knocked Brantley aside.

He fell on top of two green-covered people with an oomph. I waited for the splash of the spear hitting water. Instead a gurgling moan filled the air. I dropped beside Brantley but saw no wound on him. He pushed himself up and blanched white.

Following his gaze, I turned my head.

Navar!

Her gentle muzzle arched toward the sky, floppy ears hanging back. The spear pierced her throat from front to back. Pale, mottled fluid gushed from her wound. Pain blazed across her huge limpid eyes before long lashes lowered to hide them.

Brantley scrambled past the bodies on the shoreline and reached her only seconds after her cry, but she was already sinking. He threw his arms around her. "No! Hang on, girl." Her broad back was barely visible under the surface. He felt for his longknife, perhaps to cut off the branch. When his hand found an empty scabbard, he tugged at the spear instead.

Navar reared and shrieked. She worried her head side to side.

Brantley cast me a desperate, wide-eyed plea. "Do something."

I'd once danced beside her to heal a gash in her hide. But this weapon was still impaled through her. I closed my eyes and embraced Navar's panic, her pain. *Forsaken!* The impression rocked me.

"No! You are beloved." I touched her neck.

She calmed but sank farther. Now only her head and upper neck were visible. The ugly branch only slightly above the surface.

Her violet eyes dilated. My soul quivered with the sensations she felt. Confused, wounded, and something more besides—worry for Brantley. "Yes. You have to hold on. We need to take care of him," I whispered in her ear.

Brantley gave another tug on the branch, but it refused to move and only caused another groan of pain from both of them. He let go, and Navar's eyes cleared for a precious second. Her long muzzle pressed against his heart and she chirruped a rasping call.

Then cloudy emptiness swam over her eyes. The shimmer of her fins flattened to dull gray. Her body sank, my hope sinking into the depths with her. I reached out a hand in mindless desperation.

Then her face slipped beneath the surface, and she was gone.

BRANTLEY'S BODY HEAVED WITH RAGE.

I stared at the water as shock sent tremors through my body. A lavender slick of Navar's blood coated the water, the only evidence of her existence . . . and her death.

A wheeze sounded behind us, reminding me that danger still stalked us. I spun, ready to fight the Gardener to my last breath.

He gawked at the empty space where Navar had reared only moments before. Instead of gloating, he howled. *"No!"*

His body expanded, arms raised, gnarled fingers splayed. "Return, harbinger! You cannot leave. I am only loosed while you remain. It is my time!"

Brantley gave a feral growl. "Oh, your time has come all right." He leapt over mounds of people, right at the skeletal man.

"Stop!" My plea caught on a gust of wind and dissolved. I stumbled forward. I couldn't watch Brantley's destruction, but I couldn't turn away either. I would fight by his side no matter how many thorns or vines or numbing spores our enemy conjured.

Instead, the Gardener slid backward, still staring at the lake in horror. His arms swung side to side, and the trees along the hilltops shuddered, their branches rattling like dry bones.

Just as Brantley reached him, dead leaves and grass swirled around the Gardener. The dust drove us back, our eyes stinging from the assault. I pulled up the neck of my tunic to cover my nose and mouth. Wind and chaos built to a frenzy, then suddenly stopped.

Sound ceased. Air stilled.

I raised my head, blinking against grit that had invaded my eyes.
The Gardener was gone.

"Why did he leave?" I choked out. He had the means to destroy us. We had no weapons—other than our shock-fueled wrath. Yet the Gardener had fled. And that strange expression. He'd seemed shaken, even dismayed that his spear had killed Navar.

Brantley's fists flexed, his whole body rigid. "What does it matter?" The bleakness in his voice chilled my soul. Had spores infected him again?

I turned to the lake. "Can you dive down? Maybe she can still be saved. Maybe I can dance healing—"

Brantley aimed his rage toward me. "I'm a herder. Do you think I don't know what a stenella's death looks like? She's gone." There was no arguing against the finality in his words.

Hot tears rolled down my face. I loved Navar but had only known her a short time. Brantley and Navar had been partners for years. I stepped toward him, arms open, but he turned away.

Rustling drew my attention. A yawn, a stretch. One by one the people along the lakeside sat up and brushed off moss and vines. I watched for signs that they'd escaped the Gardener's poison. I dashed away my tears and approached one of the women. "How are you?"

She tilted her head, eyes glassy and vague. "I be fine." Then her gaze glided past me, and she ambled away.

All along the lakeshore the pattern repeated. Gradually people moved apathetically toward the trail to their respective villages. The ache in my heart threatened to consume me. The people of this world were still trapped in the wisdom of the Every, still numbed by the lies of the Gardener. Still unaware of the Maker who longed to save them.

We hadn't made a difference.

I wanted to pound the earth with my fists, to scream, to sob. But Brantley stood alone by the shore staring at the lake. He needed me. I swallowed my pain and approached him. There were no words to ease his loss. Yet I remembered the comfort his presence had been the night my mother died. So I settled on the grass near him, waiting quietly.

As the rising suns hovered above the tree line, his stiff stance sagged. Eventually he sat beside me. Plucking blade after blade of daygrass, his jaw worked, as if he were testing and rejecting words.

He crumpled leaves in his hand. "She didn't deserve such an ignoble death."

"No, she didn't," I said quietly. I wanted to add more, to tell him how much I blamed myself for coming to the island, for being called to impossible risk by the Maker, for involving Brantley and Navar. I wanted to give him permission to hate me. But I pressed my lips together and hugged my shins.

"I raised her from a calf, you know. I was a youngling myself when our village herder told me his stenella had birthed." Now that the tendons in his jaw had loosened their lock on him, Brantley's words flowed. "You've never met a boy more proud of the honor. As soon as her mother allowed it, I swam with Navar every moment I could. She was so clever, I never really trained her. It was more like she trained me." His voice broke, and he sniffed.

Tentatively, I touched his back. When he didn't stiffen, I rubbed small circles, praying my hand could offer a measure of comfort.

"We grew up together." He turned toward me, and his face hardened again. "And don't tell me I'll find another stenella."

The words bit, and I recoiled. "Of course not. I mean, one day you might, but no one could replace Navar." Tears welled in my eyes again. Even the remote hope of another stenella was impossible while we were trapped on this forsaken island.

When he saw my pain, he relented. He reached out and traced the path of a tear down my face. Then he noticed the movement of the villagers. "The people? Are they free from that . . . are they free?"

"No change. We accomplished nothing." Now the hard edge sliced through my voice. My mouth tasted bitter.

His shoulders lifted and fell in a heavy sigh. "We survived. That's something."

"Is it safe?" Morra called from the top of the hill.

We turned and waved. He emerged from the forest, followed by Harba and Wimmo and their baby. As they made their way toward us, more figures peered from behind trees and walked down the slope.

Those we'd pulled away. Those of the remnant who had no village home. And our friends. Even in my grief, Morra's round, open face coaxed a small smile from my lips.

"We be watching." He waved his plump arm over the shoreline. "You spoke truth. We be seeing how the Gardener made the people change."

Wimmo embraced me, and the downy head of her baby brushed my chin. "And the sea lord. We be seeing what he did. The Gardener harmed the sea lord. You were right. He be evil. We won't ever come to a convening again, grand or otherwise. If enough of us refuse, the Every can't punish us all. And if they cast us out, then we be a happy remnant."

I squeezed her and nuzzled the infant, drawing comfort from the smell of sweetness and milk and new beginnings.

Harba crossed ample arms over his broad chest. "And we be telling them all to stay away. Only"—he scratched his chin—"how will we be doing our making without the help of the numbing?"

A tiny kernel of faith remained in my chest and helped me speak. "Refusing the convening won't cripple your art. It will free it. The Maker will inspire new things."

Wimmo repositioned her baby against her shoulder. "And we be caring for what matters. We be naming her Makah. To help us always remember our Maker."

Harba beamed at her.

In the glow of the morning, those who had hidden in the trees drew closer.

"Tell us more about the Maker. We can be hearing now," said Morra.

Wimmo tossed her cloak onto the grass and settled, babe in her arms. "You said you be seeing the time before. All that we've forgot. Tell us again."

The others gathered around, full of new questions.

I smoothed a tangle of hair away from my forehead and looked at the dozen or so faces. Eager, awake, free. Moments ago I'd despaired, believing we'd accomplished nothing. I'd been so quick to despise this small beginning, the miracle that the Maker had done already. No, I hadn't delivered the whole world. But that was His work. I'd done what He'd asked—prepared the way.

Oh, but the cost.

Nearby, Brantley searched the withered vines until he found his longknife. With the blade back in his sheath, he braced his shoulders. I couldn't read his expression. Navar's death could rekindle all his old resentment toward me, toward the Maker. Building a new life on this island would be miserable if he hated me.

But he came and stood near me, head canted to one side. Waiting. Watching me.

"What was the world like in the time before? Please be telling us all you know," Morra asked. As much as I longed for time alone with Brantley, this duty—this privilege—required me. I talked myself hoarse recounting again what I'd learned about the Maker back on Meriel, and what I'd seen in the vision of their world's founding. The listeners' eyes sparkled as I described the early villages that used their gifts joyfully. They grieved as I told of the jealousy and conflict that drove their forebears to accept the Gardener's offer.

"But the Gardener's hold on people was limited. He only controlled those who came to the convenings. He was not given the right to control the entire island except when the harbinger arrived."

"The sea lord." Morra cast a wistful gaze toward the lake. "But she be gone."

"Yes." My voice broke. "She be gone."

Morra met my gaze. "So she saved us."

"What do you mean?"

"She came as foretold, but her sacrifice means the Gardener will not rule all. Tell us the rest."

My jaw gaped. Morra was right. I'd mourned Navar's ignoble death, but her death was everything noble. I looked up at Brantley who still stood nearby. Could he draw any comfort from knowing what Navar's selflessness had given this world? His jaw clenched, but he gave me a tight nod.

I continued telling all our friends about the vision in the willow tree. When I again shared that the Maker was planning to walk among them, Wimmo clutched her tunic with a happy sigh. "We must be telling the others."

Harba's head bobbed on his thick neck. "I be thinking we'll get more folk to avoid the convenings. When the good Maker comes, we be having more people ready to greet Him."

I plucked a small flower and stroked the petals. "It won't be easy. Not only because the others may oppose you. As you allow love, you'll face the pain that your people sought to avoid. Longings unmet. Heartache when those you care about suffer."

Brantley's features softened, and his gaze met mine. "The pain of loss."

I returned my focus to the eager faces around me. "But it will be worth it."

Sunlight glinted off the lake. No sign remained of the fog that had protected us through the night, or the enemy who had prowled in the darkness, or the gallant stenella who'd given her life to protect us. As the surface rocked gently under us, the glimmers off the water spoke to me of hope. Brantley took a few steps toward the edge. Did he see the light, or only the loss? My heart ached for him.

"Will you?" Morra asked.

I pulled my attention back to him. "What?"

"Will you be coming back to our village? We be needing your help to tell these stories to the others."

I glanced toward Brantley. Would he want to make our home there or somewhere else on the island? "I'm not sure."

He faced me. Bleakness still shadowed his eyes, but he lifted and dropped one shoulder. "For a time. But later I'd rather live closer to the water. I'm still a herder."

I nodded. "Of course." He was a man of the ocean waves, and as long as the rim barrier kept us from seeing that expanse, the lake was his last connection to the life he'd always known. Provided that we stayed far from the shore when the star rains fell, I'd gladly settle nearby. Besides, when the Maker did arrive to defeat the Gardener, this lake would likely be where He would first appear.

"We best be going." Wimmo offered the baby to Harba, then lurched to her feet. "How be your leg?"

Throbbing as always. "Fine."

Morra frowned. "Where be your walking stick?"

Lost in the turmoil of the night before. "I don't know."

"I'll help you up the hill." Brantley put an arm around my waist and guided me toward our old campsite.

Morra followed. "And I'll carve you a new one."

Various freed villagers returned to their own paths. The remnant scattered. Brantley and I filled our packs, and with a new walking stick in my hand, we set out, following Harba and Wimmo toward the green village.

Brantley's silence covered him like a shield, so I walked beside Morra. He chattered amiably, and I was grateful that it took little effort to respond during his occasional pauses.

With each stride of my good leg, I fought to kindle the tiny flame of hope. But each time my weight came down on my bad ankle, the pain mocked my efforts. This was our life now. Brantley and I on this odd world, surviving, waiting for salvation. I cast a look toward him. Every hint of playfulness had fled his features. He walked with a new heaviness. Even more than me, he'd truly lost everything. Brantley was a herder. That was his life. Now his mount was dead. The sea unreachable. And we had failed to bring valuable supplies to Meriel.

He noticed my gaze and opened his mouth. But instead of speaking, his jaw snapped shut and he strode ahead. He blamed me. He blamed me for all the loss.

I sucked in a sharp breath and stumbled. Morra grabbed my elbow.

"You being all right?"

Brantley didn't even look back.

YOU WOULD THINK THAT AFTER THE DAYS OF HIKING I'D endured back on Meriel—and the lengthy journeys to various villages I'd accomplished on this world—this half-day journey would be tolerable. Yet these were the worst hours of trudging torment I'd ever experienced. Wimmo didn't have Trilia's knowledge of herbs, but she did find a few plants to crush and apply to my wound. Morra shaped me a second walking stick. With two canes to support my weight, I was able to keep up a bit better, and Morra could bound ahead and gather fruit for the group as we walked.

I wanted to pray, to listen for the Maker's voice, but exhaustion and misery clouded my mind.

Hours later, Brantley hung back to where I took up the rear of our small group. I stared at the ground and tried to move faster. My weakness would only make him loathe me more.

He settled into a steady stride beside me and sighed. "It's so different this time, isn't it?"

That brought my head up. "Than what?"

"When you challenged the Order. Power. Wonders. Success. The whole world split open."

Sweat beaded on my temples, so I stopped to take off my cloak and stuff it into my pack. "It wasn't my power. You know that."

"I know. More than most. I saw what He did. But where was He this time?" His question didn't hold the bitter edge I'd expected. Just a confused sadness.

I thought of the hillside flowers that bloomed for a scarce minute. Of the vast seas and the mysteries that we couldn't know. Of the ache in the Maker's heart for His lost people. The images swirled through my fatigue.

"He never left us," I said, my voice breaking. "But I don't understand either ..."

Brantley's arm wrapped my shoulders, and we both stopped. He gathered me into a close embrace.

My efforts to stay strong crumbled. I sobbed against his chest. "I'm so sorry. I didn't want this to happen."

"Shh." He patted my back as if he were comforting his niece after a bad fall. "We'll bear the pain together, dancer."

I lifted my chin and studied his eyes. Ocean hues sparkled as sunlight cast green tones through tree leaves. Clear, open, and none of the resentment I expected. "Can you truly forgive me?"

Creases formed across his brow. "Forgive you?" Then his eyes widened. "You think I blame you?"

I dropped my gaze.

He gave me a gentle shake. "You give yourself too much credit, dancer. I was the one who wanted to explore this world. I was the one who called Navar. For pity's sake, you saved me when the Gardener had turned my heart to stone. I owe you—"

"But you walked on ahead. You . . . left me."

His hand found my chin and tilted it up. "I thought you needed time. To think, to pray." He shrugged. "And truth be told I had my own thoughts to give the Maker."

The corner of my mouth lifted. "Have you told Him those thoughts?"

"You best believe it." Tendons flexed along his neck.

Passion and grief still stirred in his heart, but he didn't blame me. He didn't hate me. Breath filled my lungs. "We can move forward."

"Together," he said. "Besides, perhaps now the Maker has allowed a gap in the rim. That's why I'm making haste. I want to see if anything has changed at the border of the green village."

I gasped. "Could it be possible?"

He chucked my chin. "Let's go find out."

29

AS WE ENTERED THE GREEN VILLAGE, WE PASSED THE exquisite homes, the creative gardens, and the paths lined with vibrant shops. Men and women milled around, but without bustle and chatter. I was glad for the quiet, because my head throbbed in tempo with my injured leg, and now and then my vision swam with little flecks of light. Around me, the effect of the Grand Convening blanketed everyone with listlessness. I wanted to test a few conversations, but first we had to check the rim.

Brantley's pace quickened until I couldn't keep up. "Go ahead. Run," I told him.

"I'll be right back." He raced past the last row of homes.

When I reached the clearing a few minutes later, he was striding back toward the village. One glance showed me that the tall rim trees stood fast. The vines were as thick and unrelenting as before.

Brantley forced a grin and turned me away from the sight. "Let's find Trilia and see if she has something to ease your leg. We'll rest a few days and then head back to the lake and start building our home."

"That's a . . . good . . . idea . . ." Light faded from my sight, and I searched the sky for the clouds that blocked it. My head felt strangely heavy. No clouds overhead. Odd that under a clear sky shadows shrouded my vision. The land rocked beneath my feet, and my hands reached out as it came up to meet me.

"Carya? What's wrong?" Brantley's voice was far away but full of so much caring that I smiled as darkness settled over me like nightfall.

"THAT MAN OF YOURS SURE DOES FUSS." WIMMO'S VOICE pulled my eyes open. Baby Makah cooed, and she jostled her. "I sent him to find orange tubers for soup. That's what you be needing. Overtired you be."

I pushed up to my elbows. The soft raised pallet cushioned my body. Windows let sunlight into a spacious room. A low table and a few chairs rested under embroidered tapestries. A bowl of water rested on the floor. Wimmo wrung out a cloth and blotted my forehead.

"What happened?" My voice came out hoarse, and I cleared my throat.

"I be knowing that walk were too much for you. I said the same to Harba. You be sleeping for days."

"Days?" I sat up fully, grabbing my head when the room spun. "That's not possible." But my dry throat and light-headedness attested to the truth.

"Finally!" Brantley's exasperated voice burst from the doorway. He dropped a basket of tubers and charged across the room. "Don't ever give me a scare like that again!"

Life coursed through my veins, and I opened my arms to him.

"My babe needs feeding," Wimmo murmured as she headed for the door. She scooped up the basket. "I'll be making some soup."

Brantley eased me from his tight hug and studied me. "Are you truly all right?"

I rubbed my throat that still felt dry. "Fine. Truly."

He grabbed a pitcher from the table and poured a mug of water. "Here."

Dull rainwater trickled down my throat, and I grimaced.

He grinned. "Thought you might like it filtered, since that's what you're used to."

"Not anymore."

He obliged me with a fresh mug of seawater. The citrus tang woke my tongue, and sweetness coated my throat. Brantley watched me, his eyelids heavy. With the sleeves of his tunic rolled up, his bare forearms revealed ropey muscles and the glow of years in the sunlight. I rested my hand on his arm, marveling at how translucent and pale my skin looked beside his. We were so opposite, as different as two people could be. It would take a lifetime to understand each other. But judging by the relief and love in his eyes, we would enjoy every day the Maker granted us.

"How is everyone in the village?"

Brantley winced. "The same. I guess they are waking up a little. Morra and Harba have been talking to everyone they can."

"And stirring up trouble." Trilia stepped into the room.

I held my breath. Before the Grand Convening, we had pulled her away from the lake's rim. But who knew how much damage the Gardener had done during that long night.

Trilia's eyes held some of the vacant glaze I'd learned to expect from the villagers, but she rose and lowered on her toes and smiled. "Can't be remembering much, but seems we haven't had such excitement in many convenings."

I swung my legs off the raised pallet to the floor and reached my hand to her. "You must keep your people away from the next convening. They've forgotten what true excitement can be."

She frowned, the fringe of her white hair lowering over her brows. "You be quite the spinner of tales. When you're better, I be listening." She turned to Brantley and handed him a bundle of herbs and bandages. "Keep her off her foot for a time."

I opened my mouth to protest, but Brantley spoke before I could. "I will."

After Trilia withdrew, I touched Brantley's face. "You look tired."

He snorted. "Why didn't you tell me how poorly you were feeling?"

"I didn't know. Truly. I just kept pushing and pushing."

"We could have rested. You could have let me carry you."

I poked him. "You should talk. When did you last have a good meal or some sleep?"

He looked away. "So we're agreed. We both need some rest."

"Where are you staying? For that matter, where am I?"

"We're upstairs at the central lodge—or whatever they call this building. I've been staying with Harba and Wimmo in their quarters. Between checking on you and their babe being up half the night, it's no wonder I'm looking ragged."

"Ragged looks good on you." My cheeks heated at my forwardness.

He barked a laugh, and I was glad my flirting erased the last of the worry lines from his temples. I would happily spend the rest of my life coaxing laughter from him. A new thought hit me, so obvious I couldn't believe I hadn't thought of it before.

"Brantley, how will we do a bonding ceremony? We've no matriarch to say the words. They likely don't even have bondings here."

His thumb tweaked the side of my mouth upward. "Carya, did you think I'd not look into that? They haven't done one in some time, but Trilia said she can speak the words over us, and the village will witness it."

"When?" The eagerness in my voice made me blush again.

His chuckle nourished me more than the richest tuber soup.

REASSURED THAT I WAS RECOVERING, BRANTLEY FINALLY allowed himself rest. My strength returned quickly now that there were no battles to fight or hikes to endure. My wounded ankle still made me limp, but the angry inflammation faded, and I needed to change the bandage less frequently. For the next few days, I spoke with Morra and Harba and Wimmo about the Maker. Together we all shared what we knew at the evening gatherings and in quiet conversations throughout the village.

The morning before our bonding ceremony, Trilia bustled into my room. "Will you be wearing flowers in your hair? I'll fetch some if you tell me the color you wish. And the musicians are ready with music for the revel after the bonding. I've asked the baker to be creating a tower of bresh with fruit inside. Unless you be objecting."

I blinked a few times. She was clearly recovering from the daze of the convening. "I love the little blue wildflowers that grow under the willows. But don't go to so much trouble . . ."

But she breezed out again. Wimmo brought me two robes with the wide sleeves that reminded me of butterflies. The first was a rich blue color—the day-before garment. The second was a pale silken robe, floor length with a high collar. She also gave me a basket of delicate threads of all colors. "You'll be wanting to stitch your dreams along the hem."

At my confused look, she laughed. "I forget how strange you be. In our village, back when people bonded, the woman sewed her hopes in tiny pictures. Your people don't do that?"

I shook my head. "But it's a lovely tradition." After donning the blue robe over my tunic and leggings, I settled on the floor to design the embroidery on the robe I'd wear for the bonding. I licked the end of the thread and guided it through a needle. But what were my dreams? I began sewing, letting my hands guide me. Tiny stitches formed a small cottage on one sleeve hem. A man and woman decorated the other, and with warmth rising along my neck, I even dared to add a babe in the arms of the woman.

But the entire lower hem mocked me. If I honestly depicted my dreams, it would be of Meriel, of Navar, of the tower, of Windswell, of family. And those were lost forever.

Was it wrong to sew emblems of what was lost? As I debated finding Wimmo to ask her, I sewed tiny ocean waves in a neat row. They demanded a stenella, so I added one, gliding over the sea. A figure stood proudly atop her.

Although I was excited and full of all the giddy love I'd never believed would be part of my life, wistfulness settled over me. I needed a break from figuring out the images in thread, and also needed respite from Trilia's energetic organizing, so I slipped out to the open field and strolled toward the rim. I found the place where I'd once danced a storm away from the village. I touched the tree that Brantley had climbed trying to find a way out. So much had happened. So many surprises. Some hard, and some beautiful. An ache built in my chest. I'd always pictured our bonding happening in Windswell, surrounded by those we loved. Bri and Orianna, Starfire and Saltar Kemp. Ginerva and—I swallowed—Navar. I'd always imagined Navar watching from the water's edge, chirping her approval.

I leaned against one of the trees and stared at the village. Wisps of smoke wafted from chimneys, music rose from the musician's hall. This island was my home now. Time to cast aside the grief. Time to begin our new life. We had a purpose here. Just as on Meriel, I could remind others about the Maker.

As so often happened when my mind turned to Him, the ache in my heart swelled into gratitude instead of sadness. Suddenly I wanted to dance. Not for any purpose. Not to stir up fog, nurture plants, or chase away storms. But simply to celebrate the goodness of the One whom I served.

No one else was wandering on the revel field, and I didn't see anyone on the edge of the homes looking my direction. Shyly at first, but then with more freedom, I danced the calara pattern—bowing like a soft reed. Then I broke from the pattern and spun, arms wide, face upturned. I let my heart, mind, and body all speak worship. I was a fragile butterfly, wings outspread. I was a minute flower, offering my tiny blossom for Him. I was a child, rejoicing in a garden with no ending.

I love You.

Was my heart speaking to Him, or His speaking to me? In that moment, it was a duet. Breathless, I slowed my movements and sank to my knees. Reaching forward, I bowed, laying down my losses, my grief, my longings. My back stretched, and my palms opened upward.

"I'm Yours, and that is enough," I whispered.

I rose and continued to improvise new shapes with my arms, my torso, the tilt of my head. I faced the trees and vines and faltered, my gratitude challenged by the sight of the obstacle that trapped me. Could I thank my Maker even while looking directly and honestly at my loss?

Yes. In His presence, even the most frustrating, crippling, imprisoning trial grew smaller. I opened my arms, accepting the bitter. I'd seen glimpses of the life to come, when all bitterness would be erased, and while I limped through this life, He would bring enough sweetness to help me endure. I swayed, leaning more weight on my good leg. I wanted to dance all day, but my ankle already warned me it wouldn't support me much more. Still, I let that leg float upward, stretching with my arms as if pointing to the lofty dwelling of my Maker.

"What are you doing?" Brantley's voice behind me broke my concentration, and I fell off balance. My bad leg caught my weight, and I winced but managed to stay upright.

"Sorry." He grabbed my arm to support me. "You're crying. Second thoughts?" Endearing insecurity colored his voice.

I hadn't noticed the tears that tracked down my face, and now I brushed them aside with a beaming smile. "Of course not. Just thanking the Maker for His blessings."

Brantley squinted past me and gasped. "Carya, look!"

I turned to follow his gaze.

A narrow path wound into the dark shadows of the rim. Thin, dangling limbs rustled, even though there wasn't a breath of wind. The vines pulled apart even more, and my eyes widened.

"Come on!" Brantley grabbed my hand and half dragged me along the path.

"Wait—" Was this a trap of the Gardener? The path could close behind us and prevent us from returning to food, shelter, people. Weren't we supposed to stay here for the rest of our days to wait for the Maker to walk among these people? And why rush to the sea when our world had long since drifted away and we had no stenella?

Brantley gave me no chance to form objections. He pulled me onward. The bracing citrus air hit my face as we emerged from the thick vegetation. The vast emptiness of waves and currents stretched before us.

Yet all was not empty. I turned my head and froze, clasping my hands over my mouth.

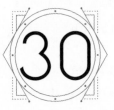

30

MY HEART POUNDED SO HARD I THOUGHT MY RIBS MIGHT break. I clutched Brantley's hand, uncertain of my sanity. Off to the left, with perhaps half a mile of ocean between us, a huge island floated serenely. Tangleroot edged the shoreline, with willows and oaks rising gently from the sea. Beyond, meadows and wheat fields colored the midlands, drawing my eye upward.

Meriel.

Home.

If I squinted hard, many miles inland, I could catch a glimmer of the white tower in the center and highest point of Middlemost. Partially around the curving shore, cottages nestled together, and smoke wafted from hearth fires. Judging from the river I glimpsed near the huddle of homes, I recognized Windswell. The mouth of the river was gently turning away from us as the island drifted. I gasped at the view of our world, so much more massive than the island we stood upon. This was a pebble beside a boulder.

I caught my breath enough to gasp. "The dancers. They found a way. To move. Meriel closer. They didn't. Let the current. Take them."

Brantley released my hand and rummaged in his pack, unearthing his whistle. He blew a piercing signal, so sharp I covered my ears as he repeated it again and again.

A speck appeared from where the river had slid from view, then another. Brantley stepped right to the edge and waved. A handful of stenella sped toward us, each carrying a herder. One of them caught a gust of wind and unfurled his fins to float against the sky.

Surprised laughter burst from Brantley's chest. "They must have called together herders from all the rim villages. And look! The others have harnesses and rafts."

So much had happened I'd forgotten our original mission. I spun and looked behind me, half expecting the path toward the green village to be closed again. If anything, the path had widened. Was the Gardener growing weaker, or was he eager for us to leave? Or did this barrier not belong to him at all?

The warm and powerful voice of the Maker welled in my heart. *I made a way for you. For three days.*

"And after that . . . are we meant to stay here?" I whispered. I wanted to leap into the water and swim for all I was worth back to Meriel. But if He asked me to remain, I would.

After the three days, return home. Your place is on Meriel.

My breathing was still shallow and fast. I stood on tiptoe, hardly daring to take a deep breath, afraid the beautiful vision of home would disappear.

As the fleet of stenella and riders drew closer, Brantley scanned the water intently. His gaze marked each creature and its rider. Then his shoulders sank. Despite his certainty of Navar's death, I knew his hope had flared and been disappointed. She wasn't among the sea creatures.

I leaned my head against his shoulder, wishing I knew how to offer comfort. "We're going home," I said quietly.

His chin lifted, and he drew a long draught of sea air into his lungs. "Yes." He turned and hugged me close, then let the realization flood him. "Yes, we are!" Dazed, joyous laughter burst from us both. Together we whooped and jumped up and down on the bouncy tangleroot.

The stenella that glided in the air was small, and when it splashed back onto the water's surface, it nearly unseated the wiry youth straddling it.

"It's Teague!" Brantley waved again to his apprentice. "Where did he get that stenella?"

Teague wiped water off his face and guided his mount toward us with a cheeky grin. When they stopped, he sprang to stand in the smooth motion Brantley had taught him. "I knew it! I knew we shouldn't leave."

"We found the parchment but thought it said you were leaving." I reached out to pat the stenella's muzzle, but it jerked away. Not all stenella were as affectionate as Navar had been.

Teague eyed the tiny opening of shoreline and bunched the freckles around his nose. "Not saying some didn't push for that. But Saltar Kemp insisted. We've had patrols circling that whole island looking for signs."

Words tumbled from the excited boy, interspersed with our questions. As the other herders drew near, we learned that the decision to keep Meriel close to this island had been contentious. "I told 'em we couldn't give up. Saltar Kemp convinced them to wait for one more star rain."

Cold prickles fluttered through my chest. We'd been within a few weeks of never seeing our world again. Even though I'd resigned myself to living the rest of my days trapped inside this world, now that Meriel was within enticing reach, the thought of losing her made me tremble. I rubbed my arms, reminding myself this wasn't mere chance. The Maker had known that help awaited us. He'd known the right time to make our path.

"And this?" Brantley perused the irritable stenella.

"Kenvo let me borrow him for my shift. All the herders have been taking shifts watching the island. Well, everybody but Goreg."

Brantley chuckled. "He's an old crank from Rippler," he explained to me. "Never had much to do with the other herders. Sounds like nothing's changed."

Teague's chest puffed forward. "I volunteered extra. Navar will be surprised at how much better I've gotten. Where is she? She was pining by the shore most days. Wouldn't let me ride her. She disappeared a few times, and I haven't seen her in many days."

Brantley, with a catch in this throat, explained what had happened to Navar. The excited boy instantly sobered and grew tongue-tied, as unsure as I was how to offer comfort to Brantley. I distracted him with more questions. The youngling relaxed as he gave us a full report. Everyone in Windswell was fine, although Brantley's family had spent many days and nights in a vigil, staring at the strange foreign island and praying for our return. Supplies were still scarce throughout Meriel. As the other herders pulled along the shore, we told them about the bounty we'd found.

"Step aboard," one herder offered. "I can bring you over."

Everything in me wanted to flee the heavy vegetation of the rim. But these herders didn't know the people of the green village or the strange problems of this island. I shook my head. "Brantley and I will bring you in to meet some of the people. I'm sure they'll help you load your rafts. But don't stray past the village."

Brantley tugged me aside, casting a dark gaze at the shadowed path inland. "We are not going back in there."

I touched his clenched arm. "Three days. The Maker told me."

His eyes narrowed as he pulled away to face me. "When?"

"A moment ago. Trust me. Please. This is our chance to help Meriel."

He rocked side to side, indecision bouncing his gaze between the sea and the path.

My heart felt tight in my chest. How dare I ask him to trust me? In spite of his assurances, it had been my decisions that led to Navar's death. What if he blamed the Maker for my actions? Had my choices that day damaged his fledgling trust in the Maker?

I chewed the inside of my lower lip, tugging on the silky sleeve of my day-before robe. He had every reason to step onto the nearest stenella and return home. And after that . . . perhaps after all that had happened here, he'd withdraw his request to bond.

His posture softened, and he offered his hand. "If you're going back in there, I'm coming with you."

His words didn't answer my deepest questions, but I managed a smile. "Then let's get started."

OVER THE NEXT THREE DAYS, WE INTRODUCED THE HERDERS to Trilia, Harba, Wimmo, and Morra. Some cheerful villagers even helped gather fruit, tubers, and seeds for the stenella to shuttle back to Meriel. Those affected by the convening showed no curiosity about the strangers or where they were taking supplies. None of the villagers dared the path toward the sea. Morra came closest, peering into the shadowed trail. But even though his mind was clear, he insisted they weren't meant to leave the enclosure of the rim barrier. And maybe he was right. In the vision I'd had of the time before, the barrier had been created as a protection—guarding out-islanders from the dangerous influence of the Gardener, but perhaps also protecting the inhabitants until the time the Maker would walk among them.

I decided not to coax any of my friends to walk through the barrier, even though I would have loved to show them the sea, my island, and the many stenella gliding through the current.

Wimmo was disappointed that the bonding ceremony for Brantley and me was postponed. I welcomed her complaints because they were such a beautiful contrast to the passivity that used to cover her every expression. No one else in the village paid much attention to the change in plans. Now that home was in our sights, I indulged in dreams of gathering with Brantley's family in Windswell, with some of the dancers and saltars in attendance. Waiting a few more days was a small price to pay.

Brantley didn't speak of our postponed bonding, which only fed my insecurities. He barely spoke to me at all. He was busy overseeing the harvesting, packing, and transporting of supplies. My heart swelled with pride as I watched the way the other herders deferred to him. Then on the tail of my admiration, the heavy wave of unworthiness would wash over me again and again. He deserved so much better. Even he had said it—under the influence of the Gardener, but still—why would he want to be saddled with a cripple? Perhaps he had only wanted to go ahead with the bonding while we were the only two from Meriel trapped on a foreign world. Now that he could return to Windswell, his affection for Brianna could blossom into more, or a strong, healthy rimmer girl could catch his fancy. And even if we went ahead with our bonding, what would happen to his grief over Navar's death? He said he didn't blame me, but in time wouldn't resentment spring up like daygrass?

Thankfully, the days were so busy I couldn't dwell on the fears that weighed me down. But I also couldn't raise the subject with Brantley. We were never alone together, working feverishly to gather all the resources our world needed before the currents pulled them apart and into their assigned paths.

On the last evening, some of the herders mingled at the revel. Bonfire smoke curled through the air. Rich stews simmered and enticed. Laughter swirled, and music stirred our hearts. The villagers danced, again reminding me of soaring birds with their vibrant robes and wide sleeves rippling. Spinning, dipping, weaving.

The herders watched wide-eyed from the sidelines, sipping punch, talking to each other and to Brantley. I was glad someone else could witness this beauty. In the coming years, there would be others to speak to as I'd remember this scene and these people.

Morra left the dancing and found me near the musician's platform. He bowed over one chunky leg, and his smile dimpled his round cheeks, florid from drink and exercise. "Be you still leaving tonight? You be welcome to stay, you know."

Weight on my good leg, I bobbed up and down on my toes. "Thank you." Then I startled him with an enthusiastic hug. "You helped us when we first arrived, and you've done so much to help our world these last days of gathering. Are you sure you don't want to stroll down the path and see our island?"

He shuddered. "My place be here. Thanks all the same."

Harba waddled over, Wimmo by his side bouncing her baby. Makah's eyes were wide, taking in the music and voices around her. Wimmo kissed her head. "We be heading to bed. Little ones need early nights, I be thinking."

Again I rose and lowered on my toes. "Your people have given us so much aid. I have a gift for you, as well." I crouched beside my pack and pulled out a linen-wrapped bundle. During all the trips between the two islands, I'd sent word asking Fiola for a spare copy of the Maker's letter. She and Brianna had organized the women of Windswell to produce more copies for all the rim villages as well as the midlands. The Order was also having novitiates dedicate an hour each day to reproducing the precious words. Although copies were still scarce, we could afford to share with these people.

"They be stories?" Harba asked, turning the parchment pages carefully against the leather cords that bound them.

"They be truth," I said. "Share it while you prepare for the Maker's arrival."

Wimmo's gaze was clear and alert. She nodded. "We will watch for the Maker and call the others to this too. Perhaps when they understand how all our villages be shrinking, how our people be disappearing, they will see the danger and listen." She caressed Makah, a new fire blazing from her eyes. "We'll speak truth so no more babes will be forgotten and lost."

I hugged them and fought a welling of tears. Saying goodbye to my new friends was harder than I'd expected.

As so often happened at a moment of ache or need, Brantley appeared by my side.

"Ready?" He grabbed my bag and slung it over his shoulder with a nonchalant smoothness. But a hint of gravel in his throat betrayed his own emotions.

I nodded, and he wrapped an arm around my shoulder, adjusting his steps to my uneven ones. I gripped the cane handle that Morra had carved. Turning back, I let a few tears fall before continuing down the shadowed path to the sea. "Is everyone out?"

"I counted heads. Can't believe none of the villagers wanted to pass through the barrier and see what's beyond."

We reached the tangleroot edge. One stenella, on loan from another herder, floated nearby. Several others with riders disappeared around the bend that hid Windswell. I looked back. Wispy branches dangled downward and swayed even though no breeze touched them. Then they reached toward each other and wove together. Soon the path disappeared, although hints of evening music reached our ears over the top of the tallest trees. "I wonder if the Maker will tear down the barrier when He comes."

"That's a better question for you to puzzle over." He swept a stray lock of hair from my face. "Having a hard time saying goodbye?"

I tightened my cloak around my shoulders. "A lot has happened. The people here have become true friends."

"True." Brantley's husky voice melded with the lapping of water against the shore. He paused. "Carya, we need to talk."

Had any conversation that began that way brought good news?

THE BARRIER TREES DARKENED WITH THE SETTING SUBSUN, reminding me of the menacing view they'd presented when we first arrived here. Perhaps I was braver than I gave myself credit for. After all, I had touched these plants, felt their pulse, heard the island's cry for help. And I'd answered in my own small way.

Yet I couldn't seem to find courage for the conversation Brantley asked for. I'd wanted time alone to talk with him ever since Meriel appeared, but now a hard knot twisted in my center. The borrowed stenella flicked an impatient fin. I looked down, my leather shoes getting damp from the water seeping up through the tangleroot. He'd said we needed to talk, but now he waited, silent. Irritating man. Clearly, he expected me to start. Still, I floundered for something normal to say. "I hope our friends will convince more villagers to stay away from the convening."

"I suppose that's in the Maker's hands now." Brantley shifted his weight, one hand resting on his longknife. "Carya, I've wanted to ask—"

"I'm not sure we gathered enough supplies. Three days weren't nearly enough time. We could have used a week or more." Now that the moment of reckoning had arrived, I pushed it away with an onslaught of words. "Once we're floating in healthy currents again, each village can plant new orchards. Of course, it will take time, but I think it will help everyone, especially the rimmers. Teague told me that there have been rumors that Saltar River has gathered a group of former dancers to oppose Saltar Kemp. I'm not sure what—"

Brantley clasped my upper arms and tugged me to a stop. "We can talk about all that once we're back in Windswell."

I pulled my gaze from my feet. When I looked up, he was studying me with a frown. The knot in my stomach pulled taut. This was it. The moment of a loss more painful than any I'd faced before. I stopped fighting it. My ribs contracted with my sigh. "Say it."

His head tilted, and that tendon along his jaw tightened. Oh, how I would miss watching the play of emotions on his face. Subsunset sparkled against his fair curls. His fingers pressed warmly into the back of my arm. I was close enough to smell his unique scent of damp leather vest and sweet citrus seawater. I inhaled deeply, tormenting myself further.

His hands dropped away, and he stepped back. "Carya, what's wrong?"

I couldn't answer. My chin dipped, and I shook my head, mute.

He took one of my hands and traced thoughtful patterns on my palm. "Have you changed your mind? Is that why you're as skittish as a newly weaned stenella?"

Stenella. We hadn't talked about Navar since that morning at the lake. A sharp sting filled my eyes. I blinked, hiding the threat of tears and keeping my gaze down. I couldn't bear to see the anguish in his gaze.

"You won't even talk to me?" His voice held a ragged edge now. "For a pair to be bonded, it seems to me we need honesty between us."

My head jerked up. "But that's just it." My throat closed, and I couldn't continue.

He drew back, dropping my hand. "You truly have changed your mind? Why? What have I done?"

I clutched my head. How could one man be so confusing and frustrating? "You've done nothing. But I know you blame me . . ."

"Blame you?" His brow puckered further, then cleared. "Are you thinking of Navar again?"

I bit my lip and managed a tight nod.

"The only one I blame is the Gardener of this accursed island." He spoke with so much heat I began to believe him. "I don't deny the shock made me angry at everyone. The Maker, the people here . . . you. I'm sorry," he said simply. "I couldn't talk about it then. It's still hard. But I shouldn't have shut you out. Forgive me?"

He reached for my hand again, and I clasped his. "Of course. But as you said, we need truth between us. Be honest. Won't you resent me for—"

"For dancing me away from the Gardener's spell? For finding resources to benefit our entire world? For bringing light and laughter to my heart every time I look at you?"

Heat curled in my chest. "But the cost . . ."

He pulled me close again. "Navar chose to save us. It was a gift of loyalty . . . and love. I'm grateful for the years we had together. A companion like that is rare." He rested his forehead against mine. "The loss is huge. But it is nothing compared to the loss I would feel if you no longer wanted to bond with me."

My heart tingled as if star rain swirled and sparked within. The warmth in my chest moved up to my face. "Truly?" I whispered.

He sighed. "That you could doubt it shows me how preoccupied I've been. Will you let me prove it every day for the rest of our lives, dancer?"

I gasped in a small sip of air, as surprise, hope, and finally delight spun inside. "You truly still want that?"

His head bent, and his lips found mine. Tender, longing, his kiss pledged things he couldn't put into words. I answered in kind, then wrapped my arms around his waist and nestled into him.

"I've never stopped wanting that, Carya. And you? Are you ready to bond with a reckless herder from a poor rim village?"

Joy emboldened me to tease. "Maybe. If you could be a tiny bit less reckless?"

His laugher spun into the sky. He stepped onto the borrowed stenella and offered his hand. "Ready to leave this forsaken island?"

"Not truly forsaken. The Maker has never forgotten them." I didn't need to look back anymore. I joined Brantley and settled behind the neck of the creature.

Instead of standing, Brantley sat behind me, wrapping an arm around my waist. "Since it's an unfamiliar mount, I figured I should hold you."

His teasing words tickled against my ear.

I sighed and relaxed back against the warmth of his chest. "If she tosses me into the water, you'll just have to save me."

"Again."

"Again? Hey, I've saved you just as many times as you've saved me."

"That you have. In more ways than you know."

The sea was still, and we glided silently as the stars emerged. The lights of torches and bonfires at Windswell drew us home.

32

"YOUR HAIR KEEPS TRYING TO ESCAPE." BRANTLEY'S mother, Fiola, smoothed the white headscarf that framed my face. "Are you sure you want to wear this?"

Her inquiry only added to the uncertainty swarming around my skull like gnats. "It's a reminder that I'm a dancer." Sinking into a chair by her hearth, where our morning tsalla brewed in a kettle, I picked at the edge of my thumbnail. "You truly think I'm free to bond now that I've left the Order? I did promise them . . ."

Fiola pulled a chair close and took my face between her soft, wrinkled hands. "Sweet child, they tore you from your home. You were indoctrinated. Lied to. If not for you, Orianna would have suffered the same fate. I think you can consider yourself free from those ties."

Her tenderness made my throat thicken with emotion. She knew my history, every confusing and ugly part. And still she embraced me as a daughter. I had to swallow to speak. "But they also trained me, taught me the patterns, showed me how our gift of movement can serve Meriel. I'm still called to dance. That's how I hope to help Windswell."

Her eyes swam with compassion and the same sea colors that always lit Brantley's gaze. "Perhaps the dancers who stay with the Order will choose to never bond. But perhaps it's time for some dancers to have families. The Maker's letter offers the blessing of family—including to those who serve with various gifts. And from what you've told me about the other island, a world without bonds is a sorry place, indeed." She brushed a light kiss on my forehead and released me. "Now eat your breakfast. Folks will be gathering. I wish I had more than saltcakes for you."

I sprang to my feet, weight automatically shifting to my good leg. Each day I learned to work around the injury a bit better. Perhaps one day it wouldn't be a constant intrusion. "I forgot. Ginerva sent a basket for us." After hurrying to the side of the room where my pallet rested, I unearthed a bundle of bresh. A day old, but still tender and flakey. I offered one to Fiola.

She clapped her hands and grinned like a child. "Such a treat! You should get bonded more often."

I nibbled on mine because it would disappoint Ginerva if she learned I hadn't enjoyed this special breakfast, but I had no appetite. There was no room for hunger in my stomach, where wisps of clouds spun in tickling circles. Even the warm tsalla couldn't calm me.

The door burst open, and Orianna scampered inside, dirt smudging her best tunic. "Two stenella arrived from Middlemost! There's a saltar and some other people."

"You couldn't stay clean for a few minutes?" Fiola scolded. "Get back out there before you touch anything."

Unfazed, Orianna grinned at me. "Are you ready, teacher? He'll be here soon to escort you."

Brantley's irrepressible niece wriggled with all her seven-year-old energy and lightened my mood. His folk had wrapped their arms around me long before this bonding day: Orianna's affection, Fiola's gentle wisdom, even Brianna's sisterly approval. What a blessing to be welcomed into this family! I smiled. "Almost ready."

After a last sip of tsalla, I put on the robe I'd brought from the green village. It fit neatly over my simple white tunic and leggings. I was grateful for something to add over my dancer garb. I didn't want to offend the saltars by dressing as if I were still in the Order. Bright thread wove across the white silk. The cuffs and hem displayed stitches of ocean waves, stenella with fins outstretched gliding above, trees, flowers, and grain fields blooming with health. A design of hopes.

"Such an unusual garment." Fiola touched one wide, bell-like sleeve that was so long it covered my hands. Orianna reached for it, and her grandmother batted her hand away. "Scoot, little one. Better yet, I'll take you over to the lodge. They'll want some time alone when Brantley comes." In the doorway, grandmother and granddaughter both threw me one more smile, noses scrunching in the same way, cheeks nudged upward, eyes sparkling.

After they left, the swirling sensation in my center grew in intensity. I took a slow breath as I'd learned to do in my novitiate classes. This was a day for joy. This wasn't some nerve-wracking dancer test or a dangerous path on an unknown island—but in a similar way, the next hours would change everything. No wonder a hint of anxiety flickered among my excitement and longing. Would I bring joy to Brantley's life or be a burden? Could we truly create a bond between a dancer from the Order and a rim herder? Such a thing had never been seen since the Order's existence. I lengthened my spine, leveling my chin. Whatever unknowns we faced, I would give this calling every ounce of commitment. Before I could finish gathering myself, a light tap sounded on the door.

"Come in." I pushed another lock of hair under the taut white scarf and tightened the belt of the robe.

Brantley threw the door open, then leaned against the doorjamb, arms crossed. "You'll make my knees too weak to walk to the lodge."

His presence chased away my lingering doubts. He wore a new tawny shirt, hanging loose to his low-slung belt. He still wore his longknife at his hip. I hid a grin. He was as committed to that weapon as he was to me. But he'd foregone the old leather vest and had new pants and kid-leather boots. He'd made an attempt to tame his golden curls, and his hair still glistened from the water. But already one lock tumbled over his forehead into his eyes. He looked so boyish and eager, I felt bold enough to tease. "You're not so bad yourself."

He grinned. "I won't ask you if you're ready for this. Ready or not, we are bonding today." Endearing uncertainty flickered across his brow. "All right?"

I limped toward him. "Do you have any second thoughts?"

"I've had but one thought since the night I saw you scampering about in the star rain in the Order courtyard."

Giggles tickled my chest. "You sure didn't show it then."

He shifted his weight away from the doorjamb, lowering his head toward mine. "You were causing a few problems in my plan. You seem to be good at that. And I'm hoping you'll trouble my plans for many years to come." His breath was sweet with tsalla, and my gaze flickered toward his lips.

He pulled back and offered his arm. "Stop looking at me that way, or the people at the lodge will have a long wait."

A delighted shiver traced my spine. My own knees were feeling a bit weak, and I was glad for his support as we walked from Fiola's cottage to the gathering hall.

"They're coming!" Orianna squealed from the top of the steps, then ducked inside.

We entered the large wooden building and stopped. Benches crowded with people surrounded the open space where I'd once shared the Maker's letter with Windswell. Torches scented the air with tallow and smoke, and cast sparkling light throughout the room, while open windows allowed in the citrus sea breeze and music of birds and rustling branches. Near the front, Brianna pulled Orianna onto her lap. Saltar Kemp's regal posture stood out as much as her formal robe. She sat on a bench with other white-clad dancers—the colleagues I'd grown up with, trained with, and served with for a time. Some of the villagers cast uneasy glances toward their row. It would take time for the tension between rimmers and the Order to heal. Thankfully, I saw no such hesitation in the gazes turned my way. Warm smiles lit the faces of Windswell. Children drummed their fingers against their benches in approval until their parents shushed them.

The village's matriarch rose and opened her arms toward us. Fiola stood beside her, a parchment in her hands—a precious copy of the Maker's letter.

As a child in the Order, I'd never dreamed of a moment like this. My heart swelled so much I was sure it would burst from my ribs and dance around the room. With Brantley guiding me, I floated past the rows to the center, my limp only a slight hitch in my step. I wanted to look around for more familiar faces—for Ginerva, Starfire, Varney. I wanted to see which dancers had made their way from the tower to be here today. Perhaps Iris had come. But I focused on the matriarch, everything around us a haze. Her wrinkled face was framed by gray hair, so sparse the pink of her scalp showed through. Her shoulders bent, but her eyes were lively and her smile reassuring.

Before the matriarch began the bonding, Fiola read a portion of the letter. "'When the ocean was vast and empty, He formed our world and breathed life into those who came before. He sets us on a blessed current and guides our course through wind and waves.'" She turned several pages. "'Love flourishes amid dedication. As the Maker has dedicated Himself to His people, He invites a man and woman to pledge a lifelong promise to each other.'"

She closed the book, and the matriarch raised her hands. "People of Windswell, Carya and Brantley seek to make such a bond. Will you support them?"

Now everyone drummed their fingers on benches, the floor, or a nearby wall—a gentle but fervent rainfall of approval. The affection and support of this village overwhelmed me almost as much as knowing that a man like Brantley could love me. I swayed, and he patted my hand where it had tightened on his arm.

"Breathe," he whispered.

Determined to display the strength he claimed to see in me, I smiled up at him.

"Do you make this promise freely?" The matriarch's voice spoke firmly, cutting through the fog in my mind.

We were supposed to simply answer yes, but Brantley and I had discussed an addition to the bonding ceremony. Together we answered, "With the Maker's care, yes."

A few murmurs sounded behind us, and more fingers drummed their approval.

"Demonstrate your unity by sharing this cup." The matriarch nodded to the side, and Orianna skipped forward with a covered basket. Instead of a plain pottery mug, Brantley lifted out a carved bowl, with delicate dancers, soaring stenella, trees, and flowers all worked into the design. The surface glistened with oil that brought out the multi-shaded wood. This wasn't created on our world. My jaw gaped. "How . . . ?"

Brantley winked at me and mouthed, "Later."

The matriarch poured water into the bowl, then sprinkled in items as she spoke. "Honey for the sweetness of love, lenka for the tang of life's challenges, persea to feed your souls and give you strength, and herbs that you may always heal each other's wounds."

My hands shook as I lifted the bowl and took a sip. The flavors swirled in my mouth as I tasted our future. It was complex, rich, and full of excitement. I offered the drink to Brantley. He reached for it carefully, as if holding something was almost beyond his capability at the moment. He didn't tremble as I had, but he stared into the water for two breaths. Then he drank a deep draught and handed the bowl back to the matriarch.

She smiled at us. "And will you be bonded?"

I faced Brantley. That muscle along his jaw twitched, showing me how hard he was working to hold in his emotion. My heart melted. I cleared my throat. "As a herder provides for his village, I promise to give love and fealty to you with all that I am."

He braced his shoulders and met my gaze. "And as a dancer gives all that she is to serve our world, I promise to give love and fealty to you with all that I am."

A shocked silence met our pledges—another change to the simple, expected response. Then a man shouted, "Well said!" Someone else whooped, and the whole lodge erupted in drumming and cheering.

My smile grew so large my cheeks hurt, and Brantley stopped fighting to hold his face still, breaking into a giddy expression of joy. Then he grabbed me and swung me around.

With my feet still not touching the ground, he spun me down the stairs and to the open area in front of the meeting hall.

Musicians set up quickly to one side, and rimmers clapped and tapped their feet when the music began. The cluster of dancers from the Order stiffened, eyes wide. Those who had lived in seclusion had only ever danced to the rhythm of drums. All other music was forbidden as a distraction. Once their shock faded, I caught smiles from some and even a bit of swaying. The first time I'd witnessed music and dance in a rim village, I'd been equally horrified and captivated. I smiled, determined to invite my former colleagues to join the dancing later.

Saltar Kemp hurried over and hugged me. New lines carved her features. The past weeks of leading the new Order, with all the changes that involved, had taken a toll. And when Brantley and I hadn't returned for so long, she'd borne the heavy decision to move Meriel closer to the strange island and wait a little longer for us. "Are you all right?" I asked. "I've heard some of the rumors. Has Saltar River caused you trouble? How can I help?"

She brushed aside my questions. "We knew change would take time and not everyone would embrace the forgotten truth in the Maker's letter. Time enough for those discussions later. This is a day for celebration." She gave a friendly nod to Brantley, who stayed glued to my side as others approached to congratulate us.

Starfire charged down the lodge steps, weaving through the crowd, arriving breathless. She'd once been so disappointed when she hadn't been selected for the Order, but watching her irrepressible movement, I realized it might have been a blessing. She needed freedom, not control and precision. We hugged tightly, then she tossed her mass of auburn hair back and laughed. "Think where we were a year ago! Could you have imagined this?"

We'd once huddled together outside the main hall, waiting for our turn to take the final pattern test before the saltars. We'd known no other life outside of sore muscles, precise patterns, and harsh competition. All our dreams had hitched on graduating from novitiate to dancer. We'd both changed, and more importantly, our dreams had changed.

I leaned against Brantley, and he tilted his head to rest on mine. Starfire grinned at us. "Make a visit to Middlemost soon, all right?"

"We will," I promised.

After she turned away, Brantley canted toward my ear. "And so it begins. You're speaking for us both now?"

I blushed. "Sorry." But when I looked up at him, his smile was teasing and warm.

He tucked a strand of hair back into my scarf and let his palm linger against my cheek. "Go ahead and make our plans. You've never steered me wrong."

Brianna approached us next. I searched her face for any sign of regret or hesitation. When her husband—Brantley's brother—was killed, she had turned to Brantley for support. I'd long feared she held more than sisterly affection toward him. But her happiness for us seemed genuine and free of guile. "I thought Orianna would race to the front before it was time for the shared cup. She was so excited to take part." She gave me one more squeeze. "Welcome, sister."

"I promise I'll look after him."

She rolled her eyes. "Good fortune with that. He's not an easy one to keep safe."

Brantley sniffed and crossed his arms, pretending to be offended. Then he directed his attention to a herder from Undertow who approached us.

The men clasped arms, and the herder gestured toward the sea. "My Javar calved last season. Pesky youngling tags along every time we are out herding and scares off the fish. You'd be doing me a favor if you'd take her off my hands."

I felt Brantley's spine tighten. Was this too soon? Would he be offended at this gift? Too heartbroken to train another stenella? I slipped my hand into his, offering support for the emotions I knew were roiling through him.

Jaw square, he gave a tight nod. "Once we've built our cottage, I'll have nothing but time on my hands. I could train her for your village."

The man clapped Brantley's shoulder. "What use would we have for a second stenella? I have no apprentice. No, if you do me the favor of taking on the calf, it's yours."

"My thanks," Brantley said quietly. He tried to respond in the same casual way that the gift had been offered and hide his emotion, but I'd known him long enough to recognize the gleam of new purpose that returned to his eyes.

I gave a happy sigh. A herder without a stenella was as limited as . . . well, as a hobbled dancer. And I didn't wish that on anyone. His joy made my spirits soar.

A new song started, and more villagers joined a group dance . . . not as elaborate as what we'd watched in the green village of the other island, but as spirited. Brantley's fingers tapped against his leg. "I'd better get that cottage finished. That calf will pick up an independent mind if she's not put to training soon."

A stenella to train was something to be thankful for, but how my heart swelled when Brantley spoke of our cottage. He had staked out a plot of land in view of the sea and had already begun construction. He'd camped there the last few nights but hadn't yet taken me to see our future home.

I stiffened. "Wait. In all the activity, I forgot. Where will we stay tonight?" I'd been distracted with distribution plans for the seeds and resources we'd delivered, messages to and from Middlemost, and organizing our bonding day. I hadn't thought beyond this moment.

He laughed. "Your face. The worry dances across your forehead. You're so easy to read, especially with your hair pulled back like that. Don't fear. We won't be camping tonight."

I elbowed him. "Well, we have spent many a night on the trail."

"One of the Windswell landkeepers has business in Middlemost. He offered us use of his cottage until he returns."

Then we were pulled apart and swept into the celebrations. Laughter, music, sunshine, well-wishes. I pushed aside my worry about the problems Saltar Kemp was facing with the Order. Time enough to help with that tomorrow. I savored the interaction with friends, although I longed to finally have a quiet moment alone with my new husband. After a lunch—lavish by rim village standards— people headed back to their work, and Brantley and I slipped away. He led me around a bend to a tiny inlet. A young stenella thrashed about near the shore, tied to a tree with a vine.

I knelt near the edge. "Poor thing. She misses her mother."

"Time to create a new bond." Brantley opened a basket that had been left near the tree and handed me a copper fish. "Do you want to try?"

Gingerly, I dangled the fish. "Here little stenella. Don't worry, we'll take care of you."

She stopped thrashing and jutted her head forward, peering at me.

"Put it in the water for her."

I lowered the fish and moved it side to side. She dipped her head and butted my hand. I laughed and dropped her meal, which she quickly grabbed. "She needs a name."

"I've been pondering that," he said. "I thought perhaps Makah would be a fitting tribute. You know Harba and Wimmo's babe may never have survived if not for you coaxing them away from the convening. Because of you, they remember to love and care for their child and each other."

His praise filled me with a warm glow. "Can I see our cottage now?"

"It's just around that cluster of willows. Not much to look at so far. We got the floor and two walls set. Wish I could build you one of those tall homes like they had at the green village. Maybe one day."

"Don't be silly."

We walked slowly on the rocking ground, and I leaned on Brantley's arm for support.

"How's the leg?" he asked.

I was grateful there wasn't a note of pity in his voice, so I answered honestly. "Tired after this morning, but I'll be fine." And I began to believe I would be.

We slipped under dangling branches, much more languid and gentle than the vines on the other island, and emerged into a clearing. Our future home nestled under a spreading pine. The lower limbs had been cleared away, and the upper branches formed a canopy over the structure. Flowers dotted the border of the foundation. I raised an eyebrow at Brantley.

"Orianna insisted." He laughed. "I warned her they'll get trampled as we finish work on the home, but she said she'll just plant more."

A fire pit stood ready on the stretch of land before the sea. "Brantley, let's not use your friend's cottage. Let's camp here tonight."

"You sure? Aren't you tired of tents and lean-tos and sleeping on bare earth?"

"Not if I'm with you."

Color rose up his neck, and I giggled. It was so fun to make him blush, I'd have to find more ways to do it.

"Look." He led me toward the tangleroot. "Our last view of the other world."

The horizon stretched straight and true, separating sky and water. The suns glinted off the still surface like golden threads on deep-jade silk. Skilled designers of the green village would have loved this view, if only they could see it.

Maker, when You walk among them, please take down the rim trees so they can see the ocean one day.

Brantley wrapped an arm around my shoulder, and I edged closer to him. For so many years my human contact had been a saltar correcting a flawed line of my body, or an attendant shoving me aside as he dragged another novitiate somewhere. I would never stop marveling at Brantley's embrace. His support and protectiveness were reminders of the Maker's tenderness.

"Do you miss them?" he asked.

"I was glad to leave. I was afraid we'd never escape. But the people became dear to me. I'll keep talking to the Maker about them."

Tiny waves licked the tangleroot. Out where the sky met the sea, a shadow like a low cloud drifted into the distance. During the last few days, the other island had slowly grown smaller as its course pulled it away from us. Meriel was finally coasting the currents again.

Brantley squeezed my hand. "Great Maker of land and sea, please save the people of that world."

I hadn't been bold enough to speak my prayers aloud in front of him. His matter-of-fact request made my admiration for him grow even more and inspired me to overcome my shyness. How marvelous that we could commune with the Maker together. "And watch over our friends."

We stood in silence for a few minutes, soaking in the warmth from the suns and watching until the vast ocean was empty again. Then we strolled to the foundation of our home-to-be. I rummaged through a burlap bag that someone had left on the steps and unearthed a soft woven blanket.

Brantley unpacked a crate, then dusted off his hands. "I'll go gather some boughs for bedding. We should be able to make our camp more comfortable than the ones we've had lately." He whistled to himself as he headed deeper inland.

I unpacked his backpack and found the bowl we'd used in the bonding ceremony. Running my fingers over the images, I marveled again at the friends we'd met and the adventure of life ahead.

Brantley returned and dropped an armful of branches onto one corner of the open floor. He helped me spread a soft blanket over the sticky boughs.

I held up the bowl. "You promised you'd tell me later. Where did this beautiful bowl come from?"

His chest lifted, basking in my appreciation. "When Morra showed me the pledging bowl he'd made, I asked him to make one for us. We kept it a secret—which wasn't easy since he was so often muddle-headed. I was afraid he'd tell you."

Moisture filled my eyes, and my smile trembled. He'd planned for our bonding when we didn't even know what our future might hold. "It's beautiful. Like nothing else in existence on our world."

He stepped closer and placed his hands over mine as I held each side of the bowl. "Exactly. Just like us."

GLOSSARY

ATTENDANTS — Servants who work in the Order.

BRESH — A flaky, buttery roll. Luxurious treat eaten by dancers.

CALARA REED — Well rooted, supple reeds growing near water. (Calara pattern is one of the most complicated.)

CENTER GROUND — The huge open field in the very center of the island, where the dancers of the Order perform the patterns that keep the island turning around its core.

CONVENING — An event in which an entire village treks to the center lake on the forsaken island, calls on the Gardener, goes into a trance, and has their cares erased. Each village goes around the time of the star rain that corresponds to their color. Green village, green star rain, etc.

COPPER FISH — Small, glittery fish that swim in large schools and provide food for rim villages.

DAYGRASS — a soft, mossy grass that springs up overnight.

FOREST HOUND — A wolflike beast almost as big as a pony, usually with amber eyes; a feared predator.

FORMS — Various levels within the Order's school. First-form children are generally around seven years old and work up through the ranks to the fifteenth form (twenty-one years of age) and if successful can join the Order as dancers. Some dancers later become saltars.

GRAND CONVENING — When the multicolored star rain happens once a year, all the villages gather simultaneously at the lake in the center of their world to be numbed by the Gardener.

HERDER — One who herds fish from the ocean waters so they can be gathered by rim villagers.

HONEYBIRD — Tiny, nervous, bright-red bird.

LANDKEEPER — A person who gardens, farms, cares for plants.

LANTHRUS — A plant with prickly leaves that cause blisters and fever, but when dried is useful for pain.

LENKA — A small, yellow, tart, and sweet fruit with a small oval pit inside. Lenka trees on Meriel have been dying off.

LONGKNIFE — Common long-bladed tool and weapon used by herders.

MAKER, THE — The forgotten one who created the oceans, the island world, and everything in them.

MERIEL — The name of Carya's world (the island floating in a vast, featureless ocean universe).

MIDDLEMOST — The largest city, in the center of Meriel, surrounding the Order.

NOVITIATES — Girls training to become dancers of the Order.

ORDER, THE — The organization of novitiates, dancers, saltars, prefects, and attendants that directs the course of the world through the dance. Located in the very center of Meriel, in a large edifice that encircles the center ground. They pass down the patterns through the generations.

PATTERNS — Precise dances and formations named for various natural elements or plants. To be accepted into the Order, each dancer must prove she can perform any pattern flawlessly.

PERSEA FRUIT — Knobby-skinned, meaty fruit with a pit.

PREFECT — Support staff for the Order school, they enforce rules, help saltars, etc.

REVEL — The all-night gathering before the convening, during which villagers share their art or gifts, drink, dance, and party.

RIM — The undulating outer edges of the island world.

RIMMERS — Sometimes derogatory term for those who live in rim villages.

SALTARS — The leaders and top teachers of the Order.

SALTCAKES — Dry, crumbly biscuits.

STAR RAIN — A periodical magical occurrence on evenings when stars burst in the air and glittering light rains down.

STENELLA — Dolphin-like sea creatures with long necks and wide spreading side fins that can glide over the water as well as dive under.

SWEET WATER — Ocean water that tastes sweet and citrusy. Loved by the rim villages but feared and filtered by those in the inland towns.

TANGLEROOT — The matted, intertwined vines that form the outer edge of the island.

TENDER — Someone who cares for domesticated animals, especially ponies.

TSALLA — Sweet ocean water brewed with herbs.

WELFEN BEAST — A forest creature with a high, gibbering howl that lurks in the deep woods and is mentioned to frighten children.

ACKNOWLEDGMENTS

MY THANKS TO MY INCREDIBLE AGENT AND PUBLISHER, Steve Laube, who encouraged this series and brainstormed a key plot point in this book. Eternal gratitude to my editors, Reagen Reed and Lindsay Franklin, who bring so much care, respect, and wisdom to making my stories stronger. Huge appreciation the amazing team at Enclave Publishing, specifically to Trissina Kear and Jordan Smith for all their hard work helping readers find these books.

Immense thanks go to the friends who have prayed with me as I work. I am blessed by every circle of support. The "church ladies," Bible study small groups, writing retreat buddies, the Dancing Realms Facebook group, my Book Buddies, family, and so many dear friends. You carried me through the years of work on this new series, celebrating the joy of a new story world, and encouraging me when the road was challenging. Special thanks to critique partners Chawna, Patti, Jenni, and Michelle for in-depth feedback.

Above all else, thank you to my Maker from whom all blessings flow. May we rejoice each day in knowing we are never forsaken.

AUTHOR BIOGRAPHY

SHARON HINCK WRITES "STORIES FOR THE HERO IN ALL OF US," novels praised for their strong spiritual themes, emotional resonance, and imaginative blend of genres.

She earned an MA in Communication (with a major in theatre and thesis in dance) from Regent University and spent ten years as the artistic director of a Christian dance company. That ministry included three short-term mission trips to Hong Kong to teach and choreograph for a YWAM dance/evangelism team. She taught classical ballet and liturgical dance for twenty years, and led workshops on dance in worship.

She's been a church youth worker, a dancer/choreographer, a church organist, a homeschool mom, and an adjunct professor of Creative Writing for MFA students. One day she'll figure out what to be when she grows up.

When she's not wrestling with words, she enjoys speaking at churches and conferences, and has taught at Minnesota Christian Writer's Guild, the national conference of the American Christian Fiction Writers, and Realm Makers.

A wife, mom of four, and delighted grandmother of three, she lives in Minnesota and is a member at St. Michael's Lutheran Church.

She loves visitors at sharonhinck.com.